# PRAISE FOR
## *What You Don't Know*

"A dazzling story, containing so much more than the width of its spine. Love is all over the place in this novel, and you don't know which way it will turn next, and you stay glued to the page to find out. Burch reminds us that life is complex and dynamic and we really don't know what might happen next."

—Nina Schuyler, award-winning author of *Afterword*

"Dreamy and poetic, *What You Don't Know* chronicles the awakening of two young women to the intertwined forces of grief and desire. Set in soul-freeing San Francisco and music-rich Nashville, this immersive novel deeply explores the hearts of its characters."

—Lucy Jane Bledsoe, award winning author of *Tell the Rest*

"Beautifully written, haunting novel by poet Beverly Burch. Atmospheric tale of a love that seeps through the life/death barrier. Strongly recommend!"

—Joan Steinau Lester, PEN award-winning author of *Loving Before Loving: A Marriage in Black and White*

"*What You Don't Know* is an engrossing story of female friendship and its power to transform. I fell in love with Chloe and Rosie and cheered—and worried—for them as they navigated work, marriage, children, and the growing feelings they had for one another. This is a tender story you won't forget."

—Frances Dinkelspiel, award winning author of NYT bestselling *Tangled Vines: Greed, Murder, Obsession, and an Arsonist in the Vineyards of California*

# What You Don't Know

*A Novel*

BEVERLY BURCH

Sibylline
DIGITAL FIRST

Sibylline Press



Published in the United States by Sibylline Press,
an imprint of All Things Book LLC, California.

Sibylline Press is dedicated to publishing the
brilliant work of women authors ages 50 and older.
www.sibyllinepress.com

Sibylline Digital First Edition
eBook ISBN: 9781960573612
Print ISBN: 9781960573889
Library of Congress Control Number: 2025931635

Cover Design: Alicia Feltman
Book Production: Aaron Laughlin

Sibylline
Press

*For every woman trying to find her own story—*

The dead don't go; they just slip into other people's heads.

—Penelope Lively, *The Photograph*

# CHAPTER 1

Chloe's parents were misfits. Kath, her mother, bought clothes at thrift shops until Chloe earned enough to buy denim skirts and black leggings from the Gap for herself. Damian, her father, was disabled by a fall from a roof and drove a truck when he could, but some days he didn't work at all. They couldn't help being poor, but it was more: they lacked something vital parents should have. Kath wasn't motherly. She didn't have friends of her own, didn't play bridge or go to PTA meetings, didn't even cook dinner some nights. Damian watched TV all day if he wasn't working.

Chloe understood that she didn't fit anywhere either.

She was only six when she made her first sandwich for school lunch. Kath had worked late again and was sleeping in. No doubt she forgot—she often forgot even when she hadn't worked late. Chloe walked herself the ten blocks to Henrietta Elementary in Tallahassee. The mashed up sandwich—peanut butter, baloney, banana on white bread—tasted like a feral animal gone sweet from rot. The girl next to her in the cafeteria asked for a bite. *Eww*! she said, but asked for a second bite.

Kath's neglect, her emotional flatness, signaled lack of interest, maybe lack of love.

When she remembered her early years, Chloe found only a few good leavings. A vintage red shirt with snaps and a long-tailed cat on the pocket she loved, though it made her uncool even in elementary school. Summers, fleeing on her bike to a sinkhole where she could swim. Dusky trees whose branches twisted into mysterious canopies. The scent of gardenias rose in the evening as she sat on her front steps and closed her eyes to let it take her somewhere else.

Never mind the snakes, the giant winged cockroaches. Her mother's thin laugh. Sundays were all alike: her parents snoozing in the living room, Kath with the comics laid over her face, a feeling of deadness in the house. That deathly quiet left Chloe feeling she'd been buried alive. She'd ride hard toward the ocean on her bicycle until exertion or sea air released her. The smothered feeling would haunt her the rest of her life.

Other emotions she couldn't explain dogged her: how scared she was of closeness with people, or the hollowness she felt in her body. She covered it well, with a smile so lovely people were drawn to her and believed she was friendly, but when someone tried to get closer, she inched away until they moved on.

She played softball, joined the swim team, but made no special friends, no children who came to her house. She remembered books, coming home from the library with armloads and characters she felt close to. Ramona Quimby, maybe she was her only friend. She, too, wanted to make money someday. Anne of Green Gables, a girl who had to muscle her way in. Then Jane Eyre, Catherine Earnshaw.

She learned the names of clouds and flowering trees. The mimosa in the backyard was good for climbing, its sprays of pink blossoms soft, feathery, its leaves so sensitive they folded if you touched them. Like me, she thought. Damian taught her names of birds who came to Kath's feeder. Naming them, knowing the sky, the weather, nature's moods made her feel more at home in the world.

Lush green exploded around her, jungly and untamed, or watery in the dark swampy areas toward the coast. Neighborhoods like hers had been dulled into servitude. She believed in something else out there, she didn't know what. Fate never meant her to live in such a world.

———

The terrible ballet costume. She begged for ballet lessons after watching *The Nutcracker* on television, to be a Snow Queen in a white tutu and tiara, her hair glistening under falling snow, violins waltzing as a white-suited prince spun her around.

Kath found a class that met in the teacher's basement on Rangle Street and gave her an orange thrift store costume, saggy on her small body. It revealed the ugliness, the girl who didn't fit. She watched other girls in pastel leotards and stood against the wall as the teacher tried to coax her into the group. She told her mother she wouldn't go back, but Kath insisted, she'd paid for a month already. So she climbed the mimosa and jumped from a high limb, spraining her ankle. Her toes were bloodied, but she didn't mind the pain because she felt the power of escape. She buried the orange outfit under her mattress.

Why did Kath not love her more? Angry frightened feelings moiled around inside. The most hideous thing, the heart of her, was the thing she didn't know how to name.

Kath's parents had died in a plane crash when she was five. Her father was a wealthy businessman, but young. He left no will, and after the crash his brothers claimed his businesses and much of the real estate. There was no one to fight back. There wasn't even a life insurance policy. *He couldn't imagine dying, I guess*, Kath said.

For two years she stayed with her grandmother, who had no money, then for unknown reasons she was sent to Tallahassee to live with cousin Dottie, who had no money either. She married Damian, whom she called Dee, a construction worker before he fell from that broken eave. Kath sold jewelry at the mall, but money was tight, and she moonlighted cleaning offices. A fading beauty, she had pale white skin and a hard look about her.

Dee came from redbone roots, mixed Native, Black, and European. Chloe inherited his tawny beige skin, green eyes, full lips, almost-black hair, and high cheek bones. A beauty also, with her striking smile that misled the people who saw openness there. She was so private even she didn't know her thoughts and feelings.

Kath and Dee moved in tandem through the house. They sat close together on the patio in dripping heat, drank the same Miller High Life. He grilled meat for dinner while Kath brought things to him. Afterward they collapsed on the sofa and watched TV. They never quarreled, they never kissed. Pair-bonded.

Was that love? Was that marriage? Why did it feel deadly?

---

Dreaming was a sure escape. Daydreams, night dreams. Later Chloe could still remember vivid dreams from her early years. There was a common theme: she was searching for something, she didn't know what, but it was imperative to find that thing. The dream always ended before discovery. In other dreams she was trying to get somewhere, a place she knew but could no longer locate. Sometimes the road to it vanished. But occasionally she dreamed of coming upon a house and realizing it was hers now, a place with lavish rooms, each leading to other rooms, a new house that felt endless.

---

At fifteen, she lied about her age to get a job at Beckman's Deli, a step toward a life of her own. Beckman's occupied the half block of Miccosukee Road cooled by sweet gum and live oaks.

Classical music played on the speakers, shelves were stocked with European beers, imported cheeses occupied the center of the store next to brined olives and pickles. Lemon aioli, mango chutney, sun-dried tomatoes gleamed in jars along the wall.

Besides Simon Beckman, who owned the deli, Yvette was the only other employee, a woman Chloe couldn't easily read. Yvette examined her nails or sang snatches of songs in French while customers waited. She came in late, kissed Chloe on the cheek, made a sad face and apologized. Customers treated her with respect anyway.

Chloe studied her, intent on learning how she worked. Yvette wasn't exactly beautiful, but she had an aura of beauty. Or magnetism. Sexiness, intelligence, or unthinkable temptation, something more than her honey-colored hair, tight skirts, deep-cut blouses. Yet Yvette befriended her. When they met, Yvette put her arms on Chloe's shoulders, looked at her, said, "A beautiful face you have."

Chloe reddened, and Yvette added, "You need to learn about that."

Learn? On her second day Yvette shooed away an older man who stared too long, scolding him at the register. "She's only seventeen, J. D.," she heard her say. It left her feeling guilty—she didn't like lying to her, but Yvette would have thought her not worth bothering with if she knew she was fifteen.

Perhaps Simon hired Yvette because she fit the fancy merchandise. Chloe herself was cheap labor and made up for Yvette's negligence. On her first day he warned her, "Yvette has good points. She'll show you around, but watch out. I wouldn't get too friendly. She's not like you and me. You know how French women are." He grinned. Chloe had no idea how French women were, or why he kept her on if he felt that way.

Her accented English? Her promise of seductions that never transpired? While Chloe waited on customers, Yvette lingered at the cash register. Men leaned forward, talked in low voices as they paid for lunch or bottles of wine. What did they say? She heard her give customers her name, but if they invited her to have a drink, she always nodded vaguely. "Maybe next time."

Chloe asked if she already had a boyfriend. Yvette laughed. "No, no boyfriend. That's maybe what you would like."

It wasn't a taunt, the way she said it, just a fact. Yvette had the answer to something Chloe struggled to name. "*Lapin,* these guys are all married. That's okay. At least with me it's okay. Probably not okay with their wives." She shrugged. "They tease you. You tease them back. They are men. You don't have to do much. Maybe just don't encourage too much, I think. They like that even more. Then you can choose for yourself."

She wished she had a mother like Yvette. Meeting Yvette felt like a stroke of destiny. She followed her around for days until Simon warned her again. "Like I said, she's a wild card. Be careful. Has an idea she's a singer. She sang for a while in a club out on the Thomasville Road. I used to go hear her. If you have a question about the store, she can answer it. But don't expect more from her."

Yvette didn't fit either, but in a good way. Maybe not fitting was fine if you did it well.

Chloe watched Yvette card someone buying alcohol. A driver's license, insignia of adulthood, she wanted that. First she needed to learn to drive.

"You want me to teach you?" Yvette asked.

"I don't even have a learner's permit."

Yvette waved her hand dismissively. "After work," she whispered.

At closing time Chloe followed Yvette to her beat-up Renault. The seats were frayed and the passenger window only cranked halfway down. Yvette started the car and drove south, changing radio stations constantly. Whitney Houston, Céline

Dion, Madonna, Spice Girls, she sang with them and flipped past male voices. The highway, a glitter-studded strip baking in the sun, passed little side roads that disappeared into pine land.

"Choose a road," Yvette said. Chloe pointed to the next one, Lace Lane, and Yvette turned sharply into the woods, pulled over, parked, and walked around to the passenger's side, waving Chloe over.

"This one is the gas, you know that? You give it gas, let up on the clutch, there, a little bit easy, and move the stick smoothly."

The gears of the old car resisted. Chloe struggled with the clutch until a nasty grinding noise drowned out the radio, and Yvette threw her hands up. She leaned close, put her hand on the gearshift with Chloe's. Chloe smelled her perfume, something French she assumed. She tried shifting again, Yvette's hand on hers. Yvette applauded. *"Bon!"*

The car lurched several times then purred slowly up the road as she moved from first to second to third gear with Yvette's help. Pine land gave way to small plots of fenced property, a few houses scattered between acres of trees, a grey horse, two scrawny goats. When the pavement narrowed at a stone bridge, Yvette said she'd take over.

"See? Not so hard. You feel it with your body. You drive a car like you play a cello."

"You play the cello?"

"No, of course not. I just mean, like, you imagine it.

The next time Yvette took her driving the Renault sputtered again, halted, and leapt forward a few times, the gears mulish, but Yvette directed her while she fiddled with the radio, switching between a jazz station and rock, then turned the radio off and began to sing, "Ooh, ooh, ooh, what a little moonlight can do. Da-da-da." Chloe's shifting smoothed out; she felt a little confidence. Yvette was right, driving wasn't so hard.

"I have all the Billie Holiday records," Yvette said. "Etta James. Ma Rainey. Buy them for yourself. That's how to learn about life. The blues, full of naughty little secrets you need to know."

Chloe dreamed about Yvette that night. They were in Paris, driving.

———

Her third week, a tall blond guy, clean-shaven, approached the counter and asked for a pint of orzo salad. She spooned it into a plastic container.

"Let's throw in some dolmas too. Six. You're new here. I'm Jamie. And you are?"

"Chloe." She wiped the edge of the orzo bowl, resettled it in the case and and turned to weigh his carton. When she looked back he was grinning. She didn't mean to smile at him—girls probably did that all the time. She re-adjusted dishes in the case, almost spilling one, and thought of Yvette. "What?"

"You. I've come here since I was eleven, picking up stuff for my mother. You're a nice addition."

Chloe pictured his mother: one of the well-dressed, entitled, designer purse types Yvette ignored. She scanned his face. She wasn't in his league, but he didn't look so arrogant. Sincere, actually.

"I'd have remembered you. I wanted to say hello, welcome."

"Thanks."

"So, Chloe, just working for the summer?"

She nodded. He reminded her of popular guys in her school. Boys who showed sly interest, but did not date her. A class thing, she knew—her family wasn't up to theirs.

"So maybe we could grab dinner? Sometime."

Startled, she stepped back, pursed her lips and turned away to think.

"I'm a nice guy, I promise. So, maybe? Thursday?"

She wavered, then nodded.

"Where do you live? I'll pick you up."

"I'll be here. I finish at six-thirty."

"Six-thirty. See you Thursday." He touched his hand to his forehead, almost a salute, then waved and left.

She didn't want him coming to her house. She'd tell her parents she'd be home late, and they wouldn't ask why. She looked at Yvette who dipped her chin and gave Chloe a knowing look.

Six o'clock on Thursday, Chloe covered dishes in the case, filled condiment jars, and wiped them down. She told Simon she was meeting someone and closed the door to the break room. Yvette had left, but her locker was unlatched. Chloe opened it, eyed the peach-colored silk shirt Yvette always left inside. She freshened her face and underarms, redid her hair, then threw Yvette's shirt over her tank top.

Jamie waited in front in a red BMW convertible. He drove to an Italian restaurant on North Meridian. She eyed the unfamiliar things on the menu. Focaccia she knew, they sold it in the deli. She let him order first. A plate of creamy burrata came with little toasts and chopped pistachios. Linguine *allo scoglio*, clams, mussels, shrimp, calamari. Grilled polenta and broccolini. Wine. Delicious, all of it delicious.

"You like the food?" he asked.

"Hmm, yes. Now I want to go to Italy and eat like this all the time."

He laughed, sweetly nodding. He was a junior at Emory in premed, at home with his family for the summer. Chloe knew they had money—there was his car, his clothes, his ease with spending. He talked about movies. She didn't go to movies except on an occasional date, so she steered the conversation to books. *The English Patient.* Wasn't that a movie? he asked. *Midnight in the Garden of Good and Evil.* Nope. *The Liar's Club?* He'd read none of them.

"You read a lot. I'd have guessed you were more the athletic type. Nice calf muscles."

Chloe flushed. "I just ride my bike a lot. And you?"

He laughed. "I don't ride a bicycle." After he paid the bill, he said, "Want to go for a ride?"

Chloe felt the old fear rising, getting too close. "Hmm. It's getting late. I left my bike at the deli. I should get back."

He looked sideways at her. "Okay. If you say so."

Relieved, she was also sure she'd blown it in her typical way, but as he dropped her off he asked for her home phone.

---

He picked her up at the deli again the next week. They rode through town, top down, sun still hot at six-thirty. "My folks are out of town. We could get a pizza and I've got tons of DVDs. Why don't we just go there and watch something?"

She felt an erotic pull between them, like heat, like physical pressure pulling on her, making her palms damp. She should not be feeling this. She'd made out with boys often enough, she liked the groping around, kissing hard, hands everywhere, but she didn't go out with anyone more than a few times. Too many of those boys reminded her of Dee anyway, guys headed nowhere. Jamie was different. Attraction overrode her hesitation.

His driveway curved from the street past live oaks hung with moss up to a large white house, a wide porch with columns, windows bowing out. It awed her. Inside, he closed the door, took hold of her shoulders, and kissed her. They staggered to a leather couch where the kisses became longer. His hands smoothly stroked her spine, behind her neck, his thumbs on her jawbone. He laid her back on the couch, leaned over, murmured in her ear as he slid his hand under her tank top and touched her breast. "You want me doing this?"

The suggestive tone stung. She was too easy. Boys pressed her to go further, they didn't suggest she stop. She shook her head, moved his hand away. He moaned, lifted his body to gaze at her. She pulled her top down and Jamie went to the kitchen, came back with a beer for each of them.

"How old are you?"

"Sixteen."

"Maybe I misread you, Chloe. I'm sorry, but you wanted to come over, so I thought, well. Look, I like you. I don't want to be doing the wrong thing."

Chloe pushed the beer and pizza away. "I need you to take me back to the deli."

Jamie put his head in his hands a moment, then picked up his keys. They didn't speak in the car, but Jamie sighed heavily. In front of the deli he said, "I'll call. Okay?"

She unlocked her bicycle and rode away without looking back.

———

The next morning she confessed to Yvette. "I borrowed your shirt to go out with that blond guy." It was too humiliating to say more, to say he made her feel sleazy, a guy who'd never take a girl like her seriously. "I'll get the shirt cleaned for you."

Yvette poured a coffee and led her to a table though Simon didn't like them sitting down together. "No worry about the blouse. I forget it's there. But the guy, if you had trouble with him, leave him alone. Wipe him out of your mind. Clean sweep." Her arm swung across the table. "That may interest him again, but it's not your problem any more. *Tu sais?*"

"How do you know that?"

Yvette laughed. "Innocence is a curse, but a better one than most of them. Have a good time. Forget the rest."

"You don't want *anyone*?"

"Who is here to want?"

Chloe understood. No one like Yvette lived in Tallahassee.

As she walked out to her bicycle after work, Jamie caught up with her and took her arm. "I'm sorry about last night, Chloe. I was clumsy, I lost my head. My fault, but I hope we can keep seeing each other. I like you a lot, really."

In spite of the heat Chloe felt a chill penetrate her skin. She held Yvette's words in mind. Clean sweep, no big deal.

"Let's walk some," Jamie continued. She looked around— there was her bicycle, she could just ride away. "When I said I plan to be a doctor, I meant a good one, not just skilled, but a good person who's also a doctor. I try to live like a good person, but I fail sometimes. I try to live as if Jesus is watching. I don't want to do anything I'd be ashamed for Him to see, but I wasn't so cool last night."

She stared down the street. Was he for real? How had she misjudged him so badly? The money and car, she assumed things, but not this, never this.

"I'm sorry. Sex is a special thing. I believe that. But well, what can I say, I'm so attracted to you. I don't think fooling around when you're young is wrong. Just certain things are reserved. You know." He touched her hand. "You never know where things will go. Maybe this is a special thing, too."

She felt a little revolted yet couldn't resist a wish to be special. Who talked about Jesus? Dee and Kath didn't even go to church. They had nothing against it—in fact, they scolded themselves for not going. So Jamie had a religion thing. At least he knew what mattered to him. He pulled her closer. Chloe resisted, but the intensity of her feelings left her unable to think. Twilight was turning the air violet.

"It's time for me to go home."

Jamie cleared his throat, hesitated. "Okay. Whatever."

"It's okay. We can go out again."

As she rode her bicycle home, she felt herself shedding Yvette's point of view. The wrong skin. She couldn't be like her even if she worked at it. She floated, she was nowhere at all, she lacked both indifference and conviction.

# CHAPTER 2

The first time Jamie picked her up at her house, he appraised their small residence quietly and made an effort to chat with Kath and Dee. They were friendly, but incurious about what he was doing in school, if he had a job, who his family was. After that first meeting they stayed on the patio when he arrived. He always came in, walked back to the patio door to wave. They seemed surprised to see him sometimes. On a Saturday afternoon Kath came into the living room with a beer in her hand "Well, hello!" she called, as if she hadn't seen him for months.

Chloe waved Kath off. "Bye Mom. Let's go, Jamie." They embarrassed her.

Jamie drove around randomly. It was an unusually dry summer, but a downpour hit as they drove through town. Jamie swerved to the curb and raised the top. The sudden shower had soaked them through, left them clammy in the steaming air. Chloe suggested they go to Wakulla Springs and swim.

He followed her directions, parked in a dusty clearing at Cherokee Sink, then grabbed a towel from the back and finished drying his leather seats. Chloe walked to the sinkhole and slid in with her shorts and T-shirt on. She swam underwater toward the other side. When she surfaced, he was sitting in the shade watching.

"Don't be a scaredy-cat. Come in."

"I don't like swimming in something with no bottom."

"It has a bottom. Somewhere. Are you afraid of snakes?"

"Yeah. Cottonmouths love sinkholes."

"No they don't. They like dark creeks and rivers with branches hanging over them where you can't see them. I grew up swimming in sinkholes." He probably grew up swimming at the country club.

Jamie took his watch, loafers, and shirt off, pulled his wallet out of his pocket, dove in and swam over, grabbed her by the waist, and hauled her out. "You don't know what's good for you. Like me." He held her wet breasts from behind and kissed her neck. They dried off with a cotton blanket from the rear of his car, then Jamie laid it on the ground for them. Moss dripped from the trees.

Unseen creatures chorused around them in the growing dark. Soon they were back where they left off the first night, as if nothing had intervened. Chloe calculated. As long as they kept their clothes on, as long as she kept hers on, it was okay. Kissing, touching above the waist, entwining, rocking, moaning, okay with clothes on.

———

"Let's get out of the city. Take the highway south, and I'll show you this place where Yvette teaches me to drive."

They turned onto Lace Lane, and Chloe sang quietly. "Mama may have, Papa may have, but God bless the child that's got her own."

"Is that some gospel song?"

She rapped his arm. "No, you dummy. That's Billie Holiday. Yvette sings it all the time."

"Billie Holiday was a heroin addict. You shouldn't listen to Yvette."

They crossed the little stone bridge where Yvette made her turn around then drove a few miles to the end of the pavement, a rough stand of aging live oaks around them. Jamie killed the ignition. They sat on his hood surrounded by moss-laden trees, pine lilies, and wild grass. Watching the sky darken, she said maybe God was the whole universe. Jamie laughed out loud, said, "God is the universe? Nope. God created the universe, every one of those little stars and set them up there. It's all in Genesis."

She wouldn't bring up God again.

Their damp hands interlaced as they talked about the future. He would be a cardiac specialist—what was more important than the heart? She would go west to college. California. She'd like to be a writer. She'd like a house in San Francisco. Money. Travel.

He scowled. "Maybe. Or maybe I'll keep you nearby."

———

"Do you think I'm ready to try the parkway?" Chloe asked.

"Yes, okay, maybe. We'll drive after work."

Yvette handed her the keys as they walked out. Chloe started the car, moved through the gears, and turned out of the lot. She felt worldly-wise now, someone who knew how to drive, as she maneuvered through town to the Apalachee Parkway. When Yvette declared, "*Oui*, you've got it, you are a driver," she beamed.

Headed back to the deli, she said quietly, "I might be in love."

"Oh no. Now you are lost, *cherie*." Yvette laughed.

They sat in the car as Yvette pulled Chloe's hair back from her ears to the crown, took the clasp from her own hair, and clipped Chloe's. "It shows your cheek bones this way. All your beautiful face." Chloe checked herself out in the mirror. Yvette was right. It flattered her, made her look older.

Only a week later Yvette didn't show up, and the silk blouse hung in Chloe's locker now. A woman named Lutrelle was in her place. Simon took her aside and said Yvette no longer worked there, but he wouldn't say why or where she was. "It was a mutual agreement. Time for her to leave. Her idea as much as mine. Don't worry about her."

"She didn't even say goodbye."

"I told you not to expect much."

It was like her, Chloe told herself. No reason to feel hurt, it wasn't personal, though she felt a sharpness in her chest, too little space between her ribs. She watched Lutrelle work the cash register. She was chilly with the customers, all business. Lutrelle was a lesson Simon had learned.

———

Mid-August, Jamie said he was going to D.C. a few days. Why D.C.? He was vague. If what she felt was love, then love made her do an embarrassing thing. She opened his backpack while he was getting them sandwiches from a bakery and found a letter. Dori. In D.C. She saw scattered words—*can't wait* and *missing you*—as if they were together. How could that be? What did they do together? More? Or less? Dori couldn't matter much, she thought, since he spent so much time with her. She folded the letter back into its envelope and zipped the backpack.

Three days after he said he'd be back he still hadn't called. A dark dog of a mood fell over Chloe. Emptiness again. Yvette. Jamie. Neither of them had really cared. Then he called. There had been a big family barbecue for his sister, home from a year in France. *Why wasn't I invited?* she wondered. The desperate feeling grew, and she wished she had someone else now, to make her not care, to feel equal to him. Yvette would tell her to shrug him off instead.

He asked about the coming weekend.

"Sorry. I've made plans."

He called at Beckman's on Monday. Simon didn't like them getting personal calls, but she told him it was Jamie Daniels, and he smiled.

"So where were you this weekend? Look, it's okay, if you had a date. I've never asked you not to date other people." As if it were up to him. She didn't answer.

"Fine. Okay then." He hung up, but called back, wanting to see her that night.

Chloe paused. "No. It would have to be Friday."

Friday night, he was silent in the car, clearly irritated. Chloe asked what was wrong.

"Nothing. I'm just quiet."

"Quiet about what?"

"Question doesn't make sense, Chloe."

He drove to Lace Lane. It was dark, and he pulled a blanket out. The air burdened their skin with its damp weight of heat. Chloe lay on her back as stars popped out, and Jamie kissed her neck. They fumbled their caresses, panting. He tugged her shirt loose, kissed her abdomen, kneaded her groin, pulled her on top of him, clutching her bare legs. Her crotch pressed against his erection, and she rocked rhythmically. He held her by the elbows, groaning. Suddenly he flipped her over, pulled her shorts down. Chloe rolled away.

"It's okay. It's okay." He pulled her back, kissed her hard and forcefully tugged at her shorts. She thrust his hands off, twisted them to the side and got up. He pulled her back down, held her, kissed her harder. It was exciting, and she bit his lip, clawed into his arm. He grabbed her wrists with one hand while he stripped her shorts off. She let him, and he released her arms, unbuckled his shorts. She cried out as he entered her. When she came, a hot spasm of pleasure overtook her, flushed through her body like quicksilver in her veins, more intense than when she made herself come.

Afterward Jamie stood, dusted off, tucked himself in, and walked into the woods. Chloe watched him sit on his haunches and look up at the trees. Moss hung like tattered grey flags. When he came back she was waiting in the car, turned away, afraid of what he would say. Her body tensed to stop the tears welling.

"We have no excuse, do we?"

Chloe looked out the window as he drove. "We'll figure this out," he said when he turned into her driveway. She wiped at her eyes, shrugged, and was out of the car.

They had sex again Monday night, then again later in the week. Furtive, fierce, something they didn't talk about. The third time, Jamie looked sheepish. As he took her home he said, "You enjoy sex, don't you?"

What did that mean? Was that the thing wrong with her? He had seen the ugliness in her. Desire. She was too sexual, an unholy animal, a dirty excuse of a girl. She cared about nothing, believed in nothing, would do unspeakable things.

He didn't call again. Chloe began to hate him, but she hated herself more fiercely, all her passionate feelings poured in that dark hole of herself. A smart girl, she'd turned out to be stupid. She sobbed in her room the night she knew he'd never call, while Dee and Kath watched TV. Kath came down the hall and opened the door.

"Something the matter, Chloe? You never cry. Is it that boy?

"His name's Jamie, Mom."

"What did he do?"

"Nothing. He's just gone. Back to his girlfriend."

"Girlfriend? He had another girlfriend?"

"He only ever had one girlfriend. And it wasn't me."

"What a rat. He acted like you were his girlfriend."

Kath came over to the bed and stroked Chloe's back. "Men are heels."

"How would you know? Dee adores you."

"I wasn't thinking of him. He was made to love someone and never think twice. I came along."

"Mom!"

"Being loved is more important than loving, Chloe."

"That sounds terrible."

Dee called out. "Where'd you go, Kath? We were going to watch *M*A*S*H*."

"Just wait a minute! I'll be there." Kath's tone was sharp. It startled Chloe to hear her mother put her before her father. "I never told you this story before, Chloe, but before, when I was seventeen, I had someone else. And he left, too. It's long story."

She went into the living room and spoke to Dee then came back and sat on the bed. Her face was very serious. "This boy and I, it's not a pretty story. I thought we were going to get married. I got pregnant, and he walked away. He had a life to live, he said, as if I didn't. Dottie helped me put the baby up for adoption. I don't know if I ever got over giving that baby away. When I met Damian, I told him, and he loved me anyway. You see now, how I know. Being loved is the most important thing. Not everyone gets that." Kath had tears in her eyes.

She was too appalled to speak. Her mother never talked like this. She'd never seen her cry or be so moved. She tried to hug her, but Kath rolled her shoulders. "It's okay. Don't feel bad. It was a long time ago, and I have Dee. He's a good man."

"Kath, it's starting," Dee called feebly.

"Go ahead, Mom. I'm okay."

"I know."

Her mother never spoke about personal things; now she had told her something big and terrible. Chloe thought hard about this new information, things about her mother shifting in her mind.

———————

On her sixteenth birthday Chloe told her mother that Yvette had taught her to drive and asked Kath to take her to get her license. When she passed, Kath offered her Corolla for the evening if Chloe wanted to go out. Dinner over, Kath brought out a carrot cake she'd made and gave her a small gift certificate to use at the mall. Chloe thanked them and drove off, no idea where she'd go. Kath's car was old, but automatic, much easier than Yvette's.

She headed south. The woods were dry, scorched by drought. Lace Lane. The grey horse behind the chain-link fence nodded toward her as she drove the narrow road. Being alone there was good. She could shake off Jamie's views of things. She crossed the bridge, parked. Moss shook in the trees, crickets tuned up, shadows disappeared into darkness, and an outsized moon hovered, lighting the road. If there was a God, it was surely the night sky.

Tears ran unchecked, for herself, for Kath, dropping from her chin to her shirt, hot and salty until her cheeks burned and her eyes were inflamed, an aching form of relief. As she drove home she hoped she was cured of love, a little.

———————

Her AP English teacher had assured Chloe she'd sail through SATs and win a scholarship to a top-ranked college. "You're a smart girl. You know? Aim high."

"Stanford," Chloe replied. Her mind fastened on her grades now and getting out of Tallahassee. She overlooked the absence of her period, and when she realized she was pregnant, she sat on the patio alone until late at night. She wouldn't re-open her mother's wound. Abortion. But how soon was too late? Who would help?

She cut school and rode to the deli the next morning, asked Simon for Yvette's number. He refused to give it to her, and she burst into tears. "I have to talk to her."

"Uh-huh, Chloe. I'm just not gonna do that." Simon put his arm around her and she shrugged him off, still weeping. "I can't do it, I'm sorry. Get yourself a Coke."

She took a Coke from the cooler, pressed it to her face, and wiped at her cheeks as Simon headed back to the storeroom. Lutrelle cleaned the counter, her constant tuneless hum maddening. Simon's office was open. Chloe slipped in and flipped the rolodex on his desk with her forefinger. There it was: *Yvette Doucette, 377 Myrtle St.*

She would borrow her mother's car. Yvette would help her.

On Myrtle Street she found a cottage with an overgrown garden, bougainvillea tangled on the eaves. The old Renault was in the driveway. A rush of longing for Yvette flooded her, but she remembered how Yvette never said goodbye. Fresh pain caught her, almost as sharp as Jamie's disappearance. It stopped her breath. She walked down the street before turning back and knocking at her door. After all, she'd left her a gift: the silk shirt.

Yvette lit up when she saw her. "*Lapin,* come in. How do you know where I live?"

"I looked on Simon's desk." She took in Yvette's appearance with a shock. "I wanted to find out what happened to you."

"Now you see." She patted her belly. "Simon sent me off with some money. He thinks it's his. I told him it might not be, but he didn't believe me. Oh well, I will stay home for a while with a lovely baby. Who would think I could be a mother?" She laughed. "I get you some lemonade."

"You're going to have the baby."

"*Mais oui*! You don't think I would get rid of it, do you? Please. I could not do such a thing. How would you think?"

Chloe's breath halted. "Sorry. Actually I can't stay. I just wanted to say hi, and, uh, that I got my license."

"*C'est merveilleux*! You come again. Only four months, I have the baby! We'll drive somewhere."

Yvette gave her air kisses and waved goodbye as Chloe drove off.

Kath wouldn't be able to stand adoption, and Yvette couldn't stand abortion. If she were as cool as Yvette, she'd have stayed and enjoyed the lemonade. But she wasn't. She'd have to do this alone. If age was a problem, she'd lie, get a fake ID. After that she'd stop lying.

# CHAPTER 3

Chloe's hands squeezed into fists and she tucked them beneath her as she lay in bed. The procedure itself was not terrible, but she was bleeding and cramping. She told Kath her period was a hard one, she couldn't go to school. For two days she stayed in bed and didn't want to eat until Kath told her to get up. It was difficult to make it to school the third day and the rest of the week. She rode her bicycle slowly and slipped into whatever class she wasn't too late for. A few days in early December she didn't go at all. She lost weight she didn't need to lose. The AP teacher sat her down after class when she failed to turn in an essay.

"You want to go to Stanford? You can do it, Chloe; you're the kind of student Stanford likes, but you seem to be in a nosedive."

Stanford had evaporated into the haze of her mind's flailing. She'd spent a chunk of her money from the deli paying for an expensive fake ID for the boy who sold drugs at her high school, then there was the abortion to pay for. She could no longer afford SAT prep. Skipping classes, not turning in work sealed her fate. Staying in Florida loomed, as horrible as not going to college at all. She'd have to get a job, save money. Maybe she could get to California when she was older. Chloe put her hands under her chair and said nothing.

"You have troubles. I don't know what. Maybe at home. I don't think it's drugs or alcohol. Boy trouble maybe. Whatever. But if you buckle yourself in and power through, you can do it. I think you know how to do that." Chloe mumbled that she couldn't afford college. "You can still get a scholarship, Chloe. Go to the library. Check out some women's poetry or a memoir. Write an essay on one of them." She named some writers.

Chloe wrote down none of the names but went dutifully to the library where she found Sylvia Plath, the one name she remembered, and took *The Bell Jar* home. Saturday morning she woke up to find Kath sitting on the floor in her room, reading the book. They looked at each other.

"I'll be okay, Mom. Really. Thanks. I'm okay. It's just for school."

By January she had gotten herself in gear and was churning out work again, words spilling onto paper with a torrent of feeling. She aced math tests the way she had before. Thirteen months later, she graduated a National Merit Scholar, but Stanford turned her down anyway. Even without an SAT prep class though, she got a financial aid package from Cal, and including loans, it would be enough. She was going to Berkeley.

———

Chloe flew west in late July, her first time on a plane, and watched from her window at the back. Rivers, prairie and farmland, mountains with streaks of snow at their peak. After camping overnight in the student lounge she bought a used bike the next day day and pedaled streets around campus until she found a cheap furnished apartment, an attic in a house six blocks from Cal, less expensive than a dorm room.

Berkeley felt like the promised land. Smart people, temperate weather, professors who respected her—the sprawling university terrified and welcomed her. She wanted it to swallow her whole, digest her past, her family, Florida, swampy weather, all of it, and spit out a new person. She enrolled in too many courses, and after attending an orientation at the Haas School, decided to major in finance and learn how to make money. Money would free her, literature would take her nowhere, a luxury she couldn't afford.

In her first months she made no friends, but she'd never had close friends. There was one woman she kept running into, an Asian woman who looked familiar and seemed to recognize her, but she had no idea why. Headed to Doe Library one afternoon, she spotted her again on the steps of Sproul Plaza, staring at her.

Her lit paper was on Emily Dickinson whose strange elliptical poetry had derailed her back to literature for the moment. Dickinson felt like an accomplice, secluding herself the way Chloe did. Dickinson had her garden, Chloe had cycling in the hills. Isolation altered Dickinson's mind, Chloe wrote in her paper. She pictured her standing in her bedroom upstairs, pierced with loneliness, emotion passing through, leaving her in a state of ecstasy and inspiration. She cited poems and letters to support this idea.

Her own seclusion was pragmatic, but she found a kind of elation there too.

At nine o'clock she left her table in the library, returned her pile of books, loaded her backpack, and walked to Blondie's for pizza, the night air turning cool. The crowds on Telegraph Avenue thrilled her, the crazies, the Jesus freaks (*ha, that's you, Jamie*), the radical screamers and hordes of students. No one paid attention to her on the avenue, anonymity so sweet and easy. Blondie's was loud as usual, people milling around in a long line to the counter. She waited, ordered a vegetarian slice, and took it with her. There was that woman again, jogging across the street.

Chloe wrote into the night, finished her paper. Her flat on Blake was easy cycling distance to campus, but it stayed warm even with her windows open until after midnight. She had a partial view of the Bay Bridge and lights of San Francisco. She hadn't been over any bridges yet, but she would. She'd live there.

Discussions in class were sharper than she was used to; they dazzled and intimidated her. She meant to blaze through core courses and finish her degree in under four years. Her advisor discouraged this. Well, she'd see. She knew how to power up.

The next time she crossed paths with that woman, they made eye contact—vaguely familiar, but from where? Then they were face to face, ordering coffee at the counter in Cafe Med. Nodding, Chloe asked, "Do we know each other?"

"We sat next to each other, the same history section, until I dropped it."

"Aha. That's why you look familiar. Sorry. I didn't remember."

"No problem. Elaine Chung. And you?"

"Chloe Berrit."

"Join me? I scored a table against the wall."

Chloe intended to get her coffee to go, but she followed.

"I was hoping we'd meet, actually," Elaine said.

"Really? Why?"

"Sorry. I'm not coming onto you. I'm not gay or anything. I just got the idea we had things in common."

Chloe laughed. "Really?"

"Maybe that I always see you alone too."

Chloe flushed. "I'm pretty focused on work. I don't take time for much else. And I live off campus, I hardly talk to anyone outside of class. Really. I plan to graduate early. I'll be happier when I can just do business classes."

"Whoa. Business school. Can't imagine it. Makes my head hurt. All those guys keeping tabs on you. You want to be a corporate or some such?"

"No." Chloe was put off by the question. "By the time I'm done, I'll have a load of debt. I'm going for finance, which is interesting I think. At least to me. What's your major?"

"Nothing. I mostly take art classes, but no money there. I'm not sure I should even be here. My parents. You know how it is. They want me to make money. I might do anthropology. I don't know. So, are you a runner?"

"Sometimes. I do better on a bicycle."

"How's American History coming? I was bored and switched to Spanish. Crazy Korean girl, speaks Spanish. I like that."

Chloe laughed out loud. She'd never had a personal conversation with an Asian woman before. "It's so gorgeous here. I look in one direction, there's the Bay, look the other, there's mountains. The weather is like heaven."

"Ha. No one thinks they're mountains once you see real mountains. We call them hills. And I don't love the weather. Fog gets to me. The days when you don't see sun until four p.m. are kind of depressing. I grew up in SoCal. I like blue sky, warmth."

"They look like mountains to me. Florida's totally flat. And cool weather in August is beyond my dreams. Try living in heat with stifling levels of humidity eight months a year. There are swamps where I grew up. I think a bank of cool air drifting down is exotic. I want to stay here forever."

"We should go for a run sometime, or even a walk. Fog's good for that."

Chloe looked doubtful. "I don't know. I'm staying through Thanksgiving. Maybe then."

"I'd rather stay, but my parents got me a ticket. Let's just have dinner. You can skip exercise, but you have to eat. I live off campus, too, and it would be nice to know someone here."

They ate together the following week at a cafe on Shattuck and talked about future plans. Elaine wanted to show her work in a gallery in New York someday. She wanted to live in a world of art and music. Emily Dickinson. too.

Thanksgiving Day, Chloe jogged around Berkeley too long. She was out of shape and the next day she ached like an aging animal. Elaine returned from break with a car and took them to a trail in the hills where they jogged and walked for miles. Inspiration Point. The Bay, all three bridges, spires of the city sparkled in reflected light, the water laid out before them. The hills were shades of beige and brown. For a moment she felt a pang for Florida. Where was the green? Nowhere.

Except for another dinner, Chloe didn't see Elaine again until they returned from December holidays. She showed up at Chloe's apartment on a Sunday afternoon and asked her to go to the marina. "The day's perfect. Come on. Get out of this cave."

Chloe stood in the doorway, hesitating, then nodded. They went to a park that jutted into the bay, the grass still not green. There had been little rain in this startling new climate. People in the park were flying kites, picking up the ocean breeze. A walker with multiple leashed dogs climbed a slight hill, skirting the kite flyers. Being by the water was like waking from a dark dream into light, what she'd felt when she first arrived in Berkeley. Blue ripples with little white tops, shore birds, burrowing owls. Wind blew her cap off and lifted her hair. Elaine chased the cap and set it back on her head, pull her hair through the gap into a ponytail. "There. It won't blow off again."

They talked about high school and old boyfriends. Chloe told her about Jamie and his religion thing, his other girlfriend, though not about the abortion and its bleak aftermath.

"What a jerk. How he could do that when you're so beautiful?" Elaine said. Chloe reddened. She was used to men noticing her, using that word, but not a woman. Except for Yvette. Elaine talked, hesitantly, about having "a thing" with her best friend Maggie when they were fifteen. "Neither of us are gay, but we did sexual stuff with each other, and it was kind of cool. I understand women being attracted to each other now." She paused to look at Chloe. "Women *are* more beautiful than men, you have to admit. They just are. I like sex with men. I just haven't met someone here yet."

Elaine said it so casually it shocked Chloe. A woman with no shame about sex. She wanted to ask questions, but everything she could think to say sounded revealing and uncool.

"Does that seem weird?"

"No. I just don't know what to say."

Elaine invited Chloe to her flat on College Avenue for dinner the next weekend. She stacked the stereo with Emmylou Harris, Annie Lennox, Sarah McLachlan, and after dinner they sat on the floor and smoked weed. Chloe had little use for weed in high school because it left her unfocused. She dropped her head back against the couch, closed her eyes, took in the music. Elaine leaned over, kissed her. Her lips were soft, the kiss tentative. Chloe kissed her back. Afterward, they didn't speak. Then they kissed again. And again. Elaine unbuttoned Chloe's shirt, whispering, "Oh honey, oh honey." Chloe felt her body soften, heat up. Soon they were on the floor taking each other's clothes off. Soon she was coming in a wave of awed pleasure.

Afterward Chloe tried to express her amazement, but Elaine hushed her, said it was where they were headed all along. She hadn't wanted to scare Chloe off. "I could tell about you. I could."

Riding her bike home that night, Chloe panicked. It was incredible, nothing like with Jamie. She didn't want to get into something though, especially with a woman. She needed to work, and she hardly knew her. How could Elaine be so at ease about this lovemaking? What was the thing she could tell about her? She carried her bike upstairs, pulled out her phone to call and say she couldn't continue it, but turned the phone off before it rang. The way Elaine swam openly with feelings made Chloe helpless.

Chloe went through classes in a fog the next day as questions peppered her thoughts and drowned out words of the TAs and professors. What did it mean? What did it mean? She liked making love with Elaine, maybe too much. Was she gay? What about her attraction to men? It had been intense at times. Was bisexuality a real thing? Was this just about Elaine, a one-off experience? Was this what was wrong with her? Her desire was always wrong. She felt giddy at some moments, almost nauseated at others.

What would her parents say, especially Kath? She could never talk to her about it. Her mother's small hard beauty and inner distance—Chloe didn't know what she thought about anything. And Kath didn't know her at all, she just readied her for the world's disregard. When she left for Berkeley, her mother had kissed her on the check at the airport, that was all, and said "Be tough, Chloe." Kath didn't see how much Chloe had toughened already.

———

In February the real rains came, downpours, turning the hills green. Plum and cherry blossoms blew all over Berkeley. Chloe admitted none of her doubts to Elaine as her anxiety slowly ebbed. They were lovers; she knew how to please Elaine now. The sweet damp flesh that heated up so quickly, this is what men thought belonged to them. How could what they were doing be wrong? Small doors were opening inside her, doors she monitored to be sure they didn't open too far, but then, why not just go for pleasure? The way they kept noticing each other out of the multitude on campus, like the hand of fate. Chloe believed in fate.

The temptations and distractions scared her though. Art shows, new food, flirtatious conversations, like rooms she'd never entered, psychological nuances she hadn't considered. How different this woman's mind was, Chloe realized. She'd never talked so much about what a gesture meant, the inflection of a word, never realized how variously one experience could be interpreted. *The Matrix* made Chloe claustrophobic while it delighted Elaine. Chloe shifted to loving the idea of it, the Platonic Cave, and how what seemed real wasn't Reality. Life felt larger than she'd imagined, loosening, opening. She'd never talked with anyone so much about anything, period.

Elaine took her to a museum in San Francisco for an exhibit of women artists. Surreal and abstract pieces left her unmoved, and she masked her bewilderment until finally she blurted out, "I don't get it." Elaine nodded, unperturbed. She felt the same about certain pieces, but in others she pointed to some idea at work, a sense of riot, of wildness, of clashing forces, aesthetic beauty, discovery. She drew her attention to details Chloe hadn't noticed. Discovering another new way of seeing kicked her interest higher, and she began to question the pieces more.

"We should go to New York," Elaine said as they walked downstairs to the cafe. "I've only been once. You can not believe the Metropolitan. Totally amazing place. We could easily spend a whole week in museums in the city."

"I'd love to. Maybe someday."

"Why not this summer?"

"I'll be in Tallahassee, working at the deli again. Making money for school."

"Not even a week off?"

"I can't afford the cost of it."

"Wouldn't your parents help?"

Chloe scoffed. "You have no idea. They don't have money like yours do."

"Sorry."

———

Chloe walked into Cody's Books, bypassed the finance section to skim the images of women in books about lesbians. She couldn't bring herself to use the word *queer* and she didn't like the Berkeley version anyway, too much of a flannel shirt and boyish jeans look. Women who wore high heels and loose pants, Marlene Dietrich and Tallulah Bankhead types, women who looked like men, their hair that short and wearing ties, buttoned-down shirts, none of them were her, just curious possibilities. She crossed the street to Supercuts and came out with a choppy bob, five-inch strands of hair left on the floor. Afterward she felt exposed, as if people would now be able to label her.

Underneath it all a current of anxiety sprang back on her, disturbed her sleep and waking hours, left her feeling that she was doing wrong. She plugged away at her courses, panicky when her discipline frayed. The first time she canceled a date, Elaine didn't complain, but the next Saturday she postponed her arrival to finish a project and Elaine was annoyed, so she promised not to do it again. After exams they drove over the Bay Bridge to San Francisco, strolled the Castro. She ordered a plate of crispy fish and slaw at Welcome Home. Elaine asked, "So what are we doing here?"

"I don't know. Just that we're having a good time together?"

"Is that it?"

"I guess. I don't know."

"Is this a relationship?"

The word startled Chloe—her "relationship" muscle barely flexed. She sipped wine slowly, heard what she'd said, how it sounded like Jamie, or maybe Yvette. That wasn't how she felt.

"I don't know exactly. I'm trying to understand. I admit it scares me."

"You're bisexual. That not a strange thing you know." Elaine scowled. "We don't spend enough time together. You're obsessed with getting through Cal fast. You need to live, to spread your wings. College only happens once. You know people spend five years here getting a degree."

"That's exactly why." She didn't trust that she belonged at Cal, she was anxious she might not finish, anxious she wouldn't get into grad school, and she didn't want to float any more loans than necessary. She had nonnegotiable goals. What if this "relationship" derailed her?

"I can't spend more time with you. I have too much work to do. I can't afford an extra year."

"Don't you want to come out of this human?"

Chloe made a face and stood up. "I'm going to the bathroom."

Elaine was a little crazy, taking school so lightly. She knew they were talking about more than school though. What Elaine might want scared Chloe. They quarreled over time together and before exams Chloe panicked, holed up with her books.

She had visited Elaine in the art studio only once. Awed by the huge images Elaine made, women in deep reds, blues, lights and shadows falling over them, women smiling artfully, she saw the playfulness that was ebbing between them was still exuberant in her paintings.

# CHAPTER 4

Summer weeks with her family were unbearable. How had she ever lived in Tallahassee? Beckman's was not the least bit cool. She vowed this would be her last summer in Florida. She called, emailed, or texted Elaine almost daily. Elaine carried the air of another climate. Early August she returned to Berkeley and got a job at Andronico's grocery, up the street from her apartment.

The day Elaine arrived she texted Chloe to meet her on the steps of Sproul at six. They waved wildly when they spotted each other, Chloe in jean shorts and a black T-shirt, Elaine's green tee splotched with paint. Chloe hugged her so fiercely, Elaine pulled back. "Whoa, girl. Yeah. You missed me. Good. Listen to this. I found out the apartment below me will be vacant soon. Let's take it. Let's live together."

Chloe stepped back.

"Come on. Why not?"

"I'm sorry. It's too big a risk. And I have a lease."

"Easy to sublet. What kind of risk?"

"I can't imagine it. Living with anyone, it's impossible. I need alone time. I'm too tempted by you as it is. You would be distracting. I have a job now up the street from my apartment now. I need money." Her words fell out, a panic of words. "And I'm starting business classes. I have to keep my grades up, keep my scholarship. I have to get a fellowship for grad school. You don't get how much work I need to do."

"Okay, Chloe, calm down. I was just floating an idea. Let's not ruin the day."

Chloe breathed deeply. Why did it terrify her? She looked at Elaine, her soft face, her look of sympathy. "Sorry. I just. I don't know."

"It's okay. We missed each other so much, I thought maybe."

Elaine sat on the steps, folded her arms on her knees and looked up. People walked past, some staring. Chloe sat beside her, rested her head on her shoulder. "Let's get something to eat. And I'll come over. maybe? We can talk about this more."

After dinner, they walked back to Elaine's in the dark, chilly even in August.

"I just want to know where we're going, Chloe. If we're going anywhere at all. Can you tell me something?"

Chloe looked off to the overcast sky.

"Seriously. I might be falling in love with you. Maybe I already have. You want me, you push me away. It's too confusing. I don't know if you want this like I do."

"I don't know. I don't know. I think I just need time. I don't mean to push you away. But we're too young to talk this way."

Their arms were entwined, but Elaine pulled hers back and put her hand in her pocket. "Maybe you shouldn't stay tonight."

Chloe nodded. "Okay."

Elaine walked in silence, then halted. "I thought you might object to that."

"I'm sorry. I didn't know what to say. It's new for me to think like this. I don't want to make you sad. Can't I stay after all?"

After that night Chloe disappeared for a week. She added a class to her fall schedule and worked alone every night. When Elaine came over on Saturday, she told Chloe things were so unclear between them, she might see other people. Chloe nodded. A few weeks later Elaine said she had gone out twice with a guy from her sculpture class. Color deepened across Chloe's cheeks.

"Does it bother you?" Elaine asked. "What's your story here? Are you really just work, work, work. Is it something else? I can't tell what you feel any more."

"Okay, maybe we should move in together. Then it wouldn't be a problem."

"Too late. The apartment's gone. And yes, it would."

Saturday nights were the only time Chloe kept free. When she got a B- on her Econ midterm, she told Elaine she had to do a deep dive. By finals they hadn't seen each other for three weeks. Chloe was a wreck over finals, hungry, weepy, and she didn't trust herself to be around Elaine. Afterward she collapsed into fourteen hours of sleep. When grades were posted, she'd done extremely well.

After more sleep, she got herself to Andronico's for a shift and brought home a sack of deli items she ate right away, then called Elaine. She left messages when she couldn't reach her, then texted: *Call Me!* Elaine didn't call. She ate out by herself, missing Elaine, a feeling like teeth gnawing at her gut, what she hadn't allowed herself to feel all fall. Finally Elaine texted and said she'd come by with a bottle of champagne.

Chloe bought chocolate truffles and an assortment of cookies. They'd have a little party to make up for missed time. She could think about what a relationship meant now, she could. She could be a better girlfriend. She put on the red shirt Elaine made her buy when they shopped on Vine Street. and a pair of tight jeans. Elaine arrived wearing khaki pants with a black pullover sweater. They popped the cork and Chloe filled their glasses quickly. "Toast. Exams are over. We can play!" She leaned over to kiss Elaine.

Elaine pulled away and shook her head. "These past months have been hell, Chloe. I bought that champagne for your birthday, and you didn't even want to see me. I've moved on. I have a thing with this guy now. What did you think I'd do?"

Chloe sucked her breath in.

"You study all the time for a reason. It's not just about the work." Elaine downed her glass of champagne. "You didn't claim me, but you don't even claim yourself, your feelings, whatever you want, you just burrow into a hole and study. You're like some kind of robot."

Chloe choked. "I know. I know. I won't be like that again. I've just been so anxious, starting business school this fall. The classes are so new, but I've got my bearings, I think. I'll be different. I promise."

"I don't believe you. Anyway I'm going to Argentina for the holidays. Alejandro's taking me to his home. Hah, I need Spanish after all."

"Alejandro? Alejandro? You have a boyfriend?"

"Don't act so surprised. I told you two months ago."

"I thought it was just someone you saw occasionally. You didn't tell me it was serious. You've gone so far with him, this fast?"

"And you've done nothing to stop me. I don't know if it's serious, but I know you aren't, and I can't do this any more. I'm done."

Chloe drew her hands down her face, closed her eyes. Elaine took her hands. "Look at me, Chloe." Chloe began to weep. "I'm sorry. You don't even know."

She turned away and let herself out.

———

Chloe's first night at home for winter break, Kath suggested she come to the store with her. In the car she turned off the radio and said, "Some boy again? You look pretty sad."

Chloe murmured. "Something like that." Kath touched her shoulder. A tear slipped down Chloe's cheek. "No. It was different."

"Remember what I told you before. It doesn't matter who you love, only whether they love you."

"I don't know. I wish it were that simple."

"Okay. We're just going to Green's Tavern."

They slid into a small booth and ordered lagers. Chloe wiped frost off her glass, drank the beer. Her mother seemed different. She never made time for Chloe. It seemed sadness was the thing that brought her close. Maybe she should have let Kath see her feelings more. "What was it like for you, Mom, when that guy left you pregnant?"

Kath grimaced. "Oh, terrible, of course. I don't think about it any more. Once it was a secret. I guess I felt ashamed."

Chloe wanted to put her hand on her mother's, but they never did things like that.

"I was a little rebel for a while." She smiled slyly. "I sassed teachers if I didn't like them. I cut school. But I changed after that, it took something out of me. Cousin Dottie didn't talk about it once it was done. Not that I wanted to either, but I got scared. She was my only real family, and if she was disappointed in me, if she didn't want me, I was up the creek.

"Dee came along when I was working at Dillard's. I didn't expect to get married. He didn't really care that I'd had a child. He's the one who started calling me Kath. Dottie always called me Kathie, but I didn't feel like a Kathie. Those days were just different. Shame about sex, about being a woman almost. I wasn't happy at first that you were a girl to be honest. I shouldn't tell you that, I guess."

Chloe exhaled deeply.

"Sorry."

"What were your father and mother like?"

"I've told you, I hardly remember them."

"You keep some photos."

"One. I only have one of my mother holding me and she has her back to the camera, showing me over her shoulder. Not much of her. If there were others, I don't know, I never had them. You've seen the photo of the house they had." Chloe remembered a big house on Habersham Road in Atlanta, a mansion to her eyes, white, columned, a long sweep of green lawn with red and pink azaleas, dogwood trees. To her, it was always spring in Atlanta. She intended to look for it someday, though there was no address, just a corner house with a street sign visible.

Kath had never said so many words at one time, and now there were tears in her eyes. She blinked them back. There was so much more Chloe wanted to know. No more asking though, she knew. When they walked to the car, Kath said, "You remember when I didn't let you go to that birthday party in third grade? How mad you were?"

"Vaguely. Not really, I guess. Why?"

"There was a boy going to the party whose family knew me when I was younger, and he called out to you once, 'Hey Chloe. Your mother gonna give you away?' You don't remember that?"

Chloe paused, searching her memory. Maybe. Yes. "I'm not sure."

"I never knew if you understood."

---

Back in Berkeley after New Year's, Chloe fell into fits of weeping. Her mind refused to analyze, calculate, categorize, absorb. She spent an hour taking notes from her Macro book then threw it across the room. She wrote Elaine's name on her thigh with a needle and ink, cutting the skin, embedding it like a tattoo. Her mind didn't work right any more. Another night she copied a stanza from Dickinson with a calligraphy pen and taped it to the bathroom mirror.

*Remorse is cureless—the Disease*
*Not even God—can heal—*
*For 'tis His institution—and—*
*The Adequate of Hell—*

It was like when Jamie disappeared, loss plus something old, primal, devastating, a conviction of being unloved. It wasn't just Elaine. Her parents loved her, but their love was something she could barely feel. The unloved feeling—that was Kath's, bequeathed to her as well.

She got through spring semester by dropping a class. She couldn't sleep well and had little appetite. Elaine passed her on campus with the boyfriend, sent her a tiny wave, but Chloe didn't wave back. They had not talked again. By May, she told herself she was through the worst, she'd survived again. She wouldn't finish early—an incomplete in Statistics loomed—but it didn't matter. She'd finish her incomplete next month, get a job, take summer classes.

Five months since they broke up. Were they ever really together?

———

Junior year Chloe met a Korean man who called himself Eddie, not his Korean name, and soon they were going out weekly. He made her think of Elaine, miss Elaine more. He wasn't anything like Elaine. After him, she dated no one until her senior year when she met Sam, a southern Californian in her Advanced Accounting class, clearly taken with her.

A late fall chill nipped at her as they hurried to his flat the night they first slept together. The sex was disappointing, chaste, a bit of a fumble. She was only mildly attracted, but if he could tell, he didn't show it. It didn't seem to bother him either that she starred in their classes, how over-prepared and eager to impress she was, and how she did impress the professors. Men competed with her, resented her, tried to undercut her, but Sam was proud of her.

Nice gifts from him—flowers, a silk scarf, a personal note-book bound in leather—pleased her. No one had wooed her with gifts before. When she turned her phone on after class, she found messages from him with hilarious impersonations of professors, TAs, other students. His face lit up, a delicately rising flush he couldn't control, as he walked toward her in the courtyard. She was with Sam when she saw Elaine on campus and took his arm, pulled him close.

His friends began saying Sam-and-Chloe like they were a unit. Almost like Dee-and-Kath. After spring midterms Sam took her to Chez Panisse for dinner. He looked so earnest that alarm bells went off. As he began to propose, she tried to head him off, but he was unstoppable. She thought of what Kath said: *It doesn't matter who you love, only whether they love you.* She wanted a few days to think. She went home and threw up—what was she doing? The thought of this life, the two of them, felt like the deadness of her childhood home. She was just bereft when he came along. It sounded like Kath's story.

She had a dream of being shipwrecked. Then another where she was marooned in a forest of barren trees.

She wasn't like Kath. Loving was as important as being loved.

She called Sam, and though she cringed as she said it, told him she didn't want to get married. He pleaded that he loved her, he could make her happy. Listening to him churned her insides like she'd swallowed something live, and it was wriggling. "It's just not right for me" sounded so lame. She paced in her tiny bedroom, then stood at the window, her eyes on the Golden

Gate Bridge to keep from saying, "Okay, okay, I'll marry you, for God's sake." That would be a fiercer churn.

After she hung up, she cried all morning. What a terrible thing she'd done. She had hurt Elaine, too. She just hurt people. Her mother was so sad when she hated those dance classes. And when she was caught once helping another girl shoplift from J. Crew, Kath was terrified. Saying no to Sam was insane, yet she felt such relief. She deserved to be lonely. Something was horribly wrong with her.

---

Two years later she received an MBA from Haas, with Honors, followed by three job offers. She accepted a position at an equity firm in San Francisco that gave a signing bonus big enough to pay off a chunk of loans. A steep learning curve waited, but she relished squaring away the borrowed money. Long hours at the computer, sometimes all weekend, much like her years of school, but now she would be earning. She didn't have to marry for money, she could make her own.

The atmosphere was even more competitive than she'd imagined. Everything outside of long hours risked losing her footing. She enjoyed poring through market trends and spotting opportunities; she was good at it. Twice she got lucky and identified a niche company that made astonishing gains for a few clients, and herself.

She observed how others handled their clients, which was not her best skill. A compelling smile helped, and her capacity for listening. She preferred to listen, realized people trusted her more when she didn't talk a lot. Maybe they were relieved that she wasn't trying to persuade them of anything. When her boss recommended her for a raise, it was more money than she'd dreamed of.

Chloe's life changed so fast she didn't know herself any more: a woman who bought designer clothes, ate in high-end restaurants. and owned a titanium bike. Everyone at her firm made mountains of money. Many of them came from money, but some were like her, displaced as she was, refugees of a sort, privileged refugees now.

The only friend she made was a colleague named Meera Bannerje. They were not close in a personal way, but Meera introduced her to opera, the symphony, theater. Chloe fell in love with the city. Asian people, Latin people, African people, Pacific Islanders, ethnicities and languages from around the world, restaurants, museums, the openness of gay culture. She had little time to explore them, but she noticed, absorbed. When she could get away, she cruised on her bike. Some hills were too steep for a bike, even hers, and they awed her. This was The City. One day she'd roam it freely.

At night she fell into bed with a novel and read until sleep took her. Some Sundays she took BART through the tunnel to Contra Costa County and rode her fancy bike over rolling hills that followed each other to the horizon, riding hard until her heart thumped so wildly it felt like a creature trying to escape. An urge to ride off the face of the earth, clear over the horizon, into nothingness, welled in her chest more and more frequently, terrifying her.

She needed to go to therapy. She'd known it a long time, but money had been her excuse. Now she could try it, and exit quickly if necessary.

———

The therapist she chose was Dr. Hannah Baylor. Her profile said she'd relocated from Atlanta for psychoanalytic training; that made them alike in her mind. In her first sessions Chloe admitted she didn't do well in relationships, describing her experience with Sam and the few men she had gone out with from work. When she talked about Kath and Dee, she rationed her history into small pieces, tiptoed past an avalanche of feelings that could crush her. It was five months before she talked about Jamie or Elaine.

When she finally told Hannah about her secret abortion at sixteen, Hannah said, "You tell me such painful things but without the pain. Like they are just facts." Chloe retreated. That's what was wrong with her. She didn't feel things right, either too many or too few feelings, empty as a kettle left on a burner too long.

"That wasn't criticism, but I think it felt like that. I'm sorry."

They began to navigate the internal maze of her emotions, the barricades she'd erected, until she finally wept, exposing her shame but feeling some relief. By the second year she was seeing her twice weekly, shocked that she wanted even more, that Hannah was important to her, that she cared that much. What felt like weakness to her, Hannah saw as strength.

In a few years she had wiped out the loans, sent money to Kath and Damian to pay for their heath insurance and property tax, built a portfolio for herself. Years of living in that frantic office: it was time to reckon with the limited life she led.

She volunteered with a bike club to teach kids who had nothing how to ride a bike. You didn't need money, just a cheap bike, which they supplied. She thought about how to change her life.

She considered resigning; there was no way to work less in a firm like hers. There had to be another life, and she had amassed enough to look around for a while. She asked for a leave of three months, for health reasons, she said, and the vice-president she reported to reluctantly agreed. Three months of freedom, loose in The City. A vacation she'd never had before, doing just what she liked. She began to feel glimmers of happiness as she explored another neighborhood, spent a whole day in a museum or an afternoon in a bookstore or a cafe.

She didn't want to go back, she told Hannah, but didn't know what else to do. When her break was over, she plugged in again. But after a few months the dreariness had taken over again, her world now a small space ready to close in on her. She told her boss she had to leave. He tried to dissuade her. Finally he suggested she check out a smaller firm with a more relaxed atmosphere and mentioned her to a colleague in Nashville. The Music City had a different work ethic. It was an exciting place, he said. People were looser in a culture of music.

———

She interviewed at McCutcheon in early April. Nashville was a city of flowering trees, gentle neighborhood streets. Friendly people, an active nightlife. The partners took her to a jazz club and an indie rock venue to show it wasn't just a country music town. She would be only the second woman at McCutcheon, but an amiable Black analyst named Geoffrey assured her it was a welcoming place, all about belonging.

Money flowed freely, as in San Francisco, but the town had a down-home feeling, an easier way of life, people with long complicated connections. She hesitated. Nashville was not Florida after all, and the South had its appeal. It was an opportunity for success that wouldn't drain the life out of her.

She wept as she said goodbye to Hannah. In mid-June when she returned to Nashville, the swelter of summer had hit its stride. A lot like Florida. Everything was green, too bright, not the subtle golds of California she loved now, and no fog for relief. There was also the food. Yes, sushi, Chinese, Thai restaurants could be found, but Nashville was a barbecue, burger-and-fried-green-tomatoes town. The culture felt alien and too familiar at once, liable to trigger memories. In San Francisco she felt herself on the brink of change, excited for it, but was this the change she'd wanted?

She missed the multiculturalism of the Bay Area. People in Nashville were entangled with the past, the land, and its disturbing legacies. Their voices sounded too much like Kath's and Dee's. Everyone was Black or white it seemed, and her work world mostly white.

Her clients came from the music world with a complex mesh of relationships, a new learning curve. Socially she couldn't find a footing. The searching dreams had come back, nightly quests for some unknown thing or something that seemed utterly trivial. One morning she woke exhausted after hunting through piles of scrap paper for a tiny broken piece of red glass. She shook herself when she got up. Enough.

The job weighed on her, plus the parties, dinners, client events, shows she needed to attend. There was of course no such thing as a low-pressure job in the finance world even if this one was more relaxed in manner. Her clients were different from those in San Francisco, many of whom had worked in tech and tracked their accounts closely. In Nashville she learned a lot of musicians paid scant attention to what she did with their money, while the business people paid a lot and spoke a new money language: album cycles, prorations, cross-collateralization, key man clauses, black box royalties.

Early January, nine months after her move, on a day when it was not raining she got on her bike and rode for hours, a series of hills and fast descents, rural roads near Franklin and beyond. Tennessee began to feel appealing. She'd made the choice. It was hers now.

# CHAPTER 5

The mid-January production party felt like a few others she'd attended. Too many jeweled vests and satin cleavages for her taste, and the music, soft country rock, didn't appeal. She knew no one except her client who'd financed the album, her boss and a colleague she rarely talked to. She roamed room to room for a quiet space to wait out her time.

On the second floor she found a paneled room with a big desk and a wall of books that looked unopened, a home office. Color photos hung on deep blue walls—the producer with Keith Urban at the Opry, Sheryl Crow kissing him on the cheek, musicians she didn't care about. She moved around the room, eyed the view from leaded glass windows behind the desk. Cold and rainy out there, grey Nashville skies. She liked this weather.

When she turned she saw a man was slumped into the couch, another trespasser. They smiled, recognizing fellow escapees from the chatter and boozy laughter. He was tapping his foot to the blues that floated upstairs, music she liked better. The man looked gaunt, though, and his eyes dulled, like someone who'd suffered some calamity. A man in need of caretaking. She felt almost protective, a feeling she was not used to. He rose and settled himself in a wingback chair, waved her to the couch

"Peter Swegan." He lifted his margarita. She raised her Diet Coke.

"Chloe Berrit."

Another man passing by looked in and said, "There you are." He asked Peter how he was doing.

"Getting by."

He noticed Chloe, nodded to her and walked on. Peter's eyes were damp. Chloe gave him a sympathetic look. What was he doing at production party? As if he read her mind, he said, "A buddy of mine played on the new album. I promised I'd come, but it's not my scene."

He produced music himself, small scale, he said, on his own label, Bluelight. Progressive blues and bluegrass. At least he used to produce music. Lately he'd done almost nothing.

"Hard times, huh?"

"Yeah. I guess I don't know what to do with myself at a party these days. Actually I don't know what to do with myself the rest of the time either. My wife died late spring and, well…"

"I'm sorry. What a loss."

"Yeah. Angie. Her name was Angie."

She nodded, shifted in her chair. Someone else looked in and waved.

"People here know you."

"Yeah. A few. I produced a couple of albums that charted. Gave me a name in some circles, a little bit." He looked uneasy, self-promotion apparently not his thing.

"So none of this music is yours."

He laughed quietly. "No. I've been dodging work for a while, but I need to work now whether I feel like it or not," he confessed. "So how about you?"

She told him she'd moved to Nashville from San Francisco to manage money for people in the industry.

"You don't look the type," he said, waving his hand at how she was dressed—black jeans and a red V-neck sweater. Her hair was pulled above her ears and held at the crown with a simple clip, not a fancy do. A platinum necklace at her throat. The jeans were designer and the sweater Gucci cashmere. She wore a pair of Louboutin boots, but he clearly had no clue.

"I'm sort of not," she said, "but I am also. I needed to make money, and I guess I make more now than is decent. I'm not used to it." She didn't like to talk about work. It bored people who weren't interested in finance, and she hated being cornered by those who wanted tips on the market.

"We could write a song," Peter said. "'New Money/No Money Blues.'"

It was good to laugh, and good to talk to someone else at loose ends. Forty-five minutes after they met, they agreed they had put in their time and could go. As they exited the house, a small crowd entered and someone slapped Peter on the back.

"How you doing, man? Hangin' in? I been meaning to call you."

"I'm managing."

A big woman with blond hair whispered to the others, and they turned to look at him. He walked Chloe to her car a block away. As she opened the door, the platinum clip she wore popped open, spilling her hair. He reached up, gathered it and refastened the clip. Then he flushed. "Sorry. That was presumptuous of me."

His gesture was the oddest, most intimate thing she'd experienced in a long while. It reminded her somehow of Elaine. "No problem. Thanks. You must be a guy who cleans things up."

"Not really. I just, well, you have great hair. I guess I was just noticing it," he said, looking foolish again. "It's been good talking to you. Maybe we could have coffee or lunch or something?"

She nodded, and they exchanged numbers. This man, Peter, felt like someone safe. It was almost like having a friend in town.

———

A week later Chloe met Peter outside a small building on a side street. The minimalist logo Bluelight was headed uphill on the side of the building, sapphire lettering against a striped background. "I wanted to show you the studio first if that's okay."

He toured her around, touching instruments as he passed; then he sat at the piano to play for her, stopped, couldn't think of anything to play. Instead he showed off several albums he'd produced, played a few selections from one, a woman singing twenties blues, lightly instrumentalized. "That's me doing the bass line."

It sounded good to her ear, interesting, not the music produced by people she handled money for. She couldn't stop herself however from remarking, "A white guy producing blues in Nashville." He didn't flinch.

"Yep. It's just always been my music. Bottom line, I never got over 'Piece of My Heart.' Not Janis Joplin's version, but the original one Erma Franklin did. Aretha's sister. It pierces you every which way. I'll play it for you."

As he hunted for the album, he turned to look at her. "Angie said that to me once. Same words. She said you were supposed to have a hard life to do blues." He pulled the album out. "I guess I'm there now, but I can't do the music anymore."

When the song finished, he broke it down for her. He'd drop most of the brass. Franklin's voice didn't need it. She didn't seem on the edge of self-destruction like Joplin, but you believed her, you felt it, you shuddered. Chloe felt it. Nice that they had similar taste.

"How'd you manage to get your own studio here? There's so much competition."

"I'm small, very small. I worked at Columbia a few years, assisted on a lot of things. Even worked on albums for Bowie and Buckley, but mostly it was albums with crappy overproduction. It paid well, but it wasn't for me. I bought this place cheap, created a couple of isolation rooms, and rehabbed the rest."

He waved his hand around. Computers, monitors, speakers, microphones, head sets, cables, amps, more equipment she didn't recognize. "I found some of it used, most I bought new. Once the piano and guitars were in, I had a studio. I rent it to other musicians when my work is slow, which it was at first. Now it is again."

His wife had mostly supported them once he left Columbia, he said. She worked at EMI so he could take risks, fail, get up again. He figured out his aesthetic years ago: highlight a strong vocal, pick songs with intense emotional arcs, let them tell their story. He tinkered with repetitions, altered minor chord progressions or blues riffs, looked for an unexpected element that might reshape the piece.

He held up another album. "This was my first release. I pulled in a bluesy rock group called Sidecar who played at local bars. They hadn't done an album yet and they were good, just waiting to be discovered." The cover featured three white guys and a Black girl sitting on the side of a pickup truck with Louisiana plates.

"Listen to her voice and tell me it doesn't remind you of Gladys Knight."

Chloe heard a resonant contralto growing raspy, dogged. She nodded to him. The album was called *South of Slidell*. Peter said it sold well at regional venues and money began to come in. A fan base built. He did a second album with them, one of the ones that brought his studio attention. He handed Chloe a CD.

"Take this. If you enjoy it, maybe you'll think of me."

———

He asked her to dinner a week later. Over plates of pasta, she invited him to tell her about his wife. He laid his fork down. "Not if you don't want. I just thought."

"It's okay."

"Was she ill long?"

"No. It was sudden. An aneurysm. That's why it's so unreal. She was fine, then she was on the floor unconscious."

"Traumatic."

"Yeah." He was silent, as if remembering it. She poured him more wine.

"How did you meet?"

"College. Kent State. Angie's twin sister Rosie was my lab partner in Biology. They grew up in Nashville."

"Hmm. Was it weird for Rosie?"

"I don't think so. We were buddies, that's all."

Chloe wondered. Men could be so dense.

"One day Angie and I were driving back to campus after a hike and got caught on a rural road by a tornado. We lay in a ditch together while everything blew apart around us. After that, we were kind of bonded."

"My God."

"Yeah. An act of God, I said. I came to Nashville with her after graduation. She was a creative herself, a dance major, but there was no good avenue for her here so she designed album covers at EMI. Once I got the studio up and running she helped with production. She pushed me to record Sidecar again and sold their CDs at concerts we hosted. She was a charmer. People could not say no to her."

"Close working relationship."

"Yeah. She also handled distribution, which wasn't a big job, but then it grew."

Fated. As if they were chosen for each other.

The chance meeting with Peter at that party had sent a twinge down her spine because it felt fated. When she realized he was not a free man, totally grief-stricken, that was okay. She wasn't looking for someone. There still could have been karma or destiny at work.

She believed in immaterial forces even at work because no matter how well she quantified risk and gain, political pressures, economic trends, world events, the market had its own irrationality. As far as love went, fate needed to have a hand. Though maybe fate had a left hand and a right one.

She saw no reason to walk away just because Peter was broken-hearted. Perhaps she'd help to set him upright again. A good deed, penance even. Perhaps that was enough for both of them.

———

She offered to cook for him the next weekend. He brought a bottle of Chardonnay. She thanked him, put it in the refrigerator, opened a chilled French white. and poured it into elegant glasses. He walked around her condo, eyed the long maroon couch, chrome and glass dining table with leather chairs. He picked up her blown glass centerpiece, touched the inlaid bone frame of the wall mirror. A huge plate glass window looked out at the city, the sun hanging low over downtown.

After dinner she opened his wine, sat on the couch with her feet up.

"Tell me about your life in San Francisco."

Chloe preferred asking questions; her skin prickled when attention focused on her. "My life was boring. I was an analyst at a large firm. It was work, work, no life, except when I escaped to ride my bike. That's why I left. Nashville's got a friendlier pace."

"You must have done something besides work."

"Not so much, but yeah, I got outdoors when I could. Went to the ballet, the symphony, dated a little. I'm a cyclist. I like to ride long distances. There are beautiful hills outside the city. The landscape's very different from here. The grass is almost blond except when it rains. Riding makes me happy. Nature makes me happy."

"I've never been to California."

"You should remedy that."

"Someday. Basically I'm a Midwesterner. I grew up in Ohio."

She asked what it like for him there. He pulled her feet into his lap and massaged one of them as he talked about growing up in Ohio. His touch gave her chills.

"Is this okay?"

"Heavenly."

"So where did you grow up, go to college?"

"Tallahassee. Northern Florida is like the rest of the South, just more tropical. I escaped to Berkeley for college. Berkeley is, well, Berkeley. Just what you'd think."

He stayed late, they drank a lot of wine, something Chloe didn't do much, and talked for hours, then ended up in bed. Their lovemaking was slow, drunkenly awkward but sweet. Afterward Peter turned away. She leaned over, looked at his face. Yes, he was weeping. She couldn't think when she'd ever seen a man cry.

"I guess I'm not really ready," he said. "It feels like betrayal. Sorry."

"It's okay. I suppose it must be strange."

She could almost feel his wife in the room. Angie. Like she was sitting on the bed with them, whispering to her. *Yes, I'm right here on the bed.*

As he dressed, threw stuff back in his pockets, Chloe didn't say anything—what could she say? She'd slept with a man who wanted to go home and be with his dead wife. It was a little weird.

*Give him time. Slow down.* Chloe felt a shiver. This man had an unearthly feeling about him.

---

Two days later he texted, asked if he could call. She debated. She was attracted: he had a quirky mind, his rangy body felt good next to hers, and he was a tender lover, his warm eagerness unlike anyone she'd met in a while. His unavailable availability appealed to her, a man who wouldn't try to rush her into a relationship. And there was no one else on the horizon.

The second time they were in bed together, Peter propped himself on an elbow. "You should know, there's another woman in my life."

She closed her eyes. She hadn't expected that.

"Not like that. Sorry, I said that wrong. I'm talking about Rosie, Angie's sister. We've kind of been joined at the hip since Angie died. I don't know how either of us would have survived without the other."

"She may have a problem with this?"

"I don't know. We're very close. They were very very close. I mean, they were twins. You can imagine. If I'm going to keep seeing you," he sat up, opened his hands out, "and I want to, then she might be upset. I know what it will feel like to her."

"Ah. Like what?"

"It will disturb her." He smiled ruefully. "She'll be scared and that will make her difficult. She'll be testy. Rosie can bite. She's doesn't get her impact on people sometimes. I don't want her to be scared. I want her to like you."

"Scared?"

"Scared I'll disappear on her."

Chloe's stomach flipped a little. Once she wanted a sister the way other children wanted a trip to Disney World. She felt a pang of envy that this woman had such a sister. She found it hard simply to be friends with women. It didn't sound like she and Rosie would be friends, though. She just liked hearing Peter say he wanted to keep seeing her.

———

Peter was in fact looking better, his posture straighter, and his torso filling out. Saturday nights Chloe cooked. Some week nights he cooked for her. He confessed he hadn't eaten real meals except when Rosie made dinner for him.

"She doesn't cook much," he said. "Too depressed now. But she's got a kid to feed and has to throw something together. Rice, vegetables from the freezer, hot dogs, pasta with a jar of sauce, it doesn't matter to me. I just want the company. I hang out with them too much, maybe. Rosie knows what I feel. She doesn't care if I'm functional."

Whenever Rosie called he answered no matter what he and Chloe were doing. "Sorry. I just worry about her," he said once after he'd left the room to take a call. "She's so lost now, without Angie. You can imagine. They were like each other's missing half." He rocked his hand back and forth between them. "She's not doing great. I want her to be okay, and she's not."

Of course she's not, Chloe thought. You're not okay, either. She never called Peter when he was with Rosie, not if she knew. When she did, inadvertently, he was clipped, and she got off the phone quickly. Roseanne's presence loomed like an invisible piece furniture in the room, easy to collide with.

It doesn't matter to me, she told herself. She was in no hurry. A bit of a challenge, but maybe she could draw out the toxin of grief. And he never called her a beauty, a word that filled her with suspicion. It helped him to talk about Angie. She wanted him to know there was space for that with her.

Was it good for her? Sometimes it toyed with the old wound, rejection, made it bleed a little. Therapy had taught her to feel it, soothe it, know that it was infected by someone else's loss. He knew little of her history, Sam being the only relationship she told him about. She liked that, and she liked a man who could cry. When his tears brimmed, she put her arm around him.

"This is okay for you?" he always asked.

"It's okay."

His memories of Angie were so evocative she felt her presence, nudging her to keep him talking, as if Angie liked hearing him talk about her.

They walked at Radnor Lake, a nature preserve, on Sundays when weather was good. Bare limbs of trees looked fragile in February, but by March they'd started leafing out. Small hawks shot through overhead branches, a turtle nudged another one off a log. Waterfowl that wintered-over were still around in early spring.

Peter kissed her when they claimed a bench, and together they admired the water's reflection of the wooded hillside. "I've been thinking about the best way for you and Rosie to meet. We could take canoes up the Harpeth. Willie's a pretty excellent kid. You'll like him. It won't be like sitting around trying to make conversation. We'll be doing something. What do you think?"

Chloe had paddled the Wakulla River and once gone down the Russian River in California with a new recruit at her firm. She liked being on a river, she just wasn't sure she was ready to meet Rosie. He was obviously nervous too.

"Not yet. Tell me some more about her."

He told her about Willie, Rosie's son who had had early developmental problems, and about Willie's father Doug, a studio musician, a drinker, a man she'd never married. "She's dealt with a lot. Raising a kid by herself, a kid with issues. She's strong, but breakable. After Doug left, I picked Willie up a lot of afternoons. I love the guy."

"You and Angie didn't want kids?"

He stared out at the lake a while. "She didn't want to. I counted on her changing her mind. But who knows? Maybe it's a good thing now, though I don't think so. I wish there were a child."

When he talked like this she recalibrated. He was either hopelessly grieving or a man who wanted a family. Neither of those fit her right now.

"But Rosie's amazing. I love her to pieces. She's really funny, she's great with Willie. She just pours herself out. Warm, really loving. Smart. She's a fabulous teacher. You need to meet her soon. Really."

"You think she'll like me?"

"Sure. I mean, I think so. You *are* pretty different. But we don't want others to be just like us, do we?"

She heard a twinge of doubt there. There's no one just like me, she thought. But enough. She didn't need to keep hearing about Rosie. She'd meet her. The first Saturday in May, they agreed, more than a month away, and they'd do the canoe trip. It will be a good day, he insisted.

She had learned to swim with sharks in school and at work. Rosie wasn't a shark, but the thought of meeting her made nervous. After all, Peter idolized her. The morning of the trip she braided her hair, feeling some confidence, but under her shorts she wore a bathing suit. If it got too hot, she could always flee to the water.

# PART TWO

# IT DOESN'T MATTER WHAT YOU BELIEVE

# CHAPTER 6

Twins were not expected. Their birth overwhelmed Ruth, but everyone else found them adorable. Angela and Roseanne. An angel and a rose, Grandmother called them. Easy toddlers, they hardly quarreled, and when they did, one cried until the other cried, and soon they resumed playing. Grownups loved that. Rosie's hair was dark and curly, Angie's lighter, a bit less curly. People treated them as special because they were twins.

When she was four, Rosie's mother explained that twins can't actually be born together—one baby comes first, then the next one. The news disturbed her. Angie was older, ahead of her. But because she was four, she forgot about it for a long time.

At seven Angie put lipstick and mascara on Rosie, pinned her hair up in a messy do, and posed her in front of their mother's mirror. "Look at you, you're a peach!" That was what their father Frank said to Ruth.

That year they discovered freedom, riding their bicycles everywhere, skimming neighborhood streets with a sense of abandon. A few miles from the house where a stream flowed through a wooded area, they found a hidden place and constructed a shelter out of fallen limbs, the floor carpeted by pine straw with a large oak as the back wall. Ferns, teaberry, trillium grew among the trees and mossy rocks. Their private den.

"We'll hide out here," said Angie, as if she knew time would pull them apart. No school, no parents, no chores, they'd only do what they wanted to do.

They spent almost wordless hours in the woods near their hideout. In summer, trees offered delicious shade and when it rained, shelter. They stored treasures inside their hut but preferred to be out in the woods. Rosie lay on pine straw looking up through the leaves for bird nests. Angie stroked her hair, privately marveling at its corkscrew turns, how tangled and deep brown the curls were. When Rosie sat behind Angie she picked through her waves, searching out lighter strands with her fingers, fascinated by a wisp of red, the smooth, silky feel of it. The mystery of each other's hair, when the rest of them was so much alike, proved they were not actually the same.

They gathered wood for no reason, picked tiny flowers, made up names for bird calls they recognized. They chased chipmunks, tracked a rabbit to its hole, and sat quietly to watch a raccoon family fish in the stream. When one girl touched the other's arm, she knew there was something to see.

Rosie stole a pack of cigarettes the next-door neighbor left on his porch, and Angie fished matches out of a kitchen drawer. They rode to the woods to smoke them.

"Tastes awful," Angie said, throwing a lit cigarette in the stream.

"I know, but let's try one more and see if it's any better," Rosie said.

When she broke an antique porcelain cup their mother loved, Angie buried the pieces near their den.

Ruth sent them to ballet classes, obligatory for girls, she thought. Angie took to it immediately, her natural grace and musicality propelling her through the routines. Near-perfect pliés drew the teacher's admiration, and she began to focus on Angie. Rosie found ballet boring—too repetitive. She'd rather be outdoors. At the end of the first year she announced she was quitting, hoping Angie would do the same. Angie was disappointed because she loved the classes. In fact she wanted to take lessons twice a week. She brushed Rosie's chin lightly. "You'll be okay if I go without you?"

Rosie turned away. "Of course."

She thought of it as their first breach.

Outside of ballet classes they were still inseparable until they were twelve and Angie began developing breasts. Rosie showed no signs of puberty, flat-chested in her T-shirts and bathing suit. Angie's body became a stranger's, with hair in secret places and the slender mystery of some female charm Rosie didn't have. Clothes no longer fit both of them. It was the second breach.

Rosie remembered then that Angie was born first. It did matter! Somehow she'd missed out. Her mother assured Rosie her body would change, but she saw no signs. She rode her bike alone, while Angie spent summer days at a neighbor's pool in a red two-piece bathing suit. Boys flocked to her as if she emitted a powerful pheromone.

Things changed. Angie became more aloof. She kept a blue diary locked with a tiny key and wouldn't tell Rosie where she kept it or what she wrote in it. They had separate rooms now, and Rosie wouldn't stoop to searching her room, preferring to act like she didn't care. She practiced not caring, but she was not good at it. When Angie got a phone call and took the phone from the downstairs hall into the coat closet so no one could hear her, a dark mood fell over her. She became spiky with Angie, sulky with Ruth.

She'd heard a friend's mother say that second-born children were more trouble. No wonder.

A few months later puberty seized Rosie. Curvier, brasher than Angie, she attracted boys herself. She wanted to be different from Angie now and studied herself in the mirror, saw soulful eyes, a sexy mouth. She bought a black bra with her allowance since Ruth wouldn't buy one, got her ears pierced and wore a pair of red studs every day. She bought products at the drug store to straighten her hair, but she left it on too long and her hair turned to straw. She had to cut it short, and soon it was a mop of curls again, nothing like the long straight hair other girls wore.

That was the year the family fractured. Ruth discovered Frank was having an affair with a young, very blonde country rock singer who came through his office at Sony. Within the week, he was moving out, and she was talking divorce. Rosie exploded at him as he packed his suitcase. "I'll never forgive you. You ruined everything. You must not love any of us." Angie came down the hall to intervene. "Leave him alone," she hissed. "Better not to even speak to him." Ruth, Rosie and Angie took turns weeping, but Rosie stayed angry longer than anyone. Their family had been a good family. How could he leave it?

At fifteen she had her first boyfriend, a thin blond junior named Harry on the debate team. Competition sprang up between her and Angie, intense and exciting. When Rosie came home with love bites on her neck, she asked Angie if she could borrow her black turtleneck and made sure Angie saw why. Angie sat her down and said in a serious tone, "You need to watch your reputation, Rosie. Boys talk."

---

Rosie discovered that working with numbers made the mayhem inside her settle down. Numbers followed rules you could grasp, puzzles you could solve. Mrs. Senter, who taught her to love even trigonometry, had gone to Kent State and offered to write a strong recommendation for her. Rosie searched the Kent website for a dance program: they had a great performance space and an audition could put Angie in Advanced Placement classes. Angie agreed—Kent, Ohio was far enough from childhood, close enough to drive home. In August Ruth drove them to college together. Rosie had cooled about her father but hadn't totally forgiven him, and she didn't want him to come. No tearful goodbye for him.

They were assigned different dorms. Before the year was over, Angie walked off campus and scouted adjacent neighborhoods until she spotted a handwritten sign in the window of an old house: "Apartment for Rent." It was a two-bedroom flat on the second floor with soiled wallpaper and an out-dated kitchen. They could get out of the dorm. Frank drove up with a truckload of old furniture and helped them settle in.

Their third year Rosie was paired in Biology lab with another junior named Peter Swegan, a music major from Cincinnati. She felt a little attraction—he was lanky, a sweet, dirty blond guy with heavy lidded blue eyes who reminded her of Harry. He hated the messy parts of lab, the sectioning into guts, deciphering squiggles on slides, which didn't bother her, and she told him to call her Rosie, not Roseanne, as she assisted him. After they put their tools away the third week he invited her for coffee.

They walked into town, the chill of fall trickling in, delicious crispness while the trees were still lush. Peter bought drip coffee for himself, a mocha latte for her. He asked what she knew about the music business in Nashville. She gave him a knowing look: so that's what this was about.

"Nashville's tough. My father's a marketing director for Sony. He always says, don't bother trying to break in there. Every other person on the street is a songwriter, a singer, a guitarist, something. I dated a musician for a while who wasn't bad at all, but he plateaued, just private gigs and a little studio work. Mostly you rely on day jobs. Sorry. Learn to do the tech stuff and try for a position at a big studio. Not enough folks have those skills."

Their hometowns were not so far apart geographically, but they came from different cultures. Tennessee was the rowdy South, Ohio the reserved Midwest. He grew up in a family with German-Swedish heritage, Democrats and Lutherans, observant but not zealous about either. She asked what he was like in high school.

"Not much to tell, really. I was a pretty good kid, got decent grades. I wasn't hugely popular, but I had friends." He sealed himself in his room to smoke weed and play music. "Weed, there was that. I made playlists and mash-ups. Learned bass guitar and keyboard. I haunted the music scene in Cincinnati. Mostly rock and heavy punk, but I found a blues club and fell in love with it. I spent so much time there they let me assist with the sound system. Basically, I was stoned a lot. How about you?"

The Fells were Anglo-Scotch, and her people were not religious. "I have a twin sister, Angie. She's my best friend, too, and she's here at Kent. We were a good family until my parents divorced. My father had an affair. Do men always keep an eye out for other women?" she asked.

"Whoa," he stammered. "I don't."

"Anyway, I love Nashville. I love living in a city all about music. The air is so sweet all spring. Fall is gorgeous, winter not too bad. Summers, you die. Now tell me something juicy. What was your worst moment as a teenager?"

"Hah. Why would I tell you that?"

"We're friends. Friends tell things. You know. Secrets. I'll tell you one. I did cocaine twice and hated it. Honest to God, it made me anxious, not high. I only tried it the second time because I was in the wrong place, at the wrong party, and everyone else was doing it. I couldn't wait for it to wear off. I'm genetically not cool. I have weird metabolism, I guess. I don't know how people get addicted. Okay, now you."

"I have to think."

"Girlfriends? Sex? Drugs?"

Yes and yes to the first two, but he didn't like to talk details. That was a good sign. He confessed that once after a gig he did heroin at a club he frequented and liked it so much he was scared to do it again. Weed was what he used. Another good sign.

Weekly coffee dates followed, and sharing notes for the midterm. She could tell he found her attractive but sensed she could overwhelm him. They were spending a lot of time together, just the two of them after labs and the occasional weekend brunch, not actual dates. Rosie weighed whether she was really attracted; she was usually drawn to guys with an edge. Yes, she thought, a feeling's growing. His laid-back cool was a nice balance. Yes, she would sleep with him. She might need to be the one to make it happen. They were having brunch again that weekend. She could invite him back to the apartment while Angie rehearsed with the campus ensemble.

They seated themselves in the cafe and ordered, then he said, "I saw your sister on campus. I thought it was you, then it wasn't you. It confused me until I figured out it was your sister. Could you introduce us?"

She spread butter on her toast, made a face when she looked in the pot of jam. "There's usually blueberry." Somehow she'd almost expected this to happen. As she spread the jam she said. "I'll see if she wants to. A warning though, she attracts guys without meaning to. I don't know what it is. She affects men that way, but doesn't seem to fall for anyone. She's never been seriously interested, even."

She invited him for dinner at their apartment, a delivery pizza, and he brought the beer. The three of them talked mostly about music, whom they listened to, whom they hated. Buddy Guy was Peter's man. "Check out Albert Collins, too." His eyes kept lingering on Angie.

———

Peter took Angie out a few times but reported that, as predicted, there was no momentum. Rosie feigned sympathy. He persuaded Angie to let him orchestrate her choreography project just to spend more time with her.

Rosie probed Angie's feelings one morning.

"He's really a nice guy." She was making coffee and turned toward her, shrugged. Nothing more.

"Yeah," Rosie said, "a WASP-y guy with some musical talent. Nice. Nothing special."

The afternoon he drove Angie to Cuyahoga Valley Park to hike to the falls, Angie didn't come home. The next day they came back to the apartment together, and Rosie knew it had happened.

"You won't believe what we went through yesterday." Angie's voice was practically breathless. "We were halfway back to Kent, and a dark funnel cloud showed up on the horizon. A tornado. It was the middle of nowhere. The sky was turning green, and you couldn't tell which way it was moving. Peter pulled off the road, but I panicked, I couldn't move, I literally couldn't move."

"I had to pull her out of the car. She just sat there. I pushed her across the road toward a ditch," Peter said. "This thing was like a train coming at us."

"You've never heard or felt anything like it, Rosie. More like a monster, coming at you from the sky. You'd have frozen, too."

Rosie shuddered.

"It was screaming. I was probably screaming."

"I pulled her into a ditch. Things were flying around, stuff was landing on us, dirt, tin cans. Hay. A highway sign slammed down a foot away, so I crawled on top of her."

"I just remembering sobbing. And holding onto you."

"It finally moved off and we sat up. The roof of a barn lay on the ground about sixty feet away, pretty intact. A tree was uprooted across the street, and rain was coming at us. It was a rough welcome to Oz." He put his arm around her shoulder, and they looked at each other. "The car was a mess. We had no bumpers and a smashed headlight, but it was drivable."

Rosie looked warily at them, at how they were together. "Thank God, you're okay. You must have been petrified."

Angie leaned over and kissed him. "I felt like I'd never really seen him before, Rosie. Things have kind of moved on from there."

Something sank in Rosie's gut. Angie had attached herself to him, imprinted, like a duckling.

Months later when they told her they were getting married after college, she felt the wrench turn. Peter had been her friend. How dare he take Angie! How dare Angie—what? Get married? At twenty-two, for God's sake. She said none of this when they told her. They looked so happy. Peter was spending time at their apartment, sleeping over. Angie stayed at his place.

"Don't you want to have a little life first? I thought you wanted a career," she asked her a few months before graduation.

"Getting married is a life." She sounded indignant. "I'll still have a career. I don't want kids." Too traditional, marrying right after college, but Angie had always been more traditional. She was always the responsible one. That was what had changed. The tornado made Peter the responsible one, and Angie had relaxed.

Spring break their senior year, she and Angie went to bridal shops. Angie swirled out of a dressing room in a vintage off-white silk gown with long, lacy sleeves, classic and gorgeous. "I think this is it."

"You look amazing in that."

Rosie was marginally happy for Angie, not for herself. She chose a skinny pink dress, low cut with narrow straps and satin flowers trailing up the left strap. She looked good in it, sexy, not so chaste. Angie studied her a few minutes. It was a small wedding, Rosie the only attendant.

"You want to look right. That's a little, I don't know. We don't look like we're going to the same event."

"If you don't like it, okay. It's your wedding." Rosie sounded pouty.

Angie shrugged. "No, it'll be fine. It's a beautiful dress."

A September wedding. The morning of the wedding Angie slid on her dress, and the stylist put final touches on her hair and makeup. A small flame had ignited inside her. She really wants this marriage, Rosie thought. Or maybe it was just a hot day.

Once the ceremony at Cheekwood was over, Rosie locked herself in the bathroom and smoked weed. People danced under the canopy, but she just wandered about in her beautiful dress, ignoring everyone, stoned to the gills. Her mind drifted, she felt herself floating over the rented rose garden and the crowd, the white satin bows and sprays of lilies draped everywhere. Van Morrison's "Brown Eyed Girl" seemed to roll down from the sky. Left behind by them. Angie was moving on.

# CHAPTER 7

Peter and Angie settled in a small house in the Sylvan Park neighborhood of Nashville. He landed a job at Columbia Nashville, but Angie found no professional troupes to join. Commercial companies hired her for two video projects, neither of them her kind of dance, and she hated it. She wasn't classically trained enough for the city ballet, which wasn't auditioning anyway. The newest company in Nashville was more theater than dance, and she didn't want to teach. She took random jobs until she landed a position as a creative assistant at EMI.

She had not left Rosie. They talked on the phone almost daily.

Rosie was hired at West End Middle School, a magnet school that drew diverse students. The principal liked her exuberance—exactly what he wanted, he said, someone eager to help raise math scores. "We're going to create a top-tier public school, and you'll be a part of it."

She had a grownup life now, a classroom of her own, a job, an apartment. For students who liked math and those who felt lost by math, she offered tutoring after school. She loved her students, and they seemed to love her back. She cracked the whip if she needed to, but cracked a jokes, too.

Rosie believed her work was significant, Angie's merely entertainment. Fine in its way, but she liked doing something that mattered. She had decided she was never really attracted to Peter and didn't understand why her sister wanted to marry him, but she envied what they had. He was a good husband.

If she wanted what Angie had, somehow she seemed to choose the opposite—guys who drank, couldn't commit. Then Doug glommed onto her, the boyfriend who put away quarts of beer, *mellowing*, he said. Rosie didn't like the word *mellow*, but she liked the way he made love, slowly, without inhibition. He cooed, hummed like an exotic animal as he stroked her body, vocalizing until she came.

"Why do you make those noises?"

"Come on. Sex can't be shy, Rosie."

They were good orgasms, worth the sound effects.

Wherever they went, Doug kept his hand on her neck, played with her curls like a child, always touching her. A sensual guy—what a sexy mouth he had—and someone who knew a lot about pleasure. She decided he was a find. He played the mandolin in a blue grass band that was not having great success, but he picked up studio jobs and Peter liked his music. They could be happy the way Angie and Peter were happy. She proposed to Doug one night as they teetered home late from a club downtown. He grinned and said, "Let's go to Vegas and do it!"

They got in the car and drove west, made it to Amarillo. Doug wanted to wake up in a sleazy Texas motel and stumble down the street to a bar, start the day with a whiskey. Just a studio musician posing as a desperado, she thought, and called Angie, sober at last and panicky. The thought of marrying Doug horrified her. "I made a huge mistake. I don't want to marry this dude. What should I do?"

"NO, you can't marry Doug. What were you thinking? Keep him in bed another day, until you're both ready to head home."

Doug was eager to drive on, but Rosie appeased him. That was likely when Willie was conceived. They drove back to Nashville late that night, arriving at dawn.

Twenty-nine hours of labor with no baby yet. The doctor was concerned for the baby and wanted to do a Cesarean. "No, *goddammit!*" She poured sweat. Angie said her skin was as red and splotched as a newborn's. "I can DO this!" Doug wasn't there. She had no idea where he was, but for sure drinking. When Willie was delivered, there was a mad scramble as he was snatched away, nurses padding things between her legs and giving her another hypodermic.

She saw Peter and Angie standing next to her, a twilight haze around them, heard the doctor speaking to them. "Low-lying placenta," he said, but she heard "low-life sinner," meaning Doug, of course.

It was odd to have a baby when Angie didn't, and didn't even want one. Maybe this was a fourth breach, but Rosie loved this little creature who slept on her shoulder and breathed into her neck. She loved feeding him in the middle of the night, even dragged out with fatigue. The apartment was quiet, Doug usually out late, while Willie nestled into her breast and belly.

For a few months she hoped they might settle into family life, but Doug was a not a father—playful if stoned, otherwise useless. He contributed money erratically. She couldn't leave Willie with him—he didn't even change his diaper. They didn't marry, they fought. Doug lost one more job, then disappeared into another studio, his mandolin suddenly in demand. So he said.

Willie showed developmental problems his first year. Possibly because of his difficult birth, one doctor said. Rosie was stricken: had her refusing a Caesarean caused his body to be this uncoordinated? The pediatrician ordered X-rays, sent her to a neurologist, who pushed and pulled at his limbs, poked him, stroked him, peered in his eyes. Willie seemed entertained by it all, babbling happily at her and the doctor. She was the frightened one. Maybe he should examine me, she thought.

The neurologist threw out terrifying diagnoses: "Odd coordination, hmmm, it could be mild cerebral palsy." Rosie looked stunned. He frowned and said, "Probably not." The words haunted her anyway. He found nothing specific, maybe just a delay, he said, and sent her on to an orthopedist.

The orthopedist ordered more X-rays. A kinder doctor she found no skeletal problems. Unfortunately some things didn't show up until later, she said, but time would tell. He might need orthopedic shoes when he started walking. That heartened Rosie. He would start walking!

After she finally fell asleep, Doug would come home, clatter through the house, waking her and Willie. Rosie got up at six to teach, dropped the baby at her mother's. Ruth took care of Willie more than Doug did.

Willie kept developing, awkwardly. When he walked at fifteen months his gait was strange. Summer, her months out of the classroom, she spent her time on physical therapy. As he pushed a plastic child's lawnmower around the house like a walker, she thought his weird little walk was getting better: he was learning to balance on those wobbly legs, to hold onto things as he moved around.

Doug showed up at her school drunk on Parents' Night. He staggered into the classroom where she sat in a student's desk talking with two parents, also in student desks. "Time to go," he slurred, colliding with a desk. Humiliated, Rosie helped him out to his truck, reached into his pocket, took the keys, shoved him into the passenger's seat, and told him to shut up as he protested.

She apologized to the parents. "That's a neighbor who's supposed to drive me home. He has a drinking problem, obviously, and I'll be doing the driving." She dangled the keys and apologized again for the interruption.

That night Rosie told him to move out. He stayed away a few days, then crept in late and slept on the couch. Peter helped her pack his things and get the locks changed. Two weeks later Doug stopped by to say he was leaving town, headed somewhere in the northwest. Idaho maybe. He promised to stay in touch with Willie. That was the last time she or Willie saw him, except for a card with a twenty-dollar bill inside on his second birthday.

Once he was gone she realized how exhausted she was. Willie's troubles made her fierce, Doug's made her angry and tired. She'd do anything for Willie. Doug was incurable, though. Angie came over and sat on the couch with her as Willie played with Duplo blocks on the floor. "You're going to be fine, Rosie. You and Willie will be fine. We'll help you, you'll manage. Remember, you're a mermaid."

A mermaid. It made her laugh. Their parents took them to Hilton Head when they were six, a beach where dolphins could be spotted offshore. They had raced far down the shoreline following a pair of them and ended up close to a marshy area Frank had warned them about—alligators lurked in there. Scared, they ran back to wait for more dolphins. When no more appeared Angie said they were mermaid-dolphins. They splashed and dived in the warm ocean until she saw a big storm blowing in. They imagined giant waves washing them into a cave on an island. Like a pirate's cave. "We don't have to worry, though," Angie said, "because we're mermaids. We breathe underwater."

———

Life was easier without Doug. She and Willie became a team. He didn't resist the doctors, the physical therapist, or the occupational therapist who came to their house twice, said he didn't need her any more. Cranky some mornings, he protested, but soon he settled into his tasks: squeeze a ball between his feet, keep a balloon afloat, walk on all fours, sit on a balance ball. Peter took him to the park or brought him home to chase bubbles, throw a ball around. Angie danced with him, teaching him to plié, jeté, twirl in his awkward way. She held his hand for a series of arabesques as *Peter and the Wolf* played on her iPhone.

Peter wanted a child, Roseanne saw it in his eyes whenever he picked Willie up and carried him around. He liked having that boy in his arms and truly was meant to be a father. Such a spoiler—whatever Willie wanted, Peter did it, bought it, fed it to him. If only Willie could have a father like Peter, she said to Angie.

He had his own studio now, Bluelight. He had produced the albums of two local groups, both of them bluesy, both good. Angie managed online media for him, designed brochures and album covers, photographed artists. He found the talent and produced them. Angie's full-time position supplied the bulk of their income. Once his label had more financial successes behind it, she planned to work for officially.

Their balance had shifted; Angie shouldered responsibility for him in too many ways, Rosie thought. Had Peter disappointed her, or was it just Angie's inability not to take charge? She liked to choreograph everything. At their standing breakfast date on Saturday mornings, Rosie's single life was now on Angie's agenda. She wanted her to sign up for Match.com, and offered to set it up for her if Rosie wouldn't.

"No thanks. I've sworn off men."

"Rosie, you're twenty-six."

"I'm not to be trusted. I don't get attracted to grownups. Maybe I'm not really a grownup myself. I don't need more drunken nights with guys I hardly know."

"It wasn't always like that."

"Often enough. Can't I just tag along with you and Peter? Willie would rather we do that." She wanted to be part of their marriage somehow.

"You don't date because of Willie."

"I didn't mean that, just that you're his favorite people. Second favorite, of course."

"It's not good for either of you. What about a father for Willie some day?"

"Someday. What about a baby for you and Peter? You see how he is with Willie. Or is Bluelight your baby? You take care of everything. Soon you'll be producing, too. I hope watching me with Willie didn't make you feel like kids are too much. You know you never grew out of managing things."

"I never ever said I wanted kids. I've never had the desire. I told you that. You didn't exactly choose a child yourself."

This was the closest they came to fighting. It was true that Angie had never spoken of wanting children, but also true that Angie wouldn't admit she didn't want another human to be responsible for. Peter and his work, Rosie and her child were enough for her list.

———

When Willie was five, he and Roseanne slapped their hands in the air and called it quits on the exercises. He could walk well enough, just looked a little sloppy. Boys could get away with that. His legs, arms, and trunk were getting strong. They celebrated with ice cream at Lulu's, then dropped by Angie's and Peter's to leave a pint of rocky road for them.

Most important, he was not like Doug. His spirit was not worn out.

Two years without drama, Rosie thought, on Willie's seventh birthday. Other kids had shunned him at first, put off by his awkwardness and habit of falling, but now they were friend-lier. No more doctors or therapists. The four of them camped out at a state park, Willie's favorite place. They canoed the Duck River together. Saturday nights they went to movies and on Sundays ate dinner at Ruth's. Ruth and Frank were becoming friends after a fashion. Forgiveness of him wavered as she heard her mother's voice lift when she spoke of him. "Don't forget, Mom. He's not trustworthy." None of them were, except Peter.

Rosie was voted Teacher of the Year and the principal gave her a fat gift certificate and a huge bouquet. Carrying home the armload of blossoms, she decided she was a grownup after all if she was such a good teacher. She missed dating and missed sex. It would be lovely to have a man call, bring her flowers, a bottle of wine. Willie might like a father for real. There had to be some good men. She would sign up for Match.com. No more musicians. No wannabe cowboys. When school was over for the year she'd think about men.

The last week of school she was on the phone with Angie for half an hour planning their birthday. Angie's idea was win-ning: an outdoor jam at Love Circle. Rosie hadn't totally given in.

"It's hard to park up there."

"You park on one of the side streets up and walk up. We'll send Peter and Willie to set things up and save some space. You can see the Nashville skyline from there. Peter's friends will bring instruments."

Back and forth they went until Rosie gave in. Yeah, it was a good idea.

———

It was after midnight when Peter called that evening. "Meet me at Vanderbilt Emergency," he said. "Angie's been taken in."

# CHAPTER 8

"What happened, Peter? You don't have a good signal." She talked to Angie a few hours ago. How could she be in the ER?

"Just come." He hung up.

"Wait!" she yelped, and started to phone him back, then cancelled the call. She sat dazed before calling her upstairs neighbor, apologized for the late hour as she hustled into jeans, retrieved a shirt from the bedroom floor.

"No need to apologize," her neighbor said, as she came into the living room, her hand up to silence Rosie. "I never sleep before one. Just go. And don't worry about things here. I'll get Willie to school if need be. You know how it goes in the ER." She picked up her keys from the floor where they'd slid off the table and put them in her hand. "Don't worry, Rosie. Really. She's too young for anything serious."

Rosie looked in at Willie, his back curled and knees pulled up the way he'd slept since he was a baby, then headed to her car. She cranked up the AC against the muggy night, backed out without looking, and grazed a pillar of the garage before she veered into the driveway and turned into the wrong lane on Dearing. The street was deserted, with little traffic until she reached 21st Avenue. Fear began to crawl up her spine.

She repeated her neighbor's words as she neared the hospital. *It couldn't be anything serious.* Peter's voice had scared her unnecessarily. She pulled into the Visitors lot. His car was there on the avenue instead of in the lot, her mother's Camry next to it. A streetlamp winked out. She opened the door before the engine was off, and the steamy night air felt like swamp breath. Urgency hit her again. She ran, tripped on the curb, landed hard on her knee.

Peter waited inside the door, his face anemic and his eyes red. Rosie gripped his arm. "What happened, Peter? You hung up on me."

"I don't know what happened. She had one of those headaches and went upstairs. That's all. I was on the computer and when I came up I found her on the floor. I couldn't wake her. I called 911. They couldn't wake her either. So we're here."

"I just talked to her. She was fine."

"She didn't respond, Rosie. She just lay there."

She tightened her grip on his arm. "How long was she up there, Peter?"

He flinched. Ruth looked up from her knitting, motioned her over. Rosie stayed where she was, gazed around. Everyone in the waiting room looked muted and distant. She shook her head, made Peter repeat how he tried to rouse Angie. Fear fluttered in her gut. Ruth motioned to her again.

Rosie sat down next to her and looked at her helplessly. "I know." Ruth said. "They won't even let me go back there with her." Her voice was shaky. Rosie got up, crossed to the alcove and knocked on the plexiglass where a clerk sat yanking her hair out of its elastic tie, putting it back in. "I'm with Angie Swegan. I'm her sister. Her twin sister. Can you tell me what's happening?"

The clerk looked too young to think about anything but her phone. She peered at a piece of paper. "I told her husband. She's back in radiology."

"But how is she?"

"Sorry, I don't know anything about that."

Rosie patted the air with her hands and went back to her mother. Peter had settled a few seats over. Ruth's hands worked strands of green yarn back and forth, rhythmically. Rosie picked up a corner of the sweater and rubbed it against her cheek, tears welling in her eyes. Her mother took it back and put a hand on her daughter's. "It's for Willie. It could be a long night, Rosie. Do you want something? Have a Valium. I took one."

"I don't need Valium. Nobody's telling us anything? This is crazy."

"I guess nobody knows anything yet." Her mother's hands slowed. She looked adrift. "It's scary. I know. Pray, just try praying. It doesn't matter what you believe."

She thought of what she'd said to Peter and moved over to sit beside him. "I'm sorry," she whispered. "I wasn't kind. You can be mad at me later, okay?" He stared at her blankly, lost in his own world. She squeezed his big hand, he squeezed hers back, looked away.

For a few minutes she did try to pray. There was no one to pray to, but it was soothing anyway, at first. *God, she's okay, right?* The chilly air conditioning made her sweaty. St. Bernadette came to mind. When she and Angie were young they watched *Song of Bernadette* on late night TV. She remembered vague black and white scenes, scratchy soaring music. She and Angie sat on the couch with a bowl of popcorn, clasping Barbies. When Bernadette saw the Virgin in the grotto, they gasped. When she dug in dry soil and water flowed, they put the dolls down and took each other's hand. The next day she decided she wanted to be holy, too, sanctified—she loved the word. She paced the school playground, spoke in a soft voice, pressed her hands together.

Bernadette's discovery healed people. She sent a prayer to Bernadette: *Remember how we loved you? Bernadette, make her be okay.*

———

Rosie couldn't sit still in the waiting room. She paced, sat again. Ruth laid her hand on Rosie's arm, squeezed it, stroked it for a while. Rosie smiled at her, but her mother's smile drooped. Only fifty-six, she looked old now. She's trying to be okay for me, Rosie thought. She knows I'm no good at waiting. She pictured a room inside a person: white walls, soft reclining couch, quiet music, a place you stepped into and were lifted out of time, out of yourself. She was all tangles inside, with no space like that.

Willie has that, she thought. He could wait like a little Buddha. How had she produced such a child? At four he played for hours by himself in the yard behind their apartment. He'd come in with dandelions, sour grass, wild onions, small yellow and white blossoms in his fist, already wilting, and stick them in a jelly jar on the table. Once she picked a new bunch so he wouldn't realize his were dead, but he spotted the imposters right away.

Now he was sleeping and his Aunt Angie was—was what? Was she sleeping, dreaming? Was she in pain? Why didn't she wake up?

Her mother noticed her jeans torn open at the knee, blood seeping from abraded flesh. She went to the clerk, asked for a bandage and an ice pack. An older nurse came in to look at the knee. "Can you walk, honey?"

She walked a few steps. "It's nothing. I just fell outside."

The nurse swabbed the exposed area and put on a bandage, waved her hand at the knee. "You'll have a big bruise."

"My knee's not a problem. Nobody's letting me see my sister or telling us what's going on."

"You're with him?" She angled her head toward Peter. "Someone'll call when you can see her. They're doing images now."

"Anything? Can't you tell us anything?"

"Sorry, honey." The nurse patted her arm and went back through those doors.

Rosie pressed her palms to her eyes. Nothing about this was real. What was real was talking to Angie on the phone. She was fine, taking charge as usual. Rosie stared at the clock's pointy arms, its lurching second hand, until the room began to swim. A sense of unreality swamped her. Which of them was in the waiting room, and which was hurt? Like the time she fell out of a tree and didn't know who had fallen until she heard herself groan.

Now strangers poked at Angie, trying to look inside her head. Rosie needed someone to talk to, to say things she couldn't say to her mother or Peter. She needed Angie. The impulse to call her was so automatic she had to stop herself from reaching for her phone. She thought of how they talked that night, half an hour. Angie was ready to get off sooner, Rosie could tell, but she hung on until Rosie gave in about the birthday plan.

"I'll find her," she offered. Her mother gave her that *don't-be-a-problem* look yet didn't say anything so Rosie slipped through the swinging doors. Behind a flimsy curtain a boy was whimpering and a woman's legs dangled from the bed. She caught a glimpse through a slit in the curtain. The woman held the child's hand. Someone needs to be with Angie. She needed to be with Angie. As children, they knew each other's minds like people who knew time without a clock, not a private language, more like a private line, invisible wires between them.

A nurse with a Spanish accent and a firm manner approached. Rosie reached for her, but the nurse brushed her hand aside. "You can't be back here, ma'am."

"I know. Okay, okay," Rosie said and turned back to the waiting room.

Her mother touched her leg when she sat down. She lay her head in Ruth's lap, a lap that once held two small heads, lying together, jabbering together on the warmth of their mother's body as she stroked them. The memory wanted to suck her back to its time.

"We have to trust she'll be okay, Rosie." She put down the knitting, laid a hand on Rosie's head. "I always expect it will be you. That you'll be hurt. Every time you took off on your bike I was afraid something would happen."

"It always was me.'

"I'll never forget that woman knocking at the door, telling me you were lying on the back seat of her car, and there was Angie holding your head and your bicycles hanging out of her trunk."

"But I was fine. I'm sorry, Mom. Don't cry, please don't cry. She's going to be fine. I'm fine." She picked up the knitting and put it back in her mother's hands. "Keep making Willie's sweater. He loves green."

She looked around the waiting room. Scuffed linoleum, a fake fern in a pot on the corner table, an outdated *Golf Digest* and two copies of *Southern Living*. The sterility of it felt almost aggressive, and the scent of antisepsis triggered dread. A sample of Nashville, minus the rich, were seated with her. They avoided eye-contact, each caught in this little spot of hell alone. Two seats over, an older Black man in an expensive leather jacket had his head thrown back, eyes closed. Gay, Rosie decided. There was a bearded middle-aged man, white, who cradled his arm, a motorcycle helmet at his feet. Others, racially ambiguous. A woman who looked like she lived on the street. A man with uncontrolled hiccups.

Radiology. She had been in radiology at Vanderbilt with Willie how many times? That was an ordeal—how did she get through it then? Over and over. Seven-year-old Willie was fine now, or almost fine. If his troubles turned out okay, so would Angie's.

"I'm going to walk around outside."

Out on the lawn she dropped to her haunches, put her arms across her knees, and let her head rest against them. She could make her way to radiology, wait for them to wheel Angie out. Maybe she could at least hold her hand. The night air had grown sweet at three a.m., heat lifting, freshened by the scent of a breeze.

*Rosie. Sweetie. Don't fret. I'm okay, just in a weird new way. Really. I see you there on the grass. Don't be scared. I'm okay. Peaceful. It's beautiful here.*

Rosie looked around, startled.

*Everyone's so busy around me. A doctor is holding something like a mask on my face. Another's doing something to my neck. He has a blue stain on his scrubs. Like ink.*

A terrifying awareness of time swept over Rosie, an electrical burn through her insides. She pushed hysteria down and called the faculty line at her school, let them know, way too late, that she wouldn't be in that day.

*Peter's in trouble, Rosie. Listen: take care of Peter. Help him.*

Rosie stood up, stared into the shrubbery, looked up at the sky. She might be losing her mind. She returned to the ER, and time seemed hardly to have moved. Peter still sat with his head in his hands. Her mother looked up, knitting again. The man in the leather jacket was gone. The hiccuping man was gone.

Maybe his hiccups just stopped. She breathed deeply. She didn't want to hallucinate again.

She moved to Peter, put an arm around his shoulders and squeezed him. He raised his face but didn't look at her. Impassive, like a stop sign. No one home. She tried again to pray, but she was praying to Angie, to that voice she'd heard, searching for the cord between them. Sitting by Peter interfered. Opening her eyes she looked at him again. She had disliked him for a while, after she liked him first—the way he looked at Angie, the way she looked at him, excluding her. She could dislike him again—all of this his fault, somehow. Instead she wanted to comfort him. And wanted comfort from him.

Minutes passed in twos: two more, two more, two more. The guy jacked up on drugs was called in. The bearded man left, his arm in a loose sling. The woman on the far wall still waited. She felt a sharp pain in her lower lip and touched it. The inside edge was a gush of red. Her mother handed her a tissue.

"What happened?"

She shrugged and tried to blot her lip. A teenager with bloody carrot-colored hair shuffled through the front door. He leered at her. God help me, maybe I'd feel better if I just slapped him, she thought. He scanned the waiting room, walked unsteadily, and dropped his head on the reception desk. In a flash she got it: the migraines. Angie had stopped taking her meds because they lowered her blood pressure. But migraines can cause seizures. God, if she had a seizure. Bad, but not as bad as some things. A seizure could leave her unconscious. The thought was a miracle drug washing through her and the ticking inside went silent, released from dread.

She sensed Angie now. After all, how would she not know if she were in real trouble? She would know. That's why she heard her. She took her mother's hand. "I think she's going to be okay, Mom. I feel it." Her mother held her hand tightly. Her new state of mind brought things into focus. She might even be able to comfort others. Soon Peter would let her talk to him, let her tell him Angie would be okay.

The school year was almost over. Two and a half months off. She and Willie would go away with them, happy days. Canoeing, camping somewhere, maybe North Carolina. The forest and mountains. She loved to cook outdoors, aromas of food and fire mingling, bacon in the cast-iron skillet. Willie and Peter would make the fires together. She'd ask him to teach Willie to fish. He was old enough, and they loved to hang out. She and Angie could relax, talk they way they liked to do, about everything, everyone. Not really gossip, she thought, just analyzing people.

A male nurse broke her reverie when he stepped into the waiting room. "Mr. Swegan," he called. Peter stood up like a soldier. Rosie and her mother pressed around him. "Your wife's in surgery. I'm sorry. I thought the other nurse had informed you, she thought I had."

"Surgery? What kind of surgery?"

"There was something on the MRI. I'll be back, I promise, as soon as it's over. I'm sorry. I just don't know more. She's not actually my patient."

Her mother sagged.

"You never told us! We didn't consent!" Rosie's voice tracked higher.

"Mr. Swegan signed papers when she was admitted. Someone should have told you, of course. I'm so sorry. We're understaffed tonight."

Rosie felt embodied fury again.

"Maybe surgery's good." Her mother's relentless hope surged back. "Whatever happened, they'll fix it."

Rosie and Peter looked at each other. He started to weep, the wrenching, gasping sobs of a man who doesn't cry often. It was brief and when it passed they sat down together. She put her arms around him and repeated her mother's words. "Whatever happened, they'll fix it."

The outside door opened and her father entered. "I drove as fast as I could." He'd been in St. Louis on business. Ruth clung to her ex-husband. "Surgery. But we know nothing. Haven't seen a doctor." Her mother hugged him a little too long and pulled him to a seat beside her. They began talking in low voices like old friends.

Peter unkinked his legs, walked to the door and went out to the night. Rosie followed and leaned her head on his shoulder. "I'm sorry, Peter. I know I was not nice to you. I'm sorry. I was so scared."

He didn't respond.

"Talk to me. We have to help each other."

"Aneurysm, that's it," Peter said.

"You don't know that!"

"They're not telling us. But I think that's it."

She punched him in the arm. "Stop saying that!"

Her body felt like she was catching fire. He took her fist and held it in his hand. That he had a stronger sense of Angie than she had, she couldn't bear it.

---

They were moved to a nicer waiting area, upstairs, private for relatives of surgical patients. Blue carpet, upholstered chairs and couches, abstract art on the walls. No one spoke much. Ruth slept lightly, Frank dropped into a deep snore. Rosie and Peter sat together on one of the couches, fidgeting, touching hands, looking at each other to see who was holding up and how. When Frank woke, he and Ruth went to the cafeteria. They returned with coffee, morning buns and fruit.

Around seven a.m. a young doctor came in to say the surgery was over. A blue ink stain on his scrubs caught Rosie's eye.

Aneurysm. The procedure seemed to go well, he said, though time would be the real test. He repaired a burst vessel at the base of Angie's brain, and she survived. He cleared his throat and looked at them with sympathy, warned there could be lasting damage, no way to know yet. She was in recovery, not awake, but if one person wanted to sit with her they could go in. Only one.

He cautioned them about how she'd look: her head had been shaved, her skull heavily bandaged, she was attached to a lot of tubes and machines. It would be awhile before the anesthesia cleared. Rosie exchanged a look with Peter. It had to be him of course. The husband took precedence. Ruth and Frank nodded.

Peter promised to come out after Angie woke. Rosie walked with him down a long hallway, through two doors. She wanted to sit outside the recovery area. As they spoke, an attendant bolted from the room, signaling to someone. Suddenly a flurry of medical people ran past them in the hallway. The attendant stopped Peter before he followed them in.

"She's had a seizure. You can't come in now. Go back to the waiting area. I'll find you shortly."

Neither of them moved. There was another flurry with medical carts and personnel. No one seemed to notice they were still in the hallway until a nurse came out removing her gloves. Peter asked how Angie was. The nurse looked at their faces, hesitated. Her dark eyes held warmth. She pulled them aside.

"It's not mine to tell you. Wait for the doctor."

"She died."

Peter's look pierced her until she nodded. Rosie's hands flew to her mouth. She shook her head back and forth, lunged for Peter, throwing him off balance.

CHAPTER 9

What her school did without her the final weeks, Rosie didn't know. She handed her principal a stack of tests to grade and told him she couldn't return. The family could bear only a small memorial, really wanted nothing, but Angie would have wanted something. Peter, Rosie, and her parents walked each other through it.

"I'll do the flowers," Ruth said. "That's all I can do." She sat on the couch and repeated that when they talked about plans. Neither she nor Frank had remarried, and now they were possibly reuniting, Rosie told Peter. His infidelity wasn't the thing that hurt anymore. Her father was the only one who hadn't cried, at least not in front of the others, but his back was stooped, his face drawn. Rosie wondered if Angie was his favorite. Of course, any parent would feel the weight. Angie might have been everyone's favorite for that matter.

She and Peter put photos of Angie on a poster board: playing in sand at the beach, singing in the school choir, a prom, Angie in a slinky purple dress. A shot of her college dance recital caught her sailing through the air, a froth of green scarf flying from her shoulders. Graduation, wedding photos in the rose garden at Cheekwood, honeymoon shots in New Orleans. Each photo left a wound. Rosie saw her future: moment after moment, memory after memory leaving her less in this world. Many photos had both of them—it was hard to find any without them together.

It's fine. Fitting, she thought. Didn't a part of me die?

*No, Rosie. Not you.*

Whispers, the voice again—she listened eagerly, and feared them. Yes, she had lost her mind.

Angie's ashes were divided between an urn, a vase, and a box, at Peter's house, at Rosie's, at her mother's, bits of her for everyone. Papers to file, people to notify. They sorted clothes and jewelry. Rosie took armfuls home. She didn't know if she'd wear them or save them or give them away, but everything held residue, aroma. A tear in a shirt from a camping trip, a note in a pocket. She wanted as much residue as she could get.

"I don't want these things," Peter said. "Take what you like, except her bathrobe. And the bracelet I gave her. On the desk." Her absence was like loss of his limbs; his memory held enough residue. He thought of her as airborne now, as in the photo.

---

"I thought people only died when they were old," Willie said.

"Mostly true, Willie. This wasn't right." He went back to drawing in his notebook.

"Where's Aunt Angie now?"

"She's somewhere out of reach. We can't understand it, but she's somewhere. Maybe she watches over us." Maybe, she thought.

After he turned the TV off one night, he looked at her and asked, "What if something happens to you?"

"Nothing bad will happen to me. It doesn't work like that." Hopefully, she thought. She wanted to believe it and also wanted something bad to happen. She imagined going in search of Angie in the wherever. Except for Willie. She had to stay okay for Willie.

The first weeks went by in a haze of things to attend to, moments of forgetting, then moments of shock, nothing real about them. She read with Willie at night until he slept, then sat up by herself, too anxious to lie down. She asked a friend to find books on death for Willie but she never opened them. If she read about death to Willie, she'd cry and couldn't stop. It would scare him. She was doing her best, but it exhausted her, trying to appear okay. Her anxiety, that was inexhaustible. It got worse, not better, until she felt herself disappearing, a sensation so extreme she doubted if she ever really had a self. She had walked around her bedroom crying so many times she might have washed her self away.

As days passed she began to feel like a truncated person, a strange, separated body after the re-sectioning of conjoined twins, like she'd lost vital organs and needed life support, unable to breathe on her own, to function independently. At best, she was incubating.

Her birthday neared, and she dismissed suggestions angrily. Nothing, she wanted nothing to do with her birthday. "Grief is so selfish," she said to Peter. "It's hard to care what's happening in the world. Things are going to pieces, and I can't find an organ in my body that cares. It's unbearable to think other people are suffering like this."

"Same. At least we can be selfish together."

Anything could happen after all. A person could vanish. The person who was your other self could vanish. There were intermittent spells of grief at first. She'd start to shudder, she knew it was coming, a sensation of someone shoveling her stomach out, followed by pain that thudded in her chest for hours. Her mind was disordered; she couldn't remember simple things: the rent hadn't been paid, laundry hadn't been done for three weeks, Willie needed lunch.

"I feel like I've been shot out of the sky," Peter murmured one night as they played gin.

"Same. Just waiting for dogs to fetch my carcass."

———

Late in July she realized Willie was starting second grade soon, and she'd be returning to teaching. She hadn't had a haircut in five months, her hair wild now, a shapeless mass of curls. As she drove to the salon on 21s Avenue and passed Vanderbilt Hospital, her body began shaking. She lifted a hand off the wheel: it was steady enough. The shaking was inside her, a rush of adrenaline coursing through. This was why she'd avoided getting a haircut, why she never drove up 21st Avenue any more.

She parked the car and walked toward the shop, the heat heavy, the worst in years. Her hair stayed in a frizz from the humidity. She heard Angie's voice over her shoulder, clear, and turned around so abruptly the woman walking behind her startled, stared as she walked around her. Angie wasn't there; the voice was in her head. She had no idea what Angie had said, the voice itself all that mattered. Angie sounded present, close, different yet the same, distant and close at the same time. She shivered.

She got a shorter cut than usual so she wouldn't have to return for a while. It looked better like that anyway.

When school resumed, the distraction of work was a relief from thinking and feeling, but she'd lost her spark, the way she engaged with students, especially girls who feared math. Work was a daily slog as she taught algorithms like they bored her, too, answered questions mechanically. Before, she'd think through a question with her students, show why it was a great question, explore alternative approaches to a problem. That was what she loved about math: look at different routes to the answer. Was one way better or did it matter? Before. Now everything was Before.

It needed to change soon; she couldn't go on like this much longer.

*It will get better. You can do it.*

---

Peter understood her as no one else did. Her grief, his grief, the same. All summer he was her mirror, perfect, like another twin. Just like me, she thought. She no longer felt tension with him. They held each other through bouts of weeping. She never imagined a man could cry so hard, with so many tears, his face wrenched up and his shoulders shaking.

"How many times can I cry on your shoulder?" he asked.

"As many as you need," she said. "As many as I need."

He slept on her couch for weeks because he couldn't step through the door of his empty house and listen for Angie again. "It was cruel for her to die so young. Cruel for her. But honestly I feel sorrier for myself than anyone else. Even you," he admitted.

Yes, Rosie thought, the same. Nothing to be jealous of any more.

*Right.*

She wondered if Peter heard Angie's voice. She was careful not to ask, because she suspected he didn't. He told her everything these days and would have said. Why didn't Angie come to him? Maybe she did and he didn't recognize her. He lived with a sense of Angie's trauma more than Rosie did. Images of her on the floor, not being able to wake her, flooded him sometimes. Like static, maybe those images blocked her out. Or Angie knew he'd be skeptical, unlike Rosie. The unseen was unreal for him.

She heard her often now, clear again, and in words she understood. A whisper, then fuller, the timbre of it, the way she trilled up at the end of her sentences. Angie. Determined. Warm. Always it knocked her back, and she'd look around, her voice so real, present, even urgent. She said odd things Rosie could hardly grasp, talked about strange weather, said there was music and light. Once Rosie thought she saw her briefly in a shaft of purplish light, like a hologram, but it came and went so quickly she didn't know if she'd imagined it. Sometimes Angie sprinkled random memories into her head.

*Remember how excited we were, packing for school, Ro? On our own. You wanted to bring your stuffed monkey. I thought your roommate would laugh at you so I hid it.*

She had forgotten how Angie used to call her Ro, how she dropped it once she met Peter.

*The blue sweater you're wearing. I found it on the back of a chair at the library, remember? You claimed it from lost and found. Shameless. Then I wore it, too.*

Rosie caught her lovely light laugh, almost audible. Why did Angie whisper pointless things? Why did she want her to remember so much?

*The night you had a history paper you didn't want to write, we watched* The French Lieutenant's Woman *twice in a row, and you made gin and tonics. I typed the paper for you while you went to math class.*

She no longer questioned that it was Angie, only why? When she talked back, Angie didn't answer. What if it was in her head? And what if it wasn't? She wanted her to answer. No, she just wanted her back. The random memories made her miss her more. Was Angie afraid she'd forget her? Never.

Keep talking, she murmured, as she drove home from teaching. I live for that.

———

Peter stopped crying with her; he was just depressed. He didn't sleep over any more and as far as she could tell, he lay on his couch all day or worse, didn't get out of bed. He said a friend stopped by and he was embarrassed to go to the door because he hadn't showered for days or changed his clothes. The friend told him to go clean up, they were going out for lunch. She worried about him when she stopped worrying about herself. He promised to get out more, make lunch dates, get a beer with a friend. He took in a few bands, sometimes with her, sometimes alone. It was good for him to see people, listen to music. Maybe it would ignite a spark. He hadn't done anything like actual work since Angie died.

They evaded the holidays except for a weak show of cheer for Willie's sake. A small tree at her apartment, dinner with Ruth and Frank, who had moved back in. Christmas dinner was simply sad. They spoke about Angie, then they stopped, to protect Willie, but there was nothing else they wanted to talk about. Her absence at the table dominated. They exchanged presents, not many, and nobody cared about the socks or the ties or nightgowns. Ruth gave Rosie a book on grief she'd liked. Rosie promised to pass it to Peter after she read it.

New Year's Eve, Peter and Rosie got takeout pizza, drank a bottle of cheap red wine and watched *Jurassic Park* with Willie again. They slumped on the couch after Willie went to bed, silent for a while, feeling bleak about the new year. Peter turned abruptly, threw his arms around her. She thought for a minute he was going to kiss her, then realized he had. Even in her drunkenness, she was shocked and embarrassed. One of them pulled away, she wasn't sure who.

She felt pleasure in the kiss. Maybe she wanted to do it again. Was this where they were finally going?

Peter went home soon after, and they didn't speak of it later, but she thought about it. Might it go somewhere? Did she want it to? She never seriously thought of Peter that way, not since long ago. But she was older now, and she needed him. What if they gave it time?

A cloud of disapproval from Angie descended.

*No, Rosie. Not that. Not that.*

She felt her, not quite speaking, hovering, scowling.

———

Early winter was unusually sunny, days that made everyone around them happy to be alive, spared the usual icy downpours of January in Nashville. Cold and gloomy was where they lived however, and when real winter returned, it was a relief. Rosie put aside thoughts of the night they kissed. Had she even kissed him back? Had she wanted to? Was it shock or guilt that stopped her? Were they both clutching at straws?

Angie had been silent lately. Rosie thought she was still annoyed about the kiss.

The second week of January he went to a party at the home of a producer he knew. She was glad he was going out, being with people. He needed to find his place again in the production world. He needed to remember what he loved to do.

She didn't hear much from him for a few weeks. In February, not even ten months after Angie died, Peter told her he had met someone at that party, a woman named Chloe.

# PART THREE

# ALMOST EQUAL

# CHAPTER 10

Rosie saw Peter's car coming, veering out of his lane as he always did on a country road. The leaden sense of dread gutted her, but she tried to breathe through it. She was farther along now, she told herself, beyond the hammering sense of loss, though pain still shook her every morning when she woke. Someone in Angie's place—he expected her to be okay with that?

He'd assured her they'd like each other. She didn't want to like her. She'd had to restrain herself from yelling, "What can you be thinking? Less than a year! You're over Angie now?" And worse, like how fucked up men were. She asked nothing about her and changed the subject when he mentioned her, but she'd promised to try today, and she would. Angie murmured to her not to alienate him. She didn't get that. Angie liked seeing him with another woman?

As he swerved into the gravel parking area, Rosie gave an almost motionless wave. He sprang from the car, grabbed her shoulders, and pulled her close, but she kept her eyes on the woman who stepped hesitantly out of his car. Kind of stunning, but not in a typical way. Braided dark hair, warm skin, full high cheeks when she smiled. Greenish eyes, thick brows, a slight notch in her chin. Nice mouth. She hated her on sight. Peter swung an arm in her direction and beckoned her over as he whispered to Rosie, "You'll like her. You'll see."

The woman straightened the straps of her tank top as she came toward them. A cool customer with that smile, Rosie thought.

"Chloe. We meet at last." Rosie willed a weak smile. "Sorry. Lame joke."

As they pumped each other's hands, she watched Chloe note the curling mess of her hair—she knew she needed a cut.

Peter loped down the river bank to Willie tossing rocks in the water, squeezed his shoulders. "Man, you're taller every time I see you. Tall as Rosie, aren't you?" The boy grinned and followed Peter up the bank. Peter gave Rosie another hug. "Good to see you. It's been weeks. You believe it?"

"Yeah. Weeks. And whose fault?" She turned away from him and spoke to Chloe. "So you're new to Nashville. From where?"

"San Francisco. Tallahassee originally."

"And you ended up here how?"

Peter put his hand on Rosie's arm. "Let's unload your car."

"It's just a small cooler. I can get it."

"I relocated for work." Chloe said casually.

Relocated. Nobody she knew relocated, they moved. "Hmm. Peter says you do money. Must be big clients if they brought you out here. Music biz people."

"Yeah, actually.

"No need to be shy about it."

"People make assumptions."

"People make assumptions when I say I teach sixth-grade math."

Willie ran up to them, stumbled, straightened awkwardly, and his cheeks flushed. "Uncle Peter! Look." He handed Peter an odd-shaped stone. "It's a fish."

Peter held it for everyone to see. "Rock cod." Rosie rolled her eyes toward Chloe and put her arm around Willie. "Peter's jokes are lame, too. This is Willie."

Chloe reached a hand out to Willie as Rosie nudged him forward. "Nice to meet you, Willie," Chloe said, withdrawing her hand when he didn't take it right away. Then he reached for her hand, and she shook his gingerly. Rosie scanned her, looking for something in her reaction to Willie she could hold against her.

"Okay, team, let's get on the water," Peter said. "Willie, I need your help." Willie ran around Peter's dusty 4-Runner, leapt up, and released bungees, straining as he and Peter hauled the canoe down and carried it to the river. From the back of Peter's car Chloe pulled paddles.

Rosie grabbed the vinyl cooler and wet bag from her car. Willie untied their canoe and trawled it towards her, but she was immobilized, watching Peter and Chloe step into their canoe and push off together.

"Come on, Mom!" Willie called. She turned to him, took the rope, pushed off and waded after. Peter and Chloe paddled well together. Her arms were muscular. Why didn't they slacken, wait for her and Willie? She and Willie were a good team but no match for them, even if the current was weak. Willie would tire way before they would.

"Hel-lo?" Rosie called. "We're here too. We can't keep up."

"Yes, we can." Willie stroked harder. Peter and Chloe stopped paddling and turned, waited for them to catch up.

Everyone was glistening with sweat already. May, a month of fiery days so far, even for Tennessee. They planned to go a few miles upriver to a wide bend with a swimming hole and a stretch of beach, picnic on the lunch she packed: tomato and avocado sandwiches, bread from Uprising on Franklin, organic carrot sticks, berries. Peter said Chloe was careful what she ate. She added a supply of Oreos and a container of peanut butter for Willie. Peter, too.

They moved past forested hills, hickory and oak, mottled greens of ash, dogwood. Peter and Chloe made an effort to stay with them, keep a conversation alive. Look at him, she thought. Happy, his face relaxed, shoulders back again. He'd gained weight. Last winter he looked emaciated, almost ashy, and walked like an old man, slow and hunched.

Soon they reached the stretch where limestone bluffs rose on both sides and the current picked up, making them work hard to move upstream. Otherworldly, this part of the river, the rocky face of the cliffs crossed with vines. Swallows flitted from cone-shaped nests. Rosie loved the sun's narrowed brilliance here, the murk of the river and its double life—the surface where nothing could hide, depths in which nothing was visible.

Chloe called out, "I love this place!"

A tourist, Rosie thought. She and Willie stroked hard, but stronger arms were clearly in the other boat. If it had been Angie instead of Chloe, Willie and Peter would have paddled ahead, she and Angie would have been chatting, relaxed. Struggling against the current with Willie, she thought how lovely it would be to disappear to the past.

Chloe and Peter were ahead again, talking quietly now. Were they saying private things? Talking about her?

Beyond the cliffs the river spread out, water shallower, the color of green tea. They relaxed as the bottom became visible, rusty ochre stones in arm's reach. A mile from the bend, the water became too shallow to continue. Rosie suggested they turn back and picnic on the other side of the bridge.

"Nah. No good pullouts for miles in that direction."

"We can portage," Willie said. "It'll get deep again."

Rosie vetoed that. Chloe suggested they float the canoes behind them for a stretch, see if it deepened. "I'll go with Willie."

Trumped, Rosie put the cooler in Peter's canoe, and picked up his tow rope.

Willie looked angelic to Chloe, a lighter, brighter version of Rosie, blond but the same brown eyes, same curls framing the same open face. Rosie had appeal. Her face at least, the sensual mouth, large brown eyes. She was pale though and chewed the inside of her cheek when they shook hands. Her mouth must be sore if she did that a lot. Maybe it was just today.

The tension between them had flipped her into business mode, her habitual shield of confidence, half fake, half genuine. She could do this.

"Come on, Willie," she said. He squared his shoulders and she moved to the rear of his canoe as they pulled it through the shallow water. She kept a steady hand on it. They trekked until the river rounded another bend and narrowed, the water deeper. Willie crowed, "I knew it would get deeper, I knew it would."

Rosie was watching her, her face shifting, as if dislike flirted with appreciation.

Chloe returned to Peter's canoe, and they paddled upriver another mile to a swath of beach, just a curve of gravelly sand, where they hauled the canoes out and secured them. Their feet crunched over bones of old twigs and chalky pebbles, littered pop tops and flecks of torn snack bags. Rosie unfolded two Guatemalan blankets. In the fluorescent brightness everything glittered.

Willie sprang off to the swimming hole. A kid who loved water, Chloe could relate. Peter had said Willie depended on adults to play with him because some of his peers thought he was strange. She sympathized. Stripping down to her suit, she waved to Willie.

"I'm coming in."

"Yay!" Willie shouted. He thrashed toward her, did a little flip right before he reached her. They slung water wildly, big splashes soaked with light, then he dove under and grabbed her feet, pulled her under with him. They bobbed to the surface, laughing and flinging water from their arms. They swam to the other side of the river, and Willie pulled himself up to an over-hanging branch, swung his legs wildly, then threw himself back in. Chloe treaded water as he did it a few more times. He tugged her under again, then she swam gently away, letting him pursue until she turned suddenly, grabbed at his feet. They had reached an area where their toes could just touch the water, so they bob-bled around like pool toys. He told her he'd started soccer last year.

"Lucky guy! I always wanted to play but we didn't have soc-cer teams in Tallahassee."

"You can come to my games. I'm the goalie."

"I will. I'd love to." Chloe suggested they float and see where the current moved them. Willie stretched out his arms and legs, looking even more like an angel. She eyed the beach: Peter and Rosie sat close, their feet almost touching. Snatches of words drifted out to her but she couldn't quite grasp them.

———

Rosie opened the cooler, keeping an eye on Willie. When he dove, his body was sleek, skinny, beautiful. He loved water, the burden of upright movement lifted. This year, second grade, he'd had his first play dates, and then he'd gone out for soccer in the spring and become goalie. He wasn't a reliable runner, so he liked being on goal. Every time he blocked a ball he was a hero. Each week Rosie waited anxiously as he jigged his legs in the goal; it was a wonder to see him out there. Peter came to most of his games. Would that change?

She prayed the days of watching children scatter across the playground when Willie approached were over. The memory of that sight still fueled an eruption in her chest. She'd learned to hold back, to pace instead of explode. She drew on the practice today with Chloe.

Sitting close, Peter poked her feet with his big toe, waited for her to speak. When she didn't, he said, "She's good with Willie."

"Yeah. You really like her, huh?"

"Haven't found anything not to like so far." He was transfixed by her out there, Chloe and Willie slinging wildly at each other again. Under the blaze of sun, beads of water flew off Chloe's arms like strings of light.

"Willie still talking about sleep-away camp this summer?"

"Yeah, but not gonna happen. He's not ready. I'm not either. Swim camp again."

"And what will you do? You think about dating?"

"No. Maybe. Who knows?" Who would she hang out with now that he had a girlfriend? His eyes shifted back to Chloe as he talked. She suspected her of trying to make everyone think she was a better deal. That Rosie couldn't forgive. Even her body was perfect.

"She's a cyclist," Peter said, as if he read her thoughts. "She used to ride those hundred-mile tours called 'centuries' with a club in California." It was clear to Rosie she was losing out.

When he told her he was seeing someone, she'd gasped. "I know. I know," he said. "I wasn't interested in dating, but it's been good for me to get out."

"Oh," she said, a deep thud registering. If she ever believed they were on the same path, it was clear now they weren't. We're not the same, you and I, she thought, never were. You'll get a new wife. I'll never get a new sister.

They still spent some evenings together, plus the soccer games, but by April the length of time in which Peter didn't call, or she didn't, had grown. The first time they didn't see Peter all week, Willie asked where he was. "Oh, doing other things." She dropped basil and pine nuts into the blender for pesto. Willie could toss it with the pasta along with the green beans. Nothing fancy, but it was nice to be making food again. She'd been such a slacker mom, nuking frozen macaroni and cheese and calling it dinner.

"What other things? I thought we were family now."

"Sort of. Maybe not his only family." She handed him a piece of garlic bread fresh from the oven. She blamed Peter, she was furious with him, but knew she'd do the same if it were possible. Anything that might let her feel slightly better.

———

Chloe and Willie came dripping out of the water. Peter stretched his limbs, walked toward her with a towel. She dried her face and a smile passed between them. Rosie grabbed Willie's towel to dry him off, kissed him on the head. She passed sandwiches around from the cooler. "Avocado and tomato? Peanut butter and jelly?"

"Avocado, please," Chloe said. Rosie passed her two apricots as well and a bottle of water. Peter and Willie took the PB&Js, apples. Oreos and a jar of peanut butter for dipping were passed around. After they ate, Peter lay back, looked pleased as a cat soaking up sun. He pointed to the cartoon-perfect clouds in the azure sky.

Rosie turned abruptly to Chloe. "Why did you even want to move to Nashville?"

She startled. "A good job offer. And I liked Nashville well enough."

"You think you'll stay?"

Peter fidgeted with the buttons on his shirt and gave Rosie a look: *You need to stop.* Rosie made a face then leapt from the blanket. "Okay guys, enough relaxation. I have things to do at home." She began to pack food cartons, throw them into the bag.

Willie groaned, gave his mother a two-syllable "Mo-om. Why? It's Sunday."

"Still have lots to do," Rosie said. "Work tomorrow. You have homework."

Chloe gathered blankets and helped pack the cooler. As they tossed gear in the canoes, Rosie eyed her. "Why don't you and I paddle together? Peter and Willie love to dawdle. Down river it's a slow drift."

Willie looked disappointed, and Peter looked worried. Rosie brushed sand from her feet, put on her river sandals, tossed the cooler into Peter's boat, and edged hers further into the water, waited for Chloe to get in. She shoved off and stepped into the stern to steer it. They synced their strokes and moved out quickly. For a few minutes Chloe enjoyed watching Rosie's difficulty maneuvering against her strength.

"Pretty warm for May, huh?" she said, and slackened her effort.

"This town cooks. Cooler in California, I imagine."

Chloe realized Rosie didn't just wish she'd go back; she feared she'd take Peter with her. That cast her prickliness in another light, one she could understand. "I'm not thinking of moving back. I love the landscape here. And the seasons, except summer. In the Bay Area you only get two sort-of seasons: rainy and dry."

They towed the canoes through the shallow stretch silently. When they reached deeper water and settled back into the canoe, Rosie said, "Let's just drift. We're ahead of them. Peter and Willie like to look for fish and collect rocks from the bottom."

Chloe dropped her paddle in the boat and turned around, gave her a sympathetic look.

Rosie trailed her hand in the river. "Peter says you're quite the athlete, a super cyclist."

"Not really. I just like to ride. You?"

"Used to. Haven't pulled my bicycle out of the basement in a long time."

"If you want to get back on your bike, I've found some nice trails."

"Thanks, but I know all the trails around Nashville. Anyway, after this year I have the muscle tone of French pastry. You know you might've even have crossed paths with Angie at EMI. She had lighter hair than I do, less curly. Prettier. Beautiful, actually." It felt stupid, bringing Angie up in that way, as if she might unhinge Chloe somehow. The woman could not possibly understand what it meant to lose someone so like yourself. Or what it meant to see someone wrong in her place.

"Peter's shown me photos. You look alike. I'd know you were twins. But I haven't met people at EMI, and I couldn't have crossed paths with her. I moved to Nashville a few weeks after she died."

She said it easily, like Angie had simply left for Bermuda or something. Rosie squeezed the back of her neck, her tension at the point of pain.

"This must be really hard. I know how close you and Peter are. I know you saved each other this year."

The words fell on Rosie like loose sparks. She panicked, words tumbling out. "I don't want to lose him, too. People really do get taken away." She shook her head back and forth, tears streaking her cheeks. "No. No more fucking tears." She wiped at her face.

"I know."

Her anger rekindled, that volcano in the chest feeling starting to rise. She wanted to scream: *You know nothing!* An explosive little sound burst from her chest, half sob, half gasp.

She bent over to relieve the tightness in her body. Chloe watched her, her mouth half open and her eyebrows lifted.

"I'm sorry, Rosie. I guess you wish Peter wasn't seeing me."

Rosie misunderstood her for a moment—was it an offer? Her perception of Chloe quickened. There was an unhappy twist to Chloe's smile when she looked at her head-on. History there, a story she'd ask about if she'd met her somewhere else, if she had nothing to do with Peter. Behind the composure was vulnerability, a fault line. She's hiding herself, Rosie thought. Holding herself together like the rest of us.

The space between them seemed to grow, as if Chloe and the canoe were moving toward the horizon without her. It made her dizzy. The sensation increased and she put her head to her knees for a minute then sat up again.

"It's just too soon. Eight months when he met you. What can he be thinking?"

"Nine. I said that, too. He wants to see me though. It seems to help him."

"You're some kind of grief whisperer?" She shrugged her shoulders. "Sorry, I'm not always rude. Just sometimes." She laughed a little. "You have no idea the nightmare this year has been. Christ, I'd date you, too, if it would help. Unfortunately I prefer men."

Chloe reddened and turned away.

"Sorry, again! I have these moments. I say things. Peter should have warned you."

She slipped to the hull on her knees, leaned over, splashed her face, dried off with her shirt and began to paddle. "I think it's the heat. Sheesh, it's only May. It shouldn't be this hot." After a breath that brought air down to her gut, she said. "So have you made many friends since you moved to Nashville?"

"Not really. I'm not so good at that."

Rosie smiled. Chloe picked up an oar and turned away, paddled steadily side to side. A shame. She knew she was primed to dislike her, but at another time Chloe might have been a person she'd like to know better.

CHAPTER 11

Rosie's bluntness was just anxiety, Peter said. Chloe read it differently. Rosie didn't necessarily dislike her—though how could she tell?—she just didn't like her relationship with Peter. She chose to believe that, because Rosie intrigued her. What she didn't know was if she liked her, or even how to know, if this wasn't the usual Rosie. She liked her directness though. No need to wonder what she thought, and her vulnerability, so apparent it was appalling, appealed to her.

She watched Rosie stroke Willie's hair, touch his arm, saw how protective she was and how easily he took it in. He was a small blond version of her except his mouth wasn't sad like hers. Rosie was a wounded creature, the kind who'd easily wound someone else in her pain. Transparent, so unlike herself she wanted to take her apart and see how she operated, a woman who attached deeply to people and let them know it. She'd never met someone who threw barbs yet was not malicious. Sharp edges, but no, Rosie wasn't a shark.

Summer, the school year over, Peter made dinner for the three of them, suggesting Willie eat at his grandmother's. The evening was uncomfortable again, with Rosie hyper-focused on Chloe and not in a friendly way.

"Nashville's just a fat-assed tinsel town. I'd think you'd prefer the Bay Area."

"It's an interesting city."

"You must miss the culture and the food out there. You've already gone back to visit."

"Yeah, I miss it, but the barbecue's better here." Rosie didn't laugh. "I like Southern food. I grew up in Tallahassee, you know."

"Tennessee people think this is God's country and California is Satan's. A lot of carpetbaggers are cashing in on Nashville, outsiders coming it, money pouring in. You know."

So Rosie thought she was a carpetbagger. It stung, but also made her laugh. In a way it was true. "That's not been my experience so far. People here are easier than on either coast. I know it's just their way, they don't necessarily like you, but then again maybe they do. Everyone's friendly. Almost everyone."

Rosie snorted. "I suppose you mean me." Peter flashed her a warning look, but she shrugged. "You think you'll stay?"

"I expect I'll stay."

Again Peter apologized afterward. "She's just sniffing you out. I warned you."

"I'm trying to have sympathy. She's afraid I'll take you to California."

"Probably, but some things she says, I don't know how you stay immune."

"I'm not immune. Survival instinct. Think of reasons beside yourself someone reacts to you. It's about them, not you. Something I picked up from my mother."

———

Chloe sat at her desk, scrolling absently through quarterly reports, when she felt a presence in the office. She looked around, feeling foolish. Her door was shut—of course no one was there but herself. *Pursue her. Don't worry about him. Think of her as a tricky client.*

The idea of inviting Rosie to lunch, the two of them, popped into her head. It wasn't her style—she wasn't one to go after someone if it wasn't business related. Pursuit was high-risk activity, walking a narrow path on the edge of a chasm. She didn't think Rosie would refuse her though, if only because of Peter.

Angie talking to her again, the voice she thought she heard before. She rolled her shoulders and stretched her arms back. Why did she have such thoughts? But she sent Rosie a text: *Could I take you to lunch?*

Rosie texted back right away. *Sure. Do we have an agenda? Something you want to talk about?*

*No. Just lunch.* ☺

Then Rosie changed the day.

Chloe arrived early at Tin Angel, a cozy place with a fireplace and brick walls not far from downtown, and seated herself by a window at the back. Rosie was ten minutes late, not apologetic. A young woman with roses tattooed down her right arm brought her to the table and handed them menus. Chloe put hers down. "My invitation, my treat. What do you suggest we get? We can share if you like."

Rosie sat forward in her chair, eyed the menu. She ordered a few things plus a glass of wine for herself, which Chloe declined. "So. Okay. Here I am. What's up?"

Chloe ignored the question. "Are you happy school is out?"

"'Happy' is not a word I use any more, but sure, I'm ready to not be in a classroom for a while, though it's impossible to know what to do with myself."

"Is it okay to talk about Angie? I'd like to understand better what you and Peter lost."

Rosie squared her shoulders. "Who, not what. Okaaay. Sort of an agenda. You want me to help you with him."

"No. Look, if you don't want to talk about her, it's fine. I'd just like to be a little friendlier."

"I know. I'm trying. Some of the time at least. And I can always talk about my sister." She took a deep breath. "She wasn't a big extrovert, I'm more that, but she could charm the silk off corn. She had a way of focusing right on you. People were drawn to her. She was kind, she treated everyone the same, no favorites, other than me, of course, and Peter. Everyone equal in her eyes. The main thing though is not her virtues but the way we were joined. That's really it. Born that way. In grammar school we used to laugh at girls who pricked themselves to be blood sisters. Being without her, well, I don't know how. She looked out for me. I relied on her more than I even knew."

Empathy and envy rose in Chloe. She kept nodding, as if she understood such a relationship. "I'm really sorry you lost her. It's hard to understand I guess, what's it's like, being twins."

"No one who's a single can understand. Sometimes we sensed each other's minds. Really. Without words, like we could hear each other think."

"I can't imagine."

"As we got older it wasn't always like that. We got competitive. That was fine too, just another way of being joined." She sighed, wiped the corner of her eye. "When she was in the ER, I tried to sense her again. I believed I would know if she was in trouble. I was wrong. I didn't know. Or maybe I knew and didn't want to know." She lifted her wine glass. "What it's like not being a twin?"

"Lonely. I had no siblings."

"Sorry for that.

Chloe waved the words aside. "Yeah. But not the loss you had. It's a wonder you've survived."

"Have I? I feel like I've lost part of my own body. I'm learning to breathe on my own again, to have a brain that functions independently. Dramatic words, I guess, but those are daily challenges."

Plates of chicken salad arrived, a platter with French bread, goat cheese, and a small dish of pickled peaches. They ate in silence until Rosie said. "Enough of that. Talk about something else."

"Work. It seems pretty challenging, teaching middle schoolers. Preteens, bursting with rebellion."

"Tweens, we call them. In fact, I'm floundering. Incompetent this year at what I once loved. I like math. It used to make me feel better inside. You know, like there's some order to the world. But now I know there isn't. It's all random. Before, I figured out how to help girls in my classes like it, or at least some of them. They got less afraid of algebra when I said equations are a code for relationships—you find the right match, it just fits. Both sides equal."

"Brilliant."

"Equal, like twins." Rosie eyed her. "Though some relationships are really triangles."

"Yes." Chloe sipped her coffee. "I liked math, but never had a teacher like you. I envy how you are with people."

"You didn't need a teacher like me, Chloe. You're too smart." She stirred sugar into her iced tea. "No need to flatter me. I'm biting the bullet. Peter has a girlfriend. What can I do? You were going to grad school while I was having a baby with a drunk. You seem like a person who excels in everything. Beauty, brains, a fat salary, athletic skill. And you have Peter. We are not an equation here, not equals."

"You're assuming a lot." Chloe paused, debating whether to say more about herself and deciding not to. "I have to say, no flattery, you're amazing with Willie. He's like the sweetest kid I ever met."

"I accept that. He is pretty great, no credit to me. Just his nature. Now that he's grown out of bigger problems, it's easier. Let's just say I balanced on a thin wire a lot of his childhood. You can't believe the way doctors talked about him. When I found one who said Willie was okay, just had a peculiar developmental history, I stuck with her. I decided whichever doctor we went to would determine what he had. It's worked out."

Rosie skewered a piece of chicken and held it in the air, ready to eat. "If Peter's going to have someone else, he is. To be honest, I don't get the attraction to him. I never got Angie's either. He's nice-looking, but too laid-back, too low-key for me. Still, aside from Willie, he's the person I love most. Next to my parents of course. But hot? Not so much. Honestly though, I thought he belonged to me. Not in that way, but I didn't expect him to be with someone else. So you could say I feel robbed."

It blew Chloe away, how straightforward Rosie was, concealing nothing, ashamed of nothing, strategic about nothing. She couldn't think of anyone she knew like that. Maybe Elaine, though Elaine seduced her, planned it. No, Rosie didn't plot her moves. Rosie's freedom from shame was a revelation: a woman could be like that.

Afterward she told Peter the lunch had been hard, Rosie wasn't warming up to her. He frowned. "Give her time. She's still pretty fractured."

———

Summer break stranded Rosie. Each morning the alarm sounded, and she shot through a tunnel of remembering Angie's absence again. She forced herself out of bed—grief in bed was risky—made Willie breakfast, dusted the corners of his mouth with her fingers and sent him to brush his teeth before she dropped him at camp.

Her mother had taught her to knit, and the year before Angie died she sponsored an after-school knitting group, six girls and one boy. They made Möbius strips—an infinity scarf. This year she'd kept a stricter classroom. Unpredictable moments were deadly, personal comments were deadly, as if the artery at the base of Angie's brain would balloon wantonly again and break open, blowing her out of existence one more time. She should consider knitting again. She needed to do something with her hands.

Willie was in swim camp June to late August. He'd be amazing by the end of it, tanned and white-blond, his body stronger, but days and days to herself now were not a good thing. Angie's absence surrounded her. She was hearing her again, the siren song of her voice:*I see you, Rosie. I know you're hurting. I miss you, too. Now get up and do something.*

Nights brought different problems, either sleeplessness or sleeping pills. Some nights she dreamed Angie so vividly her presence eclipsed reality for half of the morning. These dreams were a balm; the two of them conspired the way they used to, walked through their woods again to the secret place, lamented how there was a massive housing development there now, though there wasn't, just a few small houses. She'd wake up and be wrenched back to reality.

One night she woke to see Angie standing at the foot of her bed in a purplish light. She sat up in astonishment. Angie put a finger to her lips, *Ssshhh*. Rosie got out of bed, went to her, but Angie waved her back. She reached for her anyway. Angie shook her head and disappeared. It was unbearable.

She got Willie off to camp that morning, drove around, not wanting to go home and see again that she was not there. She found herself on Shelby Street near the bridge, a pedestrian walkway with parks at either end, then she was trudging across the bridge, leaning on the railing, looking down at the river, the green Cumberland that looked so placid yet flooded a year ago, forcing the downtown area to evacuate. Its concrete pylons gave a false sense of safety. How would it feel, she wondered, to plummet into a sheet of moving water? How cold was it in June?

Would there be a kind of mortal ascension on the way down? Was Angie waiting for her?

*Rosie, you have to take care of Peter. And Willie. You can't do this.*

The sensation of Willie's small hand reaching for her, almost as if someone placed it there, brought her back. Scary how it didn't scare her until she felt his hand. She turned back, got in her car, and drove home. In the car Angie's presence stayed with her, a phantom presence. *I'm riding with you when you're alone.*

"Great," Rosie said out loud. Angie was indeed present, not visibly, but she felt her the way a person's presence can be felt.

The next morning when she woke, nothing ached. The sun's so warm, she thought, as she opened her eyes and felt a moment of pleasure, the kind of pleasure a person feels when they recover from the flu and a body full of misery. Once she was up, gloom sullied the light again, but she liked being alive.

Willie noticed. He smiled over his Raisin Bran, and when she dropped him at his camp, he left the car with a look of curiosity, not the usual uneasy one. That cheered her, too, another good moment, one when she didn't care that she had no one except Willie. So she was a thirty-one-year-old woman who leaned on her son. Her mother said she and Willie were too close. So what? Rosie thought. I was bred on closeness.

*Go easier on Chloe. Work things out with her, for Peter.*

---

A humid Saturday afternoon, the sky looking like rain, Rosie drove down Demonbreun Avenue and saw Chloe with her bicycle upside down on the sidewalk. She circled back, parked, and got out.

"Having trouble?"

"No. Just repairing a flat."

"Where were you headed?"

"Over the Shelby Street Bridge. It has a bike lane."

"Hmm. Yeah, I know. I like that bridge. You have a classy bike." Rosie walked around, stroked the red frame. "Titanium?"

"Yes."

She squatted next to her, her face close to the tire. "Never learned to change a tire myself."

"Easy. Watch me, and I'll show you." Chloe popped the front wheel off. She levered the tire, pulled its lip over the rim, worked her way around until one side was free, pulled the skinny tire off the rim. She ran her finger around the inside and found a small tack. "There's the culprit."

"You could be icing a cake, you do it so smoothly."

"Icing a cake is harder, and you're probably good at that."

Chloe pulled a spare tube from a tiny pack beneath the saddle, pumped a little air in, slipped it inside the tire and secured the nozzle on the wheel. She worked the rim back under with her fingers, pried it into place with the lever, snapped the wheel back onto the bike and began inflating again.

"See? Pretty simple. I'm sure you could do it."

"Don't bet on it. I'm desperately inept. Don't think I'm equal to you."

"How about almost equal?" She looked up. "That was a joke, Rosie."

"I'm not joking." She looked toward the bridge. "I'll tell you something you can't tell Peter. I was headed to the bridge, too. I go there sometimes and just stand on that bridge, looking down into the water. Thinking of joining Angie. Remembering Willie, that's all that stops me."

Chloe drew her breath in, reached for Rosie and hugged her.

# CHAPTER 12

A week later they greeted each other outside a cafe, Rosie's invitation, milling around and staring awkwardly until they were seated. Rosie laughed. "We look like cats checking each other out."

Chloe laughed, feeling a moment of bravery. "I like you, Rosie, independent of Peter."

"So you're a tough cat. So am I, even though I'm in pieces." She put out her hand for a high five. Chloe considered, then slapped it.

"I know you're sturdy. You raised Willie alone. Peter said his father wasn't much use. Or is that too personal?"

Rosie made an exasperated sound. "Nothing's too personal for me. The truth about Doug? He was a very mellow guy, aside from being an alcoholic asshole, but he was a good lover, and that worked for a while. Once I had Willie, I didn't want that man around my child, but he was the father. Willie's troubles showed up, we started rounds of doctors, and Doug disappeared. We never married, we just fought."

"You know how much I like Willie."

Rosie waved her coffee cup at a waitress passing by. "You plan to have children?"

"I do. Maybe three. I grew up alone. I don't want that for mine. Not yet, though. I have to be plugged in at work right now."

"I can't imagine how you do your job. The stock market makes my head hurt. I like numbers that are predictable. But you probably make like a billion dollars." Chloe flushed and Rosie paused. "Sorry. You must know by now I've lost any social skills I had."

"I never had them." Chloe smiled ruefully. "Honestly, people are like a project for me. Sometimes I even plan what to say." She couldn't believe she confessed that.

"I can sort of tell."

Chloe tossed her napkin at her.

"So what exactly do you do all day?

"Oh, boring stuff, you might think. Read a lot of reports, digest fund strategies, go to meetings, conferences. I talk to a lot of fund managers, clients, take a lot of calls. It's interesting to me. I have lunches, dinners, etc."

"What do you like about it?"

"The psychology. I like that the most. I'm not so naturally skilled with people, but I'm a good observer and a quick study. I like listening, seeing how they act and react, how they decide things. I slow them down, speed them up. Primal emotions are at work in investing. Fear, greed. It's enough to make you turn spiritual, but it's also fascinating."

"You could be a useful friend."

"See—fear and greed."

Rosie laughed out loud. "Yeah, I guess. Tell me about yourself."

"You want to hear about me?"

"I do. I wouldn't have asked otherwise."

"It's not my favorite subject." She added more milk to her coffee and sipped it, taking a minute. "I grew up in a family that didn't have much. On any level. My mother had a hard life. She lost her parents early and was raised by relatives, passed around. My father had an accident that pretty much disabled him. He wasn't much of a father anyway, and she wasn't much of a mother, but I guess they tried. I spent a lot of time outdoors.

On my bike, swimming. Summers I paddled around in sink-holes, trying to stay cool."

"Hard childhood. No wonder you want money."

"Yeah. I need to help them. And I wanted out of Florida.'

"Florida's pretty weird."

"Oh yes. I had enough Florida for a lifetime by the time I was sixteen." Chloe curled her lip. "I'm sorry but, speaking of work, I need to meet with a client soon. Thanks for calling me, Rosie. You're a fearless woman."

"Before you go, I just want to say, I've decided to forgive you for taking Peter. Maybe at some point you'll forgive me for being such a bitch."

"There's nothing to forgive."

"Yeah, sure. Be in touch."

She called Chloe a week later for an opinion on buying a CD for Peter. It was a diplomatic concession: it wasn't hard to figure it out herself, he liked Americana and roots music.

---

Peter and Chloe arrived at Rosie's the morning of Willie's eighth birthday with a pair of bicycles on the back of her BMW. Fall colors were popping out, and Rosie had yellow, orange, and red balloons flying in the yard. A few of his friends were coming over for cake in the afternoon. Willie circled the car with appreciation and stroked the bicycle. "You going for a ride?"

"Yes," Chloe said. "We brought a bike for you to try out."

Rosie scowled, pulled her aside, and walked down the sidewalk arm in arm with her. She spoke quietly. "Willie doesn't ride. You know he has a poor sense of balance. He doesn't even know how. I didn't get him a bike on purpose."

"I'd like to teach him. I taught kids to ride through my bike club in California. Give him a chance. He'll find his balance."

"He'll injure himself. He'll just be embarrassed."

"I'll make it okay for him, I promise."

"Okay. It's on you."

"Right. On me. Don't worry. Let's just see."

Chloe pulled a helmet out of the car for Willie, put one on herself, and they walked the bikes down the street. Rosie watched until they were out of sight before she turned to Peter. "You should know better!" He shrugged.

They went inside for coffee then waited on the front stairs. Willie and Chloe seemed to be gone a long time. Rosie fidgeted with her hair, went out to the sidewalk, looked, paced back and forth. Peter called her back and rubbed her shoulders. Finally they heard a loud whoop. Willie was riding the bike down the street, a little wobbly and his knees were bloody, but he was beaming. Chloe trailed a short distance.

"Unbelievable. Great going, guy." She hugged Willie, turned to Chloe. "Like I said, you're good at everything."

"I'm not! I'm good at a few things. You're way past me. You just don't know it."

The snazzy bicycle, metallic blue with a computerized speedometer, was a birthday gift. Rosie protested, but Chloe insisted. "I make more money than a person should be allowed to. Let me spend it on him. Such a great human being he is."

She saw softness in Rosie's eyes. She was winning her over.

———

In the early weeks of November, between the summer heat and the start of another winter, Rosie discovered more days, or parts of days, when she walked with energy in her arms and legs, life moving back in rushes between recurrent dark static. She laughed in class twice in one day and hadn't been back to the bridge. One Friday morning, she celebrated by calling in sick and keeping Willie home. They'd have a long weekend and be lazy animals.

All morning they played rummy and listened to old Beatles albums then made brownies. After lunch Willie wanted to show the brownies off to Peter. Why not? she thought. Like he'll think I'm a bad mother for letting Willie skip school? Peter was working again, another sign that Chloe was good for him. They didn't find him in the sound room, where he did most of his work, but sitting in his small conference room with a man she didn't recognize. Willie raised the plate of brownies in front of him as Peter waved them in.

"Uncle Peter, Ma let me stay home from school, and we made awesome brownies." Willie slid the plate across the table, spilling a few off, and jiggled his feet while Peter tried one of the spilled brownies.

"Awesome indeed."

The visitor rose to meet her, his eyes fixed on her mouth. She stared back at him: a nicely tanned guy, blue-gray eyes, shaggy brown hair, a rough shave. "This is Jarrett Allen," Peter said. "He writes a column for the Asheville *Citizen-Times*, and he's interviewing me. This is my sister-in-law, Rosie Fell, and her son Willie."

Willie nodded at the man, grabbed a brownie, and shot out of the studio. He liked to climb a large old live oak outside the conference room, one of the few left in Nashville. Rosie sat facing the window to keep an eye on him as he flung himself limb to limb, a brownie stuffed in his mouth. She turned to the stranger, raised her eyebrows. "Peter's known in Asheville?"

"Right." Peter laughed.

Jarrett continued to stare as he spoke. "I'm looking at an Asheville-Nashville connection, blues and such, since they sound like twin cities. Someone gave me Peter's name."

"You're a journalist?"

"Yeah. And you are?"

"A foot soldier in the education wars."

He looked puzzled at first. "Aha. A teacher. That's what my mother wanted to be, but she never made it to college."

"Saved herself a lot of woe."

Peter put his hand on the recorder. "Jarrett and I are just finishing, Rosie. If you can hang a few minutes, we'll be done, and I'll get us coffee."

"Don't hurry. We just stopped by. We should be going." She waved to Willie to come back in, wincing as she saw him hanging by an arm and a leg from a branch.

Jarrett rose, packed in his notes, and nodded to Peter. "It's okay. What I've got is good stuff. Thanks for your time. You've been generous enough."

Willie stomped back in, and Jarrett held his hand out. "Willie. Nice to meet you, man. I used to like climbing trees myself. Haven't been up one in years. I had a tree house once. Lots of climbing trees where I live."

"That's what I want." Willie lit up. "A treehouse. But we live in an apartment."

Peter started to speak, but Rosie gave him a look as Jarrett followed her out the door. She felt vaguely triumphant. If this man wanted to go with her, why not? He was interested for some reason. They chatted in the parking lot a while. Jarrett told her he was planning to drive around Nashville and take a look. If she and Willie were free to guide him, he'd take them to dinner. Again, why not? She looked back toward the studio. Peter was watching as they got into Jarrett's black Cherokee.

Jarrett drove downtown along Music Row and Broadway as she directed him, pointing to record companies, instrument stores, museums and night spots he should visit, then to Ryman Auditorium and across the Gateway bridge. He admired its swooping arches and confessed to being a bridge nut, so she directed him to Shelby Street. They parked and walked onto the bridge. It struck her as a sweet place to be after all, and a lovely day to be outdoors with other folks, enjoy nice views of the city.

Their conversation drifted from music to movies, lingering on *Men in Black*, as movie talk with Willie did these days. "I can't count how many times he's seen it."

Willie raised seven fingers. "If I love something, I never get tired of it."

"Ah. We should all be that way," Jarrett said, causing Rosie to look away.

"He can repeat most of the dialogue, can't you?" Rosie flung an arm around Willie.

"'*There's only one way off this planet and that's through me!*'"

"Hmm. Through you, I see," Jarrett's eyebrows went up.

Rosie directed him to Spats for a barbecue dinner. "They have great Brunswick stew."

"Sounds perfect. If you ever come to Asheville, I'll take you to 12 Bones. Best barbecue in North Carolina. No joke."

They dropped Willie at her mother's after dinner. The plan was to drive back to Peter's studio, pick up her car, get a drink at Sadie's, the bar in his hotel. Her mother was startled to see Rosie in a man's car. "Who's that out there? You have a new friend?"

"Peter's friend, Mom. Nothing to get excited about."

After they settled into a booth at Sadie's, she ordered a vodka crush, he ordered a Jameson.

"Peter wasn't happy we left together."

"And why would that be?"

"The thing with Peter is, well, he gets a little unhinged by similarities between me and Angie, my twin sister. She was his wife, he sees her in me. Twins, you know." Extraordinary. She hadn't thought of her all afternoon.

"Was?"

"She died sixteen months ago."

"Sorry." He put his hand on hers, but she pulled it away. "Losing a twin. That's a whole other kind of loss."

"You said it. Peter and I were like married for a while, you might say, wedded by trauma."

"So he's jealous when he sees you with someone?"

Rosie paused. "It hasn't come up. I haven't been with anyone since she died. Haven't felt like it. He has someone new, but that's different to him of course."

Jarrett took her hand again and stroked a finger gently. "We drank a lot. You shouldn't be driving now."

She didn't answer right away. Two vodka crushes on top of beers at dinner, she was definitely intoxicated. It felt reckless to go to his room, but reckless to drive off. Peter wouldn't like it, but she didn't care what Peter thought. She was ready for reckless. After all it wasn't like going off a bridge. She excused herself and called her mother, arranged for Willie to stay overnight. Her mother's enthusiasm was annoying. She returned to their table and said, "Willie's going to stay with my mother."

She woke in the dark of his room in the Marriott, a quarter of a mile, she realized, from where Angie died. Maybe she was still drunk. She'd never made love with a total stranger before. A man she'd known a few weeks, yes, and one after a few days, but not one night. He was from out of town, though, and she didn't need to explain herself to anyone.

Jarrett was a decent lover, a little quick, though they were both drunk. She'd been the more assertive one and would bet a winning lottery ticket he'd done this a lot more recently than she had. She liked the way he talked about random things while they were entangled, not as if distracted but as if they'd known each other a long time and what they were doing was natural.

Four a.m. was very quiet in the hotel. Insulation, she thought, a great invention. I need more of it. The quiet was seductive, not the same quiet as her apartment in the middle of the night when her ears strained at the silence, druggy with Ambien or Valium. She'd slept soundly a few hours, no pills.

*Get out of there, Rosie.*

She slipped on her clothes and took the elevator down to the parking garage, searched for her red Jetta, no idea where she'd left it. As she walked around looking for it, the elevator opened again, and Jarrett stepped out in his boxers and a shirt. Rosie laughed. "You'll get arrested like that."

"What are you doing? Driving off without waking me? Leaving me no way to contact you unless I call your brother-in-law who won't want to give me your number?"

My God, she thought, he looks hurt. "I'm sorry. I need to go home."

"Why?"

This was not something she could explain. Standing in the chill of an underground garage in the middle of the night, she worried he'd get cold and that he really might get arrested, or at least thrown out of the hotel. He fixed his gaze on her mouth like he had yesterday. Rosie got back into the elevator with him, went up to his room, and they started kissing again.

Over breakfast he asked for her phone number.

"You're thirty-six and never married?"

"Right."

"Long time girlfriends?"

"Well, let's see. Lived with my cousin Hillie for years until she moved to San Francisco. So, not a girlfriend. I did live with a girlfriend after that, not for long though. That's it."

"Hillie. That's a name? You play around."

"Hillary. Is this a deposition? You're not wearing any ring."

"No, never married. Unwed mother. Willie was an accident, and his father was, let's just say, not a father. But your track record's doesn't sound good enough to keep this going." She'd been down the male immaturity road too many times. Besides, her current state was shaky.

"My resume's not really so bad. You haven't actually seen it." He laid his hands palms up on the table. "And I'm willing to overlook yours."

She tilted her head to the side, thought about how much she missed sex, more than a vacation in Hawaii or the four-percent raise she didn't get this year. He passed a napkin and a pen to her, and she scribbled a number for him.

"I'll be coming over again in two weeks to do more interviews."

"So tell me something. When I met you at Peter's, you kind of stared at me. A lot."

He looked sheepish. "Can't really say why. You just look like my kind of person."

She shook her head and fixed him in her gaze. "Nope."

Jarrett rolled his shoulders. "You kind of reminded me of Hillie."

Rosie laughed out loud. "I knew it. Does it make this sleazy?"

"Not really. Turns out you're nothing like her, just the mouth."

She left with his number and a plan. She noticed two messages on phone. Peter. None of his business.

---

"You'll never guess. Rosie came by the studio yesterday while a journalist from Asheville was interviewing me. I think she put a spell on him."

"I know. She spent the evening with him." Chloe input figures on her computer as she talked on the phone.

"She told you? You're kidding. Since when does Rosie confide in you?"

"She called this morning. She thought you'd be upset. And I told you, Rosie likes me now."

"Yeah, okay. But she wasn't interested in meeting anyone. She hasn't looked at anyone for a year and a half."

"So this is good news."

"I called twice last night. Now I find out why she didn't answer."

"Hold on a minute." She waved to her assistant, who'd brought a stack of forms to sign. "You're upset?"

"Not upset. It concerns me. Her head's not on straight. Easy pickings. I don't think you should be encouraging this."

"You *are* upset."

"I worry about her, is all."

"Think about it, Peter. Are you going to react like Rosie did when you started seeing me?" Peter protested, but Chloe told him she needed to get back to work.

When he learned Jarrett was returning two weeks later, he grumbled again.

"I know it's strange to see Rosie with a man, but she wants a life again, Peter."

"It's unexpected, that's all. I don't want her to be hurt."

They had been together close to a year, the sex and overnights still mostly initiated by him, but they never spoke of the future. They hung out by themselves, with Rosie and Willie occasionally, never with his musician friends—she wouldn't like them, he said, a bunch of stoners and drinkers, though he wasn't like that himself.

They'd gone to the mountains for a weekend in July, to California in September, two days in San Francisco, walking through the Mission, Japan Town, Golden Gate Park, When they saw *La bohéme* at the opera, it left him in tears. Wow, this man can cry, Chloe thought. Of course the opera would be about a woman who died. She'd begun talking back to Angie. Did you arrange that, too?

She'd left him at SFMOMA while she met with a fund manager, then drove them north to Jenner where the highway became a narrow strip of asphalt with a drop to the Pacific on one side and steep coastal hills on the other. Orange poppies and purple lupines still tossed color along the sides of the road in this warm October. From their cottage on the hillside she showed him where the Russian River emptied into the ocean.

He was moody, happy-sad over their lunch at a seafood restaurant on the edge of a cliff. From the deck, they watched a fat ribbon of seals haul out on the beach to sun themselves. It evoked a "Wow, I've never seen seals in the wild." He looked lost as he stared out at the water. She wondered if she had miscalculated—too soon for a trip together, too painful a difference in their finances.

Or was Angie jinxing it? *I told you to slow down.* It was hard to shake the notion that Angie had a grip on him. She understood something of how people got taken with Angie. She was taken a bit herself.

When they made love the last night he seemed ardent enough, but afterward he walked out and sat on the deck. It reminded her of their first night together. She waited before following him out. He was staring at the night sky and didn't acknowledge her. Stars were thick, depths of sky unraveling behind them. Even if he seemed interested, what could it amount to? A man so broken-hearted he couldn't enjoy a trip with her. She liked him, at least she thought so. What would he be like when he recovered? At least he wasn't pushing her.

When they returned to Nashville he was better again. She heard him whistle as he walked through the studio one afternoon when she stopped by. He really liked her. She felt the same. They didn't use the L-word though.

It shouldn't have surprised her that he reacted to Rosie seeing someone.

# CHAPTER 13

Almost noon. Rosie watched from the window: Jarrett was forty minutes late. It annoyed her, not that he was late, but that she had let someone make her worry again. She waited fifteen more minutes, called. It went to voicemail. Either he'd had an accident, or he was ducking her calls. Either way, a disaster. She cursed him, cursed herself.

"Maybe he's not reliable. You'd think I'd know better," she said out loud to Angie. Maybe Angie didn't like him. Then again, she didn't think about Angie as much as she used to.

He called ten minutes later to say there had been an accident, a big traffic pileup in the mountains. No cell coverage, and it took an hour to clear. She breathed deeply, letting go of the impulse to pummel him. When he arrived, his things in a backpack plus a soccer ball he brought for Willie, she said, "Willie's at a friend's house for another hour. We could just wait in the bedroom."

Willie came home a little early, and she hurried to the bathroom. When she came out, Jarrett was talking to Willie about a trampoline park he passed on the way in. "Ever been there? "

Rosie scented risk. She didn't let Willie do risky things, still anxious whenever he rode away on his bike. Overprotective maybe, but years of protecting him had laid deep ruts in her neural pathways. She was not losing Willie.

"I can't watch. You go without me," she said. An hour and a half later they strolled back in the door, Willie shadowing Jarrett like a puppy with a ball in his mouth.

The next day she drove them along Natchez Trace Parkway to the famous bridge: a double-arched eight-mile span over a sloping valley. Jarrett whistled. "Amazing construction. Like the car ads where a fancy vehicle cruises the California coast."

Bored by the bridge, Willie turned back to the car, scrolling something on his phone.

"What's your thing with bridges?"

"I just like them. I worked on a road crew in the mountains after high school, and always parked next to a bridge for lunch. They're works of art."

"You built roads?"

"Hah. No, I removed branches and rocks and stuff after storms, plus roadkill. Our bridges aren't as impressive as this, but they're pretty cool. Come to the mountains with me. You'll see."

"Hmm. How'd you get to be a journalist?"

"I took the long road. Hated school. That's not a good thing to admit to a teacher, is it? I never planned to go to college, but Hillie pushed me. And an editor I knew. I worked in the classified department of the newspaper through high school, so I knew the editor. While I was on the road crew I hiked my way back into the mountains and met people I wrote about later. I showed them to the editor. He liked them and said I needed to study journalism. When Hillie came back from college, we lived together a while. She got married and moved to Chapel Hill. She wanted me to come with her, so I went to community college there until I got into UNC."

"Interesting path." She pointed to a section of the bridge. "People have suicided there."

"Ouch. Not the way I'd want to go. Too much hard ground down there."

"Me either. I'd choose water."

Jarrett drove over again the weekend of Willie's last soccer game. Rosie was the snack mom, but Peter and Chloe brought everything: bagels, cream cheese, apple and orange slices, water bottles for the team. Rosie contributed a soft-sided ice chest with bags of frozen peas to ice injured body parts. "Third grade boys are drama queens when they get clobbered on the field," she warned Jarrett. "That's what the frozen peas are for. Like ice packs. Or they eat them. Frozen. Even if they won't eat them cooked."

Angie didn't come to Willie's games often, Rosie recalled, then tossed the thought to the trash heap of things she wouldn't think about.

Willie's team lagged in their league. After every game she reassured him, "No goalie blocks all the balls. It's up to the team to stop them from getting down there."

When Rosie followed the team down the field, Chloe sidled over to Jarrett to get a read. He was a good-looking man. "Rosie says you write for the paper in Asheville. You have an area of special interest?"

He stared at her curiously, a lingering look. "The mountains. People who live there. Southern music. That's why I interviewed Peter. He did a nice bluegrass album a few years ago. I hope he'll do another one."

"Me, too. Encourage him. He needs that now."

The opposing team scored. Willie spotted Jarrett and suddenly looked alert, or panicked, Chloe couldn't tell. The other team charged downfield again, booting the ball wildly left and right, zinging it at the goal. Willie did a great belly flop and landed with his hands clutching the ball in the air. Everyone whooped and clapped. "Willie! Willie!" After the game they all trooped back to the apartment with a couple of pizzas and a few extra boys. Willie handed out slices before they settled in front of the TV. Jarrett slid his arm around her waist, looking almost proud as Willie recapped his save. Chloe watched Rosie remove it and clear away pizza boxes.

Once the house was free of boys, and Willie had gone to a friend's, Peter started questioning Jarrett.

---

"Why do I get the feeling your people are checking me out?"

"Because they are. Sorry, but I come with complicated ties. We're family, an enmeshed family, only they're more watchful than my parents ever were."

"So I answer to them if I misbehave?"

"For that you answer to me."

They had gone to bed for the afternoon. The ease of it and sense of transgression competed seductively. "I feel like I should not be having such a good time. Like Angie will think I don't care anymore. Do the dead think?"

She had her own opinion on the matter, but she wasn't going to tell Jarrett she heard Angie sometimes and even saw her once.

"Sure they do." He shifted so she was lying across his chest and wrapped his arms around her. "When I was nine, my mother died. I believe she's had opinions about everything I've done since."

"Nine. That's so young. Tell me a story about you and your mother."

Jarrett sighed. "Okay. Well. I'll tell you the lemon cake story. I had a bad temper as a kid. One day, I was a little younger than Willie I guess, I was playing in the kitchen with a kid from the neighborhood and something he did got me riled up. I held him down and doused him with hot sauce until he started bawling.

Don't know why I did that, but I also poured hot sauce on this cake she'd just made. Go figure.

"My mother came in, wiped the boy off and sent him home. She was pissed. I couldn't explain myself. I would just get mad. It took me by surprise—something would pop in my head. So I told her I'd make her another cake, and I went to the pantry and pulled out a bag of flour. 'Then do it, buddy,' she said. She got some eggs, salt and sugar and a couple of lemons, she showed me how to use her mixer, squeeze the lemons. It was a pretty decent cake for a seven-year-old. She was never much for punishment. Could not say no to me either."

"Nice story. I like your mother. Sorry I never met her. How's your temper these days?"

"Think I grew out of it. I learned to cook a lot of things from her. I like cooking."

She liked the idea of a man with a little fire in him, but one who could cook, too—heaven-sent.

"What happened to your father?"

"A useless man. Came home from work and got drunk in front of the TV. That's why I lived with Aunt Laraine and Hillie after my mother."

"They took you on. You're still close?"

"You bet. Aunt Laraine's a character. Dresses like a forties movie star. Come to Asheville, you will meet her. And Hillie's a soul sister, if I can use that term. Smartest woman I ever knew." He looked at Rosie and lowered his chin. "You're the second smartest, of course. If it weren't for Hillie, I wouldn't be a journalist. She turned me on to books. She and Laraine didn't, don't, get along. For some reason my aunt's very critical of her daughter, a bit of a flame thrower actually, and Hillie does like to provoke her. I mediated between a lot. And I was Hillie's protector. She needed protection from some of the men Laraine took up with. We talk every single week."

Rosie felt her jealousy muscle throb. "Is Hillie married?"

"Twice already. She prefers being single."

———

Mid-December Rosie packed up and left school early to drive I-40 east to Asheville. He'd come to Nashville four times. It was her turn. She brought Willie, as Jarrett insisted, though her mother offered to keep him. He had a small house surrounded by poplars and oaks, winter bare. Two bedrooms and a study with framed awards on the walls, a photo of a teenage Jarrett and Bill Clinton at the *Citizen-Times* office. She surveyed the kitchen. It was well-stocked, not like a man's kitchen, especially a man who played around. She opened the pot on the stove, lamb stew. There was a bottle of wine on the table. She searched for the opener.

Willie was in high spirits at dinner, funnier than she'd seen him in months, doing his imitation of Forrest Gump. She stayed in the back bedroom as he fell asleep. He was used to Jarrett sleeping over at their apartment now, but he didn't like sleeping anywhere else except his grandmother's. When she emerged from his room, Jarrett waved her into the living room with the open bottle. She lay on the couch, her feet in his lap, and he refilled her glass.

"I'm tired of driving over the mountains, and I'm tired of missing you." He traced his lower jaw with the back of his hand, the way he traced her flesh after they made love.

"Watch out. You're making me nervous."

"Me, too." He laughed his low little laugh. "Still, I've been thinking. Maybe we should consider ... "

"Consider what?"

"This might be a for-real thing."

"You? Determined single guy? I don't want to talk this way, Jarrett. Let's not ruin the weekend."

"You say stop, I stop. But … "

An awkward silence hung in the air until Rosie went into the kitchen and loaded the dishwasher. They didn't talk about it further, and the weekend was fine, great, actually. They hiked into woods off the parkway. Willie raced ahead and hid in a cave, a deep opening in a rocky wall. She called his name twice, then Jarrett whistled like he was calling a dog, and Willie burst out laughing. In Jarrett's yard he got his fill of tree climbing. Later they played Monopoly, and Willie won, gleefully stacking up piles of bills.

Driving out of Asheville on Sunday the unfinished conversation troubled her. She'd wanted to grab Willie and get in the car if Jarrett was getting serious on her. He'd invoked a possibility, a murky mass of potential change in the weather. He wanted her there, in his house. All the time.

Past Canton the road swerved appealingly back and forth through the mountains. The prospect of a new city began to seize her. New people. A vague chance of a future. No Nashville dreariness. No jab of pain when she passed Angie's old office building or Vanderbilt Hospital or their childhood playground. A city not geared to trigger misery at every turn.

Ribbons of ice decked the trees as the highway wound higher into the mountains and icy patches sparkled on the asphalt. The bridge across the Pigeon River shimmered, and the car suddenly skidded toward the guardrail. She wrenched it back just in time, and then went into a tailspin. Adrenaline weakened her limbs as she clutched the steering wheel, tried to control it, ending on the wrong side of the road, headed back to Asheville.

"Whoa!" said Willie.

"Yeah, whoa."

She drove to the pull-out just past the bridge and leaned back against the seat, breathed deeply. Willie looked alarmed, but she assured him everything was okay, she just needed to chill for a minute. He went back to his video game. She imagined the iciness of that water. She hadn't thought of the Shelby Street Bridge in ages. How close did I come? Without Willie, would I have done it?

Instantly she was furious. Not once had she been angry with Angie for dying, but fury blazed up now. Angie was an undertow, pulling on her. If you wanted to have an aneurysm, fine, but I'm not through here yet. Why should I want to be with you now? I've met someone. Stop this!

Close as pages in a book, but Angie was the one who broke away, got married. She professed to love Willie so much, but forgot his birthday once and put Peter on duty when they babysat. Sure, she was a good sister, the better one. Nicer than Rosie, too. Skinnier for sure, with better hair and perfect skin. I never felt so great about myself because of you. I skated on your popularity in school. You knew it. You never asked me once if I was interested in Peter. And I thought I was the narcissistic one. Guys had liked her, but Rosie waited for them to discover Angie. Sometimes they did, like Peter.

She remembered Angie ignoring her when the most popular girl in their class walked out of homeroom with her. Rosie called to her, but Angie could apparently no longer hear her sister's voice. It wasn't the only time. It might be pathetic to care about stuff like that now, but I never ignored you, not for anyone. Ever.

With Jarrett, there would be no triangle. She could have another baby, might stop teaching for a while. She felt him moving toward settling down, with that house that looked like a family home, not a single man's house. He had embraced Willie. Possibly he'd be a soft landing. She started the car again, debating which way to go, Asheville or Nashville. Finally she turned back around toward Nashville.

Headed slowly into the next hairpin curve, she wondered why she'd been so angry at Peter for wanting to keep living after Angie died. It just seemed normal now. Cresting the Swannanoa Gap, she thought, If you don't like what I'm doing with Jarrett, I'm not listening any more. I'm done with the grief business. I'm moving on. You can just go away now.

Once they were out of the mountains, she pulled out her cell to call Peter, thought better of it. If she shouldn't ask Peter what to do, she could ask Willie, her little wise man, her home base. She handed him her phone and told him to search for ice cream in Knoxville. As he poked around on the screen, she silently practiced sounding neutral, innocent enough to ask, "How do you like Asheville, Willie?"

# CHAPTER 14

Chloe bought a pregnancy test, but she knew already. Six weeks since her last period. She used a diaphragm, believing hormones brought unnecessary risk, and she trusted her habits. Ominous things stirred in her chest, traces of the past as she made the appointment, old bones being disturbed, trying to unearth themselves. She harbored no regrets about that early abortion, but it carried traces of misery, and the idea of a second one hurt.

Rosie came by that evening to return a cookie tin left at a soccer game. Chloe looked uneasy standing in the door, and her lack of eye contact alerted Rosie. Like a cat sniffing an alien scent, she asked, "What's up? Something's wrong."

"I didn't expect you, that's all."

"Come on, Chloe."

Chloe let her in and offered a drink. Rosie declined but sat on the couch, clearly planning to stay. "Okay. I'm getting an abortion on Friday."

Rosie's mouth fell open. She shook her head. "You haven't told Peter. That can't happen without him knowing, Chloe."

"You can't tell him."

"I won't, but you have to. That is, unless it's not his."

"Of course it's his! But he doesn't need this now."

"If he ever finds out, ever somehow finds out, not from me, but because you can't stand keeping it from him any longer, or if anything happens, he'll never forgive you. You know how he wants kids."

"But not now."

"Think of yourself, too, Chloe. Is this something you want to do alone? You have a choice. Alone is hard."

"I know. I've been there."

"When? Talk to me," she said, patting the couch. When Chloe sat down, Rosie moved closer.

"A long time ago. I was very young. Fifteen."

Rosie looked dismayed. "I know so little about you. Tell me."

"I was young and stupid. I was dating this guy who was gorgeous and smooth, and I was smitten. I thought I was in love. I thought—that is, he said—he was a righteous guy. He talked about Jesus and all and didn't believe in sex before marriage. It was against his religion thing, his great view of himself as this good man. We'd be making out and he'd pull back, and I'd feel ashamed. But he had another girlfriend all along. And then suddenly, when he thought *I* was seeing someone else, he got forceful. I couldn't think. It wasn't rape. Though maybe it would have been if I hadn't given in. We even had sex two more times. I knew nothing. I thought it meant something, but it meant something else. He looked down on me after that. He never called again. Then I discovered I was pregnant."

"What a shit." Rosie put her arm around Chloe. "What a crappola guy."

"I trusted him, and he made me ashamed of *that*." Chloe looked young as she said it. Rosie stroked her back.

"Oh, Chloe. That's so terrible. I'm so sorry."

Chloe wiped a tear and smiled gruesomely. "I was desperate because I couldn't tell my mother. Or anyone." She took a deep breath then told her everything. What her mother was like, how Kath had given up a child, all about Yvette.

"So I had to get a fake ID and go to an abortion clinic alone."

"At fifteen."

"Yeah. Afterward I lay in bed and cried, for weeks. I felt so stupid. I was furious, but really I just felt hopeless."

Rosie rocked her a little with her arm.

"I've never told anyone all this, except my therapist a lot of years later." She apologized for her tears. "Maybe this is just me hormonal already."

"This is you with a heart that got crushed by everyone. I had no idea. No idea. You never talk about yourself."

"I don't know what to do. I mean, I do. But..." She pulled away and drew a hand down her face.

"Peter's not like that asshole who disappeared. He'll want to be part of this, one way or the other. He won't leave you alone with it. Don't make yourself go through that again."

Chloe nodded. Peter wasn't like that.

"Think about what you want. Are you sure you don't want a baby?"

It was unthinkable.

After Rosie left, Chloe curled on the couch. Those early days she'd crawled into a hole, dark feelings seizing her insides, and now she felt them again. She tried to speak of them once to Elaine, but choked. In therapy she pictured herself crawling out of that hole. Now Rosie had gone there with her. She wished Rosie had stayed. Her heart strained toward her, as if it could actually move in her chest.

The next day Rosie called. "What are you thinking now?" They talked it through again. She promised to tell Peter that afternoon. When she went to his studio, she found him on the phone. She paced the sound room. Maybe she shouldn't tell him. He was working again.

He bounded into the room with a handful of notes. A new distributor wanted several of his albums. He'd be making money after all. "Let's go out and celebrate."

"Sure."

"I can foot some bills now. What are you doing here anyway instead of making someone even richer? What's up?"

She led him to his favorite chair in front of the controls, pulled up a chair for herself. "I'm pregnant, Peter. I just want you to know. I don't know what happened. I never forgot the diaphragm." Was that true? Suddenly she wondered. Had she slipped, and why? He looked at her like a child about to be punished. "You don't have to go there. I already scheduled an abortion."

He fidgeted with the switches as if that would tell him something. "Wait. So we could be having a baby."

"That's not what I meant."

"You're moving too fast for me. Let's think about it."

"I can't wait long. It will just be harder."

His eyes scanned the room. He took a deep breath and leaned back in the chair, gave her a sheepish look. "Maybe we can do this."

"We've known each other, what—not quite a year? You're not ready for something this big. I'm not either."

"Life doesn't wait for ready. If your vehicle's moving, you fasten your seat belt." He stared at her for a long minute.

"I've thought about it. A lot, Peter."

"You haven't thought about it with me." He put his jacket on. "Let's go for a walk." As he locked the studio behind him, he asked, "What if we just go ahead and get married?"

Chloe looked at him. She hadn't expected that. Her heart flip-flopped because she was thrilled and also frightened. She took his hand. "We're too new, Peter. We're still getting to know each other. It's not something to rush into."

He nodded. "I know. But I don't know. I don't know. I really don't know, Chloe. It might not be something to rush out of either."

A year and a half since Angie died, he was still grieving. She was getting her bearings at work. Should she have told him? Was Rosie right? She stalled, no idea which way to go. She agreed to wait, not very long, though.

"I want a child. Angie didn't. I banked on her changing her mind."

"You'll have other chances."

"You don't know. Things happen."

"We can't make up for that, Peter. This is about us."

"Of course. Of course it's about us. And about the baby."

Did he want this? He seemed to, but should she trust it? She didn't know. Did she want it? She couldn't tell. Did he realize neither of them had ever said *I love you*?

She stewed all evening, trying to imagine telling her office she was having a baby. She tried to imagine being married. An investment, perhaps, that might pay off in time. A man she liked, a man who wanted a baby with her, who didn't ask for more time or devotion than she could give.

She fished through a box of old things from the past—her National Merit pin, her Phi Beta Kappa pin, an envelope of cycling ribbons. At the bottom she found the gold locket inlaid with tiny diamonds her mother had given her when she graduated from Cal. "We don't have much for a present, Chloe, but this is yours now. One of the few things of my mother's I have."

They opened it together and admired the lock of Kath's baby hair. "You can take that out of course. One day you can put a lock of your own baby's hair into it."

"No, I want it in there." She snapped the locket shut and thanked her. Why had her mother not put a bit of her hair in there when she was a baby? She didn't ask Kath questions like that. Kath looked dazed and hurt if Chloe complained about her, and any question about Kath as a mother was taken as complaint. She had given her so little. She had been given so little herself. Chloe put the locket beside her bed.

Did she love Peter that way, was she *in love*? She cared about him, and she trusted him. He was a good man. They had fun together, liked a lot of the same things, and there was good sex, good enough sex. Maybe that was love. It wasn't like with Elaine, but that was youthful infatuation. Possibly she didn't recognize mature love. She wished for Hannah to talk to, but it didn't occur to her to call.

Peter phoned every day. She kept telling him she was thinking. It was time to tell him more about her. More of Kath and Dee. About Elaine. Even Jamie. She had told him so little. She went to his house that night, ready to reveal her painful story.

He nodded as she talked, expressed surprise, empathy. He held her close that night and said he was glad to know her better.

He still loved Angie of course. Would he ever love her like that? He did seem to love her, in a different way perhaps. Would they ever have a marriage that didn't include Angie? The laughable idea that the pregnancy was Angie's doing, her gift to Peter, unsettled her. She wanted to banish Angie.

*You don't need to banish me. This is good for you.*

The next morning she told Peter she was ready. They talked all morning, and he said it. "I do love you, Chloe." That's how he said it. "I know I'm all tangled up inside, but I want a life. I want you. I want a family." It felt like there was love in it. Did she ever say she loved him? She didn't think so and didn't think he had registered that.

They started thinking about dates.

———

A wedding. Chloe watched Rosie's face as she told her Peter wanted to get married.

"Holy Bejesus! I wondered if that might happen."

"I should thank you."

"He should thank me! I'll be an auntie! And Willie will have a cousin, sort of. Oh my god, will *he* be thrilled."

Rosie's enthusiasm warmed Chloe. Affirmation. But again, all about the baby. Well, it was all about the baby, not her and Peter. Babies are healing, babies fill everyone with love, hope. They'd decided on early May. She didn't care if people knew she was pregnant, but she would not have a quickie wedding.

"I could be maid of honor!"

Chloe hadn't asked her. Her one friend in town, aside from Rosie, was Meera Bannerjee, whom she'd lured to Nashville from her old job in San Francisco. Meera hated the pressure there as well and was curious about the South. Now they ate lunch together and schemed around certain male colleagues. Once she went to Meera's office, shut her door behind her and show an email from one who'd breached a client's confidential file, claimed it was an accident, but made a few suggestions. "He wants her for himself. Really I'd be happy to hand her off. They're both a pain. But Arthur wants me to work with her for some reason."

"I can't believe he did that. He should be fired." Meera had a strong sense of propriety. "He doesn't work well with female clients, we all know that. That's why Arthur won't let him have her." Meera would be invited to the wedding, of course, but their relationship wasn't warm, not the sort to include her in the ceremony. Other than Rosie, there was no one to ask.

They were becoming family. Marrying Peter came with benefits. She already felt allied with her, no, something more tender or deep than alliance. She didn't want to give it a name. She insisted on paying for Rosie's dress, and they scrolled photos, designer dresses that Rosie eyed eagerly, choosing a silk indigo gown with an asymmetrical hem. Chloe's dress was a high-waisted, almost off the shoulder, pale cream satin that draped gently and heightened her tawny skin and green eyes.

"These dresses are gorgeous together," Rosie said. "We'll look stunning."

Chloe flushed, thinking something like that herself: *we would look stunning together.*

---

They sat at Rosie's dinner table as Rosie took apart a roast chicken and told Willie to pass the mashed potatoes. Chloe showed Ruth the sapphire ring she and Peter selected. Ruth admired it and sighed. "Life really does go on."

"Rosie likes you. That's a top endorsement," Frank said.

Ruth wiped at her eyes. "Imagine, both of you planning weddings." Rosie kicked her under the table, shook her head.

"Weddings? Both?" Peter queried.

Ruth looked apologetically at Rosie. "I didn't know you hadn't told them."

"Well, it's no secret now. I didn't want to upstage them. This is their celebration. Yes, I have news. Jarrett and I are getting married. We just decided a few days ago, but this evening is about you." She put the chicken wings on Willie's plate.

"Yup," said Willie. "And Jarrett's building a tree house for me."

Chloe stared. Peter's mouth hung open wordlessly.

"You're moving to Asheville," Chloe said.

"Everything changes so fast," Frank said, reaching for a slice of meat. "We get used to one thing, then there's another." He put his fork down and patted Rosie's hand. "Cat's out of the bag. Ruth didn't know you hadn't told them, honey. Just as well, huh? So we have two things to celebrate!"

Ruth was tearing up. "You've waited a long time for the right one, but I hate that you're moving. I'm happy for you, honey, but I can't help it, I don't want you to go."

"It's not so far, Mom, really. I'll come back a lot. You'll come to see me."

Peter had gone pale, walloped-in-the-gut pale. Chloe excused herself from the table, went to the bathroom and sat on the toilet with the lid down until she composed herself. Something was unraveling inside her. Rosie not here any more. Just her and Peter. And the baby, of course. She stared in the mirror. *You're overreacting*, she told herself.

When she returned, Rosie was speaking earnestly to Peter. "I know it seems sudden, but I love this man. Willie loves him, too. He wants us to live together. Jarrett and I plan to have a baby." She didn't tell them that she might already be pregnant.

"I'll have brothers and sisters," Willie raised his arms like a winner.

"Happy news, Rosie. Well done." Chloe lifted her glass of iced tea for a toast. She did not feel upstaged, she felt robbed. Weird synchronicity between them, but it was pulling them apart. After nibbling at a slice of buttermilk pie, she carried plates into the kitchen and began loading them in the dishwasher. Rosie followed.

"Leave this mess. It's a party for you."

"You're really running off to Asheville? Just when we've started to care about each other."

Rosie put her hand over Chloe's mouth, kissed her on the cheek. "We'll visit so much. You'll see."

Peter was not so gentle. "I don't understand. You're marrying a basic stranger."

"He might be a stranger to you, Peter. He's not to me."

"Why haven't you talked to me about this?"

"We don't talk, Peter. Not any more. I'm closer to Chloe."

"Ouch."

"Well, really. Look, I wasn't keeping it secret. I was planning to tell you."

Silence.

"It's not Mongolia. Only four hours away."

"*Four hours.* You're four minutes away now."

"And when was the last time you came over?"

Silence again.

"You have no idea. Okay? The telephone is how we talk, Peter. And it connects to Asheville."

"Yeah. Okay."

"Can you be happy for me? I'm happy for you. You're going to have a kid. You'll be a father. It's what you've wanted. I hate leaving all of you, but honestly I'm happy to get away from this town. It's all painful memories. A new city appeals to me, and Asheville's a cool place. You'll love it there. The bluegrass music, the people who play, they're the real deal and Jarrett knows some of them. You have to come a LOT."

"Who is this Jarrett?"

"You'll like him. He's a decent guy or I'd never marry him. Willie adores him."

"It didn't work when I said that about Chloe."

"But you were right. It took time. You see how I love her now. Take time to get to know him. You'll be friends. I have a feeling."

Peter's jealous, she thought, as they returned to the living room where her parents sat. Fine. His turn. But why did every relationship turn into a triangle?

———

When she told Kath she was getting married and also pregnant, Kath offered a little money for the wedding. "Better you should spend it on yourselves. When have you taken a vacation? Go somewhere after you come up here."

"Maybe," Kath said.

"Come early so you can meet Peter. We'll go out for dinner and have a few drinks. I'll show you around Nashville."

Kath said they couldn't get away early. They'd arrived just in time for the rehearsal dinner, and when Chloe introduced Peter, Kath said, "You seem like a very nice man. We're happy for you," polite things that sounded empty to Chloe.

His people were hearty, warm. They had driven down once before to meet her, but unlike her parents they were not cowed by the money, her car, her condo, her job. His mother approved of Chloe. Chloe flinched as she hugged her. Mrs. Swegan asked a lot of questions, beaming and chuckling at her, patting Peter on the shoulder. The effort to be at ease made Chloe long for it to be over.

Mrs. Swegan took over the rehearsal dinner. She herded Kath and Dee to their seats, cued the waitstaff to serve, to clear. His father was genial, happy to have his wife run things.

At the wedding Kath and Dee walked around staring, awed by the elegance of Belmont Mansion where the ceremony and reception were held. Chloe had sent her mother a light blue silk sheath with a jacket and Dee a new suit, an elegant cane. Still slender, Kath looked good in her dress and kept stroking the material. Chloe felt the familiar void of oxygen around them, but it was her wedding—she had a roomful of people to pay attention to her, colleagues, some clients, Peter's friends and a raft of musicians.

A string quartet played Mozart and Vivaldi. No giving-away-the-bride bit, she walked alone down an aisle of yellow rose bushes in silk-draped pots and stood beside Peter. As she turned to him, she caught Kath's eye. Kath gave her a thumbs up. She looked happy for her.

———

Rosie and Jarrett married in early June in the sunken garden at Centennial Park. A bluegrass trio, Peter's friends, played, Willie served as ring bearer and Chloe as matron of honor. Jarrett's cousin Hillie came from San Francisco to be his "best person." She and Chloe wore matching halter-necked flowered dresses. Aunt Laraine from Asheville, flashed around in an off-the-shoulder yellow dress, hugging everyone, all strangers to her. Ruth wept and smiled through the ceremony. She was going to be a grandmother again, but at a distance.

Rosie wore a spaghetti strap mid-calf dress in pale green, full below her breasts as her pregnancy was beginning to show. Summer heat curled the leaves of the poplars and wilted the ginger lilies, but Rosie kicked off her shoes and danced on the grass. Chloe spent much of the party with Hillie, Jarrett's cousin, talking about the Bay Area. Hillie had a bookstore in Noe Valley near where Chloe once lived. A bookstore sounded like an oasis to Chloe. "I'd love to spend my days with books."

"It just sounds idyllic. It's not easy, not these days. We host a lot of events to bring people in. If you get to San Francisco, stop by."

Chloe was intrigued—an Asheville native who made her way to California and opened an independent bookstore in a tough economic climate. She asked a lot of questions and said she'd definitely visit when she came to California.

After a few drinks Hillie confided that she never thought Jarrett would marry. "He's a restless soul, and loves women, maybe too much."

Chloe looked alarmed.

"I shouldn't have said that. Jarrett and I grew up together. I still think of him as a teenager I suppose. He wants to settle down. Rosie's a great match, a woman with a lot of spirit."

Chloe's feelings about Jarrett were impossible to separate from the loss of Rosie. Something she sensed about him though was confirmed by Hillie's words. He'd been a player.

Before Rosie left with Jarrett for New Orleans, she pulled Chloe aside and compared their bellies. "Remember when you were changing a bicycle tire, you said we're almost equal? Now we are!"

# PART FOUR

# BABY, BABY

# CHAPTER 15

Six months pregnant on their Jamaican honeymoon, Chloe began cramping. A doctor said it was heartburn, spicy Jamaican cuisine the likely culprit. She had doubts. They flew home early, but when her OB concurred with the Jamaican doctor, they drove over the mountains to Asheville.

Jarrett toured them along the Parkway and up a steep narrow road into the Blue Ridge, pointing out ancient trees, rare wildflowers, naming birds by their calls, but it was hot, and the two pregnant women with their shared pregnancy woes—swollen feet, constant need to pee—just complained when he pushed them to hike. They shopped in town for tiny items of clothing while Jarrett took Peter to meet a fiddle player in Black Mountain.

Real labor began ten days before Chloe was due. Not to worry, the doctor said, the baby was ready. For hours she followed her doula's directions, breathing, walking, panting, using the birthing ball while Peter massaged her back and legs. At the end, she streamed tears as intense pain pushed through her body with the baby. Peter lifted the infant like Mufasa. She was gorgeous—perfect Cupid's-bow mouth, coarse dark hair of Chloe's redbone ancestors and white plumpness of his German ones. Then a nurse whisked her away.

Peter wanted to name the baby Jennifer. Chloe wanted something less common. "Why not Jenner?" Jenner was where they probably conceived her. When the nurse returned with the baby, he took her in his arms, nuzzled her, kissed her belly. "What a little miracle you are, Jenner."

Together they thrilled over her tiny hands, how slender her fingers were: guitar fingers, he said, as they strummed the air. She gurgled, she farted, she cooed, she spit up on them. Chloe was awed and intimidated by this tiny vulnerable creature. How could she think she knew what to do for her? She stared as the baby slept. Her own baby. Did she really grow inside her? It felt more like she'd discovered her, found this baby who could not really be hers, especially when Jenner wouldn't latch on. She wasn't surprised. She always suspected she'd be a bad mother.

A nurse guided the baby's head to her breast, told her to cradle her just so. Finally, on her second day, Jenner nursed.

The first weeks were a daze of sleeplessness and diaper changes, quick showers, take out food or Ruth's deliveries. Nothing had felt so sensual, intimate, private as nursing her baby. Peter hovered until she sent him away. Holding her close, carrying her against her shoulder, she wondered how it had been for Kath. How could it be that she didn't remember her mother ever holding her?

Peter's delight reassured her though. Their marriage was still an amazement. He was unoffended by any bodily fluid that came out of Jenner, and the sheer animal essence of her left him faint with pleasure. He practically gave off light. "Life has paid me back at last."

At six weeks he lifted Jenner's tiny sausage legs off the changing table to pull a wet diaper out and she let loose, shot green slime across the room, almost hitting him. "Chloe, come look!" he called, delighted by a closet door dripping with projectile diarrhea. Chloe gave a gruesome smile and cleaned it up, staggered back to her computer. Barely capable of adding numerals, she had only two more weeks of maternity leave and felt compelled to try to work, even in her sleep-deprived state.

Her love for Jenner didn't look like Peter's, not ecstatic and vocal, but calmer, held at bay even as she felt its profundity. She didn't need to compete with his joy. Time ran backwards on his face, the pained man she'd met at that party was flushed now, peaked with pleasure. And Peter took to her so easily.

Rosie visited, seven months pregnant. Jarrett persuaded her not to let the doctor reveal the sex, but intuition said it was a girl, and she hoped for a girl. She crowded next to Chloe and Peter over the crib at five a.m. as Jenner wailed. Chloe threw her hands up and stalked back to bed.

"Good thing she's pregnant," Chloe said. "Or she'd steal Jenner and we'd be on the front of *People* magazine."

She expressed milk the week before she returned to the office and reluctantly let Peter bottle feed her. Her first day back, she took Jenner with her, showed her off, nestled in a sling, then tried to work as the baby slept. Peter picked her up at noon, then eleven the next day, ten the next. She started pumping at the office, her assistant on guard against intruders, so she could leave Jenner with Peter all day.

While everyone grabbed their lunch delivery of crab ravioli in the kitchen, a colleague pulled a bottle of breast milk out of the fridge and held it to the light. "What's this?" Chloe snatched it from him and put it back. He could figure it out.

Financial news, movements of the markets, endless details to track, were hard to follow with her brain awash in maternal juices. A chance at a partnership loomed, but it was permissible to draw limits, refuse calls while she nursed or rocked Jenner. What she couldn't do was relax. It was like having two babies. She vowed to cut her hours for the next one.

It was hard to escape Peter's vigilance too. He preferred to hold her, change her, feed her. Chloe never dreamed a man could be so absorbed in a baby. In the middle of the night, he began feeding her himself. "You have to sleep, hon. Let me do this."

Rosie's baby arrived late, her labor difficult, the baby "stuck," according to the nurse. How could a baby get stuck? She groaned and sweated, cursed Jarrett and the baby who was killing her. The doctor said she needed a Caesarean to get him out. *Him.* The baby was a boy. Woozy, she wailed. "I don't want a boy." And *he* refused to come out, *he* knew how she felt. As the doctor prepared her for surgery, the baby began to move again and entered life with a series of sharp tearing lunges.

Jarrett wanted to name him Brian Fredericks, his mother's father's name. "Fine," Rosie said, turning to the wall. Why did Chloe get the girl? She gets everything! she thought, like she was five again, and Angie had something she didn't. She nursed the baby, but rarely got out of bed. Postpartum depression, the doctor said. She hadn't been depressed with Willie, and life was so much harder. Unlike Doug, Jarrett coached her through the birth, took care of the baby while she turned inward, waiting to hear from Angie. But Angie had gone silent since the day Rosie spun out on the bridge and told her to go away. She asked her to come back: I'm sorry. Are you annoyed? Do dead people pout?

Silence from Angie weighted the scales. A boy, not a girl. She had been hoping for a little Angie back in her life.

Jarrett eagerly showed Brian off to everyone. Nine-year-old Willie carried him in his arms, changed diapers, read to him, clapped in his face to make him smile. When Ruth arrived, Rosie let her take over. She called Chloe and sobbed intermittently— she couldn't manage to get up before noon, their household had fallen apart. After Ruth left, Aunt Laraine tottered around in high-heels shoes cleaning up, clucking and sympathizing in turn.

Rosie avoided Chloe's calls, but Chloe persisted until she finally answered. "I'm a pathetic mother," she moaned. "The baby screams like a character in a slasher film. I can't help it, I don't know how to love him."

Chloe started packing. Peter wanted to come with her. "Nope. You need to spend time in your studio, and I want time with Jenner." Mostly he seemed upset that Chloe was taking the baby. "She's too young, and it's December. You'll hit ice. "

"There's no weather coming. We'll be fine. You need to get working again."

She put her assistant in charge at the office, left instructions if anything was urgent, loaded diapers, stroller, gifts, and tiny clothes Jenner had outgrown. Halfway between Nashville and Asheville, she nursed Jenner in the rear of a hotel parking lot while rain swept across the highway. Bliss to be alone with her again.

The mountain roads were slick with rain, but there was no ice, and she was cautious. Spooky clouds of mist hung in the valleys and climbed the road ahead of her. Walking into the house with Jenner in her arms, she found Rosie still in bed, hair uncombed, covers piled on.

"You shouldn't have come," she grumbled. "We aren't fit for company."

"That's why I'm here."

Willie brought Brian into the bedroom, changed his diapers, put him in his crib. Chloe put a sleepy Jenner in the crib with him and curled up next to Rosie.

"Jenner's so easy. You have everything now."

Chloe shut her eyes, tightened her arms around Rosie. Rosie began to weep, open-mouthed quivering sobs that made it hard to breathe. She clutched at Chloe, buried her face in her shoulder, soaked her blue sweater. Chloe felt an electric sensation run through her torso and arms. Suddenly every part of her felt alive, alert, thrilled. She couldn't tell if the trembling she felt was

Rosie's or her own, and the effort to remain still almost brought her to tears, too. The sensuality disturbed her, a taboo feeling.

Jenner fussed and Brian began to roar. Chloe disentangled from Rosie and brought him over then picked up Jenner. They sat up in bed together feeding the babies, a swirl of joy running through her body, clearly erotic. Neither spoke until Jenner broke away and gurgled. After Brian finished, Chloe switched the babies and played with wisps of hair on Brian's scalp. He gave a rambunctious baby smile.

"Look at his eyes," she said. "Blue-grey. Jarrett's eyes."

A sweet baby, and he had Jarrett's mouth, too. Rosie watched him in Chloe's arms, and a new feeling jolted her. She lifted a strand of his hair and ran it over her finger. She began to love him, a small Jarrett.

The next day she roused at seven and slowly made her way through the house picking up discarded jackets, returning shoes to closets, and announced she'd cook breakfast for everyone. Chloe was carrying garbage out when Jarrett emerged from the garage. He stared at her, an unreadable expression in his eyes, or maybe she didn't want to read it.

"Thank you."

His stare unnerved her. "I didn't do it for you," she snapped.

He halted. "What's your problem with me?"

Chloe dumped the bag into the can, fled to her car and sat there with the doors locked, pretending to be on the phone. She hadn't meant to speak to him like that. What she had meant she didn't know. His stare, it suggested something—he suspected what she felt for Rosie and her retort confirmed it. She breathed deeply. Impossible of course. Jarrett had always kept his distance with her—or was she distant with him? She'd apologize, he'd dismiss it. But why had she lost it like that? He took Rosie away.

Jenner wanted to be in motion and fussed if they weren't jiggling her, rocking or strolling her, sailing her through the air like a glider. At six months they discovered the miracle of the jumpy-chair where Jenner bounced for stretches of time. Chloe cooed to her, tones that felt strange to her, and when her arms were free, she did other things. Peter bought a second jumpy chair and set it up in his studio so he could take her with him. There would be no nanny for Jenner.

He lamented his lack of productivity. A few of his albums were making money, but basically Chloe paid the bills. Sharing her wealth felt thorny: a relief to have no worries, to buy nice things, but a prickling of guilt disturbed his ease. His reputation as a producer had dimmed, though he muddled on, relying on the fact that he was mostly raising Jenner to justify his existence. He called her Bananaflower.

"Are you sure banana trees have flowers?"

He showed her his computer screen. A brilliant purplish-red blossom had become his screen saver.

He pureed bananas, carrots, pears, spinach, applesauce which Jenner took to eagerly. She slurped and slapped the food around, looking like an abstract canvas when feeding time was over. Chloe guided Jenner's hand to her mouth as much as she would let her, but Jenner preferred to bang the spoon on the high chair tray. At seven months she fussed at Chloe's breast, refusing to nurse.

"She's just not as hungry," Peter said, "with all the solid food she eats now."

"No, she's on strike. I've read about that. It happens. It passes."

It was a relief, though she hated to admit it. Breast-feeding's claim was so intensive, devouring her time off work, evenings swallowed whole by Jenner's sporadic nursing. She latched and unlatched, distracted, smiling, fussing. Chloe fretted, dogged and patient at first, finally frustrated, which made Jenner fuss more until she weaned herself at eight months and refused to nurse even at bedtime. Chloe's breasts hurt, she was weepy, and once her milk let down at work before she could pump, staining her blouse. Jenner was rejecting her. Peter said it was Jenner's independent streak, or her precociousness, or how she loved being active.

"Look how early she crawled, and she already stands in her crib when we put her down. It's crazy to take it personally."

She kept pumping, hating it, plugged into a machine instead of her baby. Easier and faster, but she hated it. She wouldn't admit that weaning had its consolations or that she was glad to be done with nursing. The downside—Jenner seemed more than ever like Peter's child—triggered more doubt and growing discomfort about work. She moved some of her clients' accounts into index funds and passive investments—better for them, better for her.

She needed to change things up before she had another baby. When the market got volatile, she moved investments around. Otherwise it helped that these accounts required less, and they seemed to do as well. The urge to create fireworks, skyrocketing gains, risky guesses that paid off big, the kind of thing that had gained her kudos but kept her on edge, waned. Better to be a good manager than a wizard, one of her professors once said.

She turned down a rising guitarist who wanted her to take on more risk. "Let someone else handle him," she told a senior partner. "We're not suited to each other temperamentally." Those clients were the first to turn on you when things went south, but she wouldn't have dared to turn him down earlier.

A large house off Hillsboro came on the market, and she persuaded Peter that they should make an offer. He was satisfied with Chloe's condo, Jenner's room next to theirs. She had finally settled into her room, out of their bedroom, over objections from Peter. "I need a home office," she said. "And so do you. Soon Jenner will want siblings." Never mind what she herself wanted, the way to persuade Peter was through Jenner.

She hired a decorator, and they moved on Chloe's thirty-second birthday. Jenner got a child bed near her crib and started napping there. Downstairs was Chloe's office, plus a den insulated for Peter's sound system. Walking past Petco she saw a black and white fluff of kitten in a cage with other rescue cats. She paid the fees, bought supplies, and carried the little guy home, presented him to Peter and Jenner. "Francisco." Francisco turned out to be a girl, a Maine Coon mix. She attached herself to Chloe, slept at her feet every night, dropped soft fluffs of black and white hair on the new bedspread and upholstered chairs. Family. She held her breath when she thought the word.

Kath and Dee didn't meet the baby until Jenner was nine months. They drove up from Florida and only stayed two nights. Chloe was quietly furious they hadn't come sooner and fed them take out food Peter picked up at a Thai restaurant. Kath wouldn't hold Jenner, insisting the baby wouldn't like it. Finally Chloe put Jenner in her arms. Jenner looked at her curiously, looked back at Peter, then Chloe, and began to cry.

"I told you," Kath said as she handed her back.

"It's just stranger anxiety, Mom. At this age babies realize they don't know you. She'll get used to you, and she'll be fine. Play with her a little while I hold her."

"No, no. I don't want to upset her."

Kath asked if she had put Jenner's hair into the locket. Chloe realized she had forgotten about the locket. She dug it out and while she read to Jenner, Kath quickly snipped a piece of her dark hair. Jenner patted her head and turned to see what Kath had done then broke into a wail. "You see. She's scared of me," Kath said.

"It's not you, Mom. She just doesn't understand."

Dee spent most of the visit watching TV. Chloe was relieved they only stayed two nights.

# CHAPTER 16

"She'll be fine."

"Look at her."

Two-year-old Jenner cried wildly: they were leaving without her. Ruth tried to soothe the child but she wouldn't quiet. Peter turned back, took her from Ruth, held her close and talked to her, then looked plaintively at Chloe. Chloe paced and circled, finally peeled her from Peter and handed her back to Ruth, took him by the arm, and headed to the car. Jenner was still reaching frantically when Chloe backed the car out. She pulled over once they were out of sight and asked, "Do you really not want to go?"

She'd lobbied for a second honeymoon, back to California to the cottage on the coast which Chloe thought of as theirs now. Peter had postponed it twice already.

"Of course I want to go. It seems harsh to just drive away, though."

"We spent half an hour there."

He looked miserable. She drove around the block and stopped far enough down the street that Jenner wouldn't see them. She was picking flowers from the front garden and handing them to Ruth. Chloe turned the car around and headed for the airport. It took Peter most of the flight to settle, but by the time they drove up the Pacific Coast he was humming. Four days.

They floated on the Russian River, walked in a redwood forest. They had not been good lovers the past two years, with the demands of pregnancy and nursing, lack of sleep and Peter's absorption in Jenner. The first morning, passion sparked like loose flint, a brief fire. It had not been totally lost. It wasn't only his loss of interest she feared, but hers. And, she thought, Now maybe I'll get pregnant again.

When they returned, Jenner insisted on sleeping in her big bed. "Not yet, missy," Peter said. Jenner yelled, "But I *want* to!" Chloe came into the room, sided with her.

"Her independent streak," she reminded him.

Chloe tucked Jenner into the new bed and read *Goodnight Moon*. Jenner drifted off the second time through, arms around Hugo, her plush purple elephant. She turned the nightlight on, tiptoed out, leaving the door ajar, and secured the child-proof gate at the top of the stairs. The monitor was on—Peter could check on her in the night if he was worried.

She didn't tell Peter when she missed her next period. Not yet. He wouldn't be as thrilled as he was the first time. He'd think it was too soon, Jenner might feel displaced. Three weeks later Chloe woke in the night, her belly cramping hard, her period after all, though inexplicably late. She had been bleeding heavily each month, but this was different, too much blood, too much pain. A miscarriage? She was up the rest of the night, blood soaking through a pad every half hour. Twice she looked in to see Jenner sleeping soundly. At six a.m. Peter found Chloe doubled over on the bathroom floor and called Ruth to come.

"Probably a fibroid," the ER doctor said as Chloe lay on the table. "The uterus is enlarged, but it's probably not a sarcoma."

Peter stared at him. "Sarcoma?"

"Not likely, but biopsy's the only way to be sure."

"Biopsy it."

"We'll have to do a D&C."

"Do it."

"Wait a frigging minute," Chloe shouted over them, foggy from medication. She sat up, and Peter put his arm around her as the surgeon arrived.

"We should do what the doctor suggests, Chloe. You don't want to take a chance."

Chloe tried to reassure him—it was a fibroid, benign. He kept repeating, "You don't know that. What if it's cancer?" This doctor sided with Peter too.

Post-surgery she fought back to consciousness through a thick batting of anesthesia, vaguely conscious when the doctor appeared. She asked if she could go home.

"Good news. It was benign."

"I knew it." She lifted her hand, let it drop limply back, closed then opened her eyes again. The doctor lingered, looking unhappy.

"There's bad news, too, Chloe. The procedure was difficult. There was severe bleeding. More than expected. We had to do a hysterectomy."

"NO!" Chloe said. She bolted upright, but a jagged sharpness pierced her gut. She lay back and put her hands on her face.

"It was the only thing to do. That was a very big fibroid, too big just to take it out. You'd have had trouble."

"You can't do this! What about what I want?"

"I didn't expect this, but you were hemorrhaging. Turns out you were pregnant, too. I'm so sorry. Did you know that?"

She nodded, but she didn't believe him. Surely there were other options. Peter came in with Jenner. She felt dizzy looking at him. He'd made her do this. It was all about losing Angie. He had a fault line in him, seismic vulnerability too easy to trigger.

She wouldn't speak to him afterward, roaming the house in her pajamas, weeping, the sutures like little knives. Francisco followed her room to room, sat in her lap when she exhausted herself. Chloe left her diaphragm on Peter's pillow one morning for him to dispose of, then retrieved it and tossed it into the garbage with the plastic wrap, the cat litter and the empty blister package for the estrogen pills she took now.

She wouldn't talk to Rosie, either. Angie was responsible, somehow, but she couldn't say that to Rosie. She knew it, though. Angie was still around. Why? She asked. Why this? Not that Angie would answer. Or maybe she had already. Peter wasn't ready for another child.

———

"How's Chloe dealing with the hysterectomy?" Jarrett asked as they passed the outskirts of Knoxville.

"What are you talking about? Wait a minute," Rosie paused. "Chloe had a hysterectomy?"

"Yeah. I thought you knew. Something went awry, Peter said, and they had to."

They were driving through farmland, the Cumberland plateau toward Nashville. Rosie's mood was buoyant since they left Asheville, but now she thumped her head against the headrest and exhaled heavily. A few miles east of Lebanon she grabbed her phone and called, practically shouting at Chloe. "I just learned you had a hysterectomy. Why did you not tell me? I can't believe it. That is so wrong!"

Jarrett motioned her to tone down, pointing to Brian in the back, collapsed against his carseat, napping.

"Of course! Of course I mean the hysterectomy. And I'm also really hurt you didn't tell me. Why did I have to learn this from Jarrett?"

Rosie's huff was evident when they arrived. She embraced Chloe stiffly, did not look at her or smile. Jarrett tried to ease the tension by suggesting the guys would cook a big dinner. "I'll do a rack of lamb and Peter can make his fancy blistered beans. You take the kids to the park while we make a quick run to pick up meat and produce. We'll have a feast."

Chloe said they should go to Bare Bones, ask for Clyde. "I think you know him, Peter. He'll choose a good one."

"I want to go with Peter." Rosie said. "Jarrett, do you mind?"

Punishment, Chloe knew, leaving her with Jarrett. As they drove off, Jarrett called the kids out to the yard, picked up a ball, and tossed it toward Jenner. Alone in the kitchen, Chloe understood: he didn't like being stuck with her either.

———

Peter picked up the meat, then swung by an outdoor market and Rosie went in, returned with a sack of green bean, new potatoes, and a blackberry galette. Instead of heading home, he drove to the house where he once lived with Angie and parked. They sat in front, staring. A tricycle lay on its side on the porch and a soccer goal was set up on the lawn. "You come by here often?"

He shook his head. "Too painful. I thought maybe you'd want to see it."

"Not really. I don't like being in Nashville. It brings it all back. I go down the rabbit hole again, asking why Angie's not here. What are those people doing in her house? Don't they know she's coming back?"

"That's what I mean. I miss you being here."

"I miss you, too. It's why I'm here now. I need to see everyone, I just don't need to see Nashville. Better for me to be in a new town." She turned away from the house. "Even if I don't want to live here, I hate what it's done, me leaving. Everything feels fucked up again. Look at what happened to Chloe. I ask myself if it would have happened if I'd been here."

"Oh. You think I failed her."

"I don't mean that. I don't know, I can't explain it." Peter had started the car, idled in neutral, still staring at the house. "I'm upset she didn't tell me. It makes me feel like *I* failed her in some way."

"Nobody failed her. It was a matter of saving her life, for God's sake. You don't know. You weren't there."

"That's what I'm saying. I wasn't there."

"What do you think you could have done? When the doctor came out after the D&C and said she was bleeding heavily, you think I was going to let her bleed out? What would you have done?

"I don't know. You had to agree, of course. I would have done the same."

"This is what you did when Angie died, Rosie. Like I could have saved her."

"You're right." Rosie covered her face. "I'm sorry. I'm so sorry. What's the matter with me?" She looked at him with her pleading eyes. "I can't stand it that we have no control over things. That bad things happen and we're helpless. I can't stand it. I have to imagine what if's."

"Nobody can stand it."

"You must hate me. How self-centered I am."

"I could never hate you. You know that. I know too well what you feel. Life's too fragile. If I were in your shoes, I'd probably blame you." He eased the car slowly forward. "We're a pair."

"I don't know why I flip so easily and turn into a bitch." She touched his arm. "It's complicated between us, you know. Once I thought we might be a thing. A possibility, always off in the distance, I guess. Before Angie, after Angie. What a mess we would have made, though. So much better for you to be with someone like Angie or Chloe who can pick up the reins." Peter flinched. "Come on. You know it's true. And I need a durable guy like Jarrett."

Peter scowled.

"Here's another reason I'm being difficult. I'm pregnant again, and I can't bear to tell Chloe."

———

Chloe threw toys and snacks and water bottles into a back pack. "Come on, Rosie. Let's walk the kids to the park. We need time."

"You might want to ask Peter first. He'll tell you what kind of company I am."

"Go," Peter said.

They got the kids out the door but neither would get in a stroller, so they ambled down the sidewalk, stopping when Brian stood transfixed by a dog in a neighbor's window. Jenner pulled him on. She wanted to get to the swings.

"He wants a dog but, no, not yet."

Chloe pushed both children in the swings while Rosie watched. She helped Jenner climb the slide, clapped for her her at the bottom as she landed gleefully on her bottom. Brian wanted Rosie to catch him when he came down, but he wriggled away and stood on his feet, raced back to the stairs, went down faster, and raced back again. Jenner toddled off to the climbing structure, Brian waddled after her. The climbing structure was too high for them so Chloe led to a sandy area, and Rosie sat on a bench to watch, hoping the amount of sand that was flung or swallowed wouldn't require someone to intercede.

Jenner told Brian they needed to make a mountain. Their little hands worked hard to create a huge heap of sand, almost as tall as they were, running back and forth with a bucket some child had left behind, patting it into a cone shape.

Chloe joined her on the bench. "You're still mad at me."

"You bet. No. I'm hurt. It's such a big thing not to tell me. I don't understand, Chloe. I know you're upset, but we talk when we're upset, don't we?"

"This was different."

"How?"

"I couldn't bear it. I was pregnant, too. I couldn't speak about it. And I was so furious at Peter, I couldn't even talk to him. Finally he just left me alone, and that's what I needed. I felt like I'd been assaulted. No more children. I can't accept it. "

"I don't want to leave you alone. I want you to talk to me. You have to talk about it."

"Actually I don't. There's nothing left to say."

The children ran over and pulled toys from a bag Rosie brought. Jenner raced a car up and over their mountain while Brian stuck little sticks in, making a tree-lined road for her car.

"I'm trying not to sink into a hole. I should probably go to therapy again."

Rosie moved closer and put her arm around Chloe, who had tears in her eyes. Jenner looked at them, a question on her face. "It's okay, sweetie." Rosie said to her. "Your mama just needs to cry a few minutes. She'll be okay."

Chloe wiped at her face. Too many feelings, all dangerous. "I know you're there. I appreciate it, more than you imagine, Rosie. I'm just still in a dark place with it. I don't want it to be real. I want to be angry, not sad."

"Be angry. Be angry at Peter. Be angry at me."

Chloe shook her head. "I'm angry at Angie. I didn't know how to say that to you."

"Angie!"

"It sounds crazy. I know. But sometimes I feel like she's a force in my life."

"Say more."

"Like she's around, part of being married to Peter. I feel my life steered this way and that by her. She wanted Peter to have a child, and we got Jenner. He didn't necessarily want another one though. Jenner's enough for him, and he can't imagine loving another child like her. I feel like she made the hysterectomy happen."

Rosie's eyes narrowed, her mouth skewed to one side, thinking.

Chloe wanted to explain, but how? "I'm sure you don't want to hear this."

Rosie shushed her. "Let's just sit here a minute with the thought."

"I wish I could make her go away."

The terrifying swerve on the icy bridge—was Angie trying to stop her from being with Jarrett? She told Angie to go away. She never told Chloe because it sounded so crazy. It brought up mayhem inside when she thought of having told Angie to go away, then she did go away.

"The dead seem to have their own morality," Rosie said at last. "I understand how you can feel that. Maybe loss turns us into crazy women. I've felt mad that way myself."

"You understand I don't really really believe this. I just feel it."

"Chloe, I've also heard her. I don't think she went very far away."

Chloe looked skeptically at her.

"What if she's telling us things in the only way we can understand? Things we can't see ourselves. When I was in the ER waiting for news of her that night, my mother told me it doesn't matter what you believe. I've thought about that. It does and it doesn't, but whether you believe in something isn't what makes it true. If something is, it just is."

———

Jarrett prepped the lamb, Peter chopped garlic. On their second beer already, Peter flashed the knives around. "Look at these," he held up two gleaming blades. "Hand-hammered. This set cost almost as much as a studio monitor."

"You admiring or complaining?"

"Awed. I don't complain about Chloe's money. I live on it."

"What happened to that drive of yours?"

"I don't know. It fell away with Angie. I'm trying. She was my business manager. Maybe my muse. Rosie thinks she was also my emotional manager." He shook his head, took a whiff of the garlic and sprinkled it on the pink meat along with herbs. Jarrett came behind him, salted it, and pressed the herbs in.

"She sold the CDs at concerts, made our brochures with software she picked up at EMI. We did well in those days, made actual money. She came to the studio while I recorded. She handled social media. I was grateful to be just the music guy."

"Hire some people. Get your stuff on a streaming platform."

"Yeah, yeah. I should do that, I guess. You still traveling, interviewing musicians?"

"Yup. Money's rolling through the South, and music's a healthy part of it. You're missing out. I've been meeting a hip-hop artist in Atlanta, Antwone Brown, founder of *Noize Heet*. You know the label?"

Peter laughed. "Not my music. I wouldn't be cashing in."

"You don't know what else is out there these days. Come with me next time. I interview a lot of different musicians. Might get your juices flowing again."

"Thanks. I don't think so. Jenner's at a stage. Doesn't like to be separated."

"Chloe would be there."

"No nanny."

"You guys need a nanny! If anyone can afford it, it's you."

"It's not the money. I don't like to be away. Ever since Angie, I don't know, I just…" He raised his palms helplessly. "I seem laid back maybe, but I live on an edge. I don't feel in control of anything. Maybe that's what killed my drive. I suppose Rosie's right."

Jarrett wiped off the meat thermometer and stuck it in, slid the pan into the oven.

"If I'm honest, I still hate it that you took Rosie away. When I'm with Jenner I feel at peace. Only then."

"So she's your emotional manager now?"

Peter scowled. "Please. I don't need that."

"Sorry. Just ragging you."

"Yeah. Seems to be the favorite sport today."

———

A few days after they left, Peter told Chloe that Rosie was pregnant again. She sucked in her breath. "Oh." She headed out to the backyard, began pulling weeds from the rose bed then sat in the grass and let out a wail. She didn't care who heard her. Then steady sobs, pent up since the surgery. She went into the garage and pulled her bike from the ceiling hook. Not in shape and not fully healed, it hurt to be on her bike again, but she rode quickly to Otter Creek Road and powered up a steep hill. Her hamstrings twinged into fiery resistance, and pain in her abdomen forced her off the bike. She called Peter to pick her up. Furious now, she limped around waiting. Even that hurt. She pulled out her phone and called Rosie, started in as soon as she answered.

"You let me find out from Peter. After we talked! After what you said about talking."

"I was protecting you, Chloe. You're dealing with something devastating."

"You think I'm an emotional cripple now? It's humiliating. Like when you decided to marry Jarrett, and we had to learn that from your mother. I don't want you shielding me. I'm a grownup. I deal with things." She hardly let her speak until Peter pulled up. "Were you planning to hide the pregnancy? Never see us again? If you wanted me to be angry, I am now. Peter's here. I have to go."

Text messages popped on her phone. She ignored them until they were home. *I'm so sorry.* Then *I was waiting until you felt more healed.* Then *I should know better.* Chloe deleted them.

Rosie was right. She wasn't ready to deal with this. How could she not envy her? After a few hours she gathered her feelings in and sent Rosie a text. *I'm happy for you. You deserve more joy.*

Rosie tagged it with a heart, and Chloe sent another. *Feeling better now. Call me, okay?* 🌹🌹🌹. *Congrats!* 🍾.

She would walk into this upright. She would be happy for Rosie.

# CHAPTER 17

Even swamped at work, Chloe took Rosie's calls. Even when she skipped Peter's. And Rosie, almost due, called daily. She knew the sex of the baby this time—another boy. "I'm okay with it. Three boys. I know boys."

The pregnancy was harder than the first two, more nausea and moodiness, and Brian was tearing around the house, brimming with defiance until Rosie felt she was losing her mind. Chloe coaxed her through fatigue, heartburn. "I know. I remember...I had that, too, with Jenner and had to eat a lot of little meals...Get a fatter pillow. Or sleep on two...Hire some help. An after-school teenager." The delivery was easier though, and Rosie called from the hospital. It was a girl.

"How could they make such a mistake?" Chloe asked. "I thought they saw a penis."

"No idea, but there's no penis, just all girl parts. We're arguing over her name."

Rosie had flirted with naming her Angelina, then thought Angie might not like it. *Don't tempt her*, Rosie thought with a shudder.

"We planned to name the baby Andrew. So I said, 'Let's name her Andrea. We'll call her Andie.' And Jarrett said that was a boy's name. So I said, 'Don't be so gender rigid. Who cares? And what about Andie MacDowell? What about the girl in *Toy Story*?' He named Brian. I should get to choose this one."

Still close to Angie, Chloe thought, when she heard the name. She was lying on her bed, stroking the cat as they talked.

She wanted to visit, wanted to breathe that intoxicating baby scent, but it was too soon. After Ruth had come and gone, Rosie said Jarrett was happy to have the house back to them. He probably never wanted her there, especially if she came without Peter. When they ended the call, she brooded about Peter. He still hardly worked. In fact he seemed to do little but play with Jenner and run errands for her. She went downstairs and waited for him to finish putting Jenner to bed still.

He came down late, crooning a lullaby, so she snapped at him. "You need to be producing music again. Your lull has lasted too long."

"Why are you yelling at me?"

"You're wasting your time in the studio. You take Jenner with you instead of dropping her at preschool, and I know you don't do anything but hang with her and your stoner friends." She looked at him, her eyes ferocious. "You have talent, Peter. You need to work. I could send people your way."

"Don't you dare! I feel bad enough that my wife supports me."

"Then do something about it! You're too obsessed with Jenner!"

"Don't start. I could say something about how you're always working, but I'm not going there." He walked out of the room.

"You already did!" She came after him. "Bad enough that you're a white guy who made money off Black music. At least you could do the work!" She saw it plainly on his face, his wound. She shouldn't have picked at such a tender area.

"You can have this fight by yourself."

Francisco crept over, cast inquisitive eyes on Chloe. She picked the cat up, nuzzled her, walked around the house cradling her on her shoulder like an infant. Later Peter apologized, then she did. He rubbed her shoulders. "I know how hard you work. You provide so much for us. I should do more. I'm going to do more. Honest. Trust me."

The next time she called Rosie she grumbled, "You should make Jarrett move to Nashville. These children ought to grow up together. Our lives were in sync until you left." Brian had taken his first shaky steps on Chloe and Peter's lawn as Jenner clapped her hands. "You shouldn't fight cosmic influence."

"I know. It's just, Jarrett's job's so good. His column anchors the second section now."

"The *Tennessean*'s bigger. It's won more awards and he'd probably make more money. I know one of the editors and could pass his work to him."

"He'd be furious."

"I wouldn't, if he didn't want me to."

That night she dreamed Angie was a realtor showing properties to Rosie in Nashville. Each house amazed her: spacious lawns, views of mountains and lakes, roomy closets, huge bedrooms. The next morning she woke in a fog of yearning.

———

Over breakfast Rosie said to Jarrett, "I've been thinking. What if we moved to Nashville?"

"Why? Why would we do that?"

"To be close to my parents, to Peter and Chloe. We could raise our kids together, and you could get a job on the *Tennessean*."

He stared at her, not in a friendly way.

"We need to move anyway. We need a bigger house."

Brian was in Willie's small room and could reach into his crib from his own bed. Every morning he woke Willie to play with him before their parents got up. Andie slept with them of course, but she'd need a room someday, too, even if Willie and Brian shared a room.

"You think?" Clearly he was displeased, maybe offended. She let it drop.

A week later he came home with news. He'd asked around and a friend of a friend had a house ready to go on the market who might give them a good price if it didn't require a realtor. They drove over that weekend to take a look. A long backyard opened to a wooded trail which led half a mile to a stream with small waterfalls. The rooms weren't large and the house was dated, but there were four bedrooms. It felt spacious. She sighed. She did love Asheville. Better than Nashville. A small town with city culture, progressive politics, more so than Nashville's, and the mountains. Never had she lived anywhere this beautiful.

"Honestly, Chloe, we can't give up this house. Jarrett won't leave anyway. He got majorly grumpy when I suggested it. Four bedrooms. It's not as large as yours, but roomy enough for us. Almost equal!" She sounded nervous. "They're ready to give us a good price. You'll love it, I promise. A trail runs out of the backyard all the way to Beaver Lake. And his editor agreed to turn his columns into a book."

Chloe didn't want to talk about the house. She had her doubts about whether Rosie really tried to get Jarrett to move. "How's Andie?"

"She's great, just willful. She's not an easy baby, but she laughs at everything. She thinks Brian's hysterical. For a while I tried to think of her as a little Angie, but she's so not."

"She sounds more like a little Rosie."

"Maybe. Meanwhile it's a mess here again, our house is a mess. So much to clean  before we move. If I were teaching, I'd have an excuse, but two babies feels like enough excuse. Aunt Laraine brings us dinner at least once a week, and she always tidies things. Clicks her tongue, but doesn't say a word. I truly am a lousy housekeeper."

"Maybe you should move every time the house gets out of control." Chloe's tone had a bit of sarcasm which Rosie ignored.

"Good idea. Now Brian will get a room. And you'll be able to stay at our house. No more hotel rooms."

---

Driving into Asheville after they moved, Chloe stopped at a nursery to buy a sapling. Their new yard had nice trees in front, fewer in the back. She wanted to plant something there, proof she was fine that they were never moving to Nashville. Overcompensating, she told herself. Whatever it took to keep her disappointment from causing a rift. A paperbark maple caught her eye with its habit of shedding skin in long curls, and she paid extra to have it delivered the next day. She'd put it in the ground herself.

Rosie hardly let Andie out of her arms. It gave Chloe chills. "Let me hold her. I need to hold a baby again."

Rosie handed her over with a sigh. "I don't like to put her down. Since my sister died, I forgot what happy feels like. I mean really happy. When Jarrett asked me to marry him, he promised he'd make me happy. I laughed—expecting happiness is like expecting a Nobel Prize for just existing, don't you think? But here I am."

"Can't fully relate, but I'm happy for you."

Chloe had left Jenner with Peter this trip. He was so wrapped up in her these days she doubted either would miss her. They had their daily routines, their private games. He kept a closet full of toys in his studio. When he took her to the park, he carried her and used the stroller for her gear. Naturally Jenner gravitated toward Peter.

"Oh, sweetie, Jenner will shift." Rosie said as they walked Andie in a stroller through her new neighborhood. "Children just do. You know how they are, they prefer one, then the other. Remember Willie, how he loved having a dad so much after Jarrett and I married? I thought we'd never be close again."

Twice Chloe asked Jarrett about his work, but he gave a short answer and said he had to mow the lawn the first time. The second time he shrugged. "About the same." She thought, as she often did, of the trembling sensation she felt that afternoon she lay in bed with Rosie, and felt guilt again. Whenever she tried to engage him, the memory rose. Did he know her feelings somehow?

———

Rosie and Jarrett's sex had been disrupted by pregnancy then babies, but the first years they still felt new to each other, and once they threw a blanket on the grass in the privacy of the backyard while Brian napped. Rosie had stripped off her clothes with abandon and run around the yard until he pulled her to the blanket. "Crazy woman. Stay over here, or Mrs. Magley will see you." She didn't care. Making love under a cloudless sky was maybe the best way to feel free.

That was before Andie. Sex had less allure now, and they wanted no more babies. Jarrett suggested a tubal ligation. She suggested a vasectomy. He thought it over and agreed. It seemed to light him up. That gave her pause.

Andie didn't nap much. Too many things to pay attention to, especially Brian. As soon as she crawled, she went looking for him. "Bi, bi," she called out. Rosie spent her days tracking the two of them. Andie loved nursing though and lifted Rosie's shirt to put her hands on her breasts for comfort. Rosie had to stop her from doing it in public. Body contact was the only thing that got her to sleep in the afternoons. She lay on Rosie and sucked her thumb, a soft collapse of baby flesh molded to Rosie's body that made her croon.

Angie seemed to have gone farther away.

The babies left her less shapely, rounder, and her clothes a size larger. Weight gain kept her breasts full, if more veined. Looking in the mirror she shrugged at the changes. If this was the price of happiness, fine. Jarrett didn't complain. He was preoccupied with writing his stories anyway.

They furnished the new house with a big sectional sofa and a large TV, a dining table extendable to seat ten. Dirty clothes littered the laundry area again, stacks of mail, newspapers accumulated for days before she cleared them. It didn't matter because she was happy. Each time she lifted Andie, felt the heft of her body in her arms, her little padded bottom in the crook of her elbow, a rush of pleasure surged through her. She believed she'd sprouted new receptors in her brain. As she fell into sleep at night a floating feeling streamed through her body.

Jarrett travelled to the mountains for days. At home he was often moody. Sometimes he seemed better when he returned, but if she asked about his mood, he got annoyed. Did the changes in her body annoy him, turn him off? After a meeting with Mac one day he came home and slammed things around in his study, then went outside, pulled out the power saw to cut wood for the fireplace. Rosie worried he'd lose a finger in that state.

Once a week he talked to Hillie. The voice she heard from the other room sounded like a different Jarrett, quiet, intimate, close, then a loud hoot of laughter. Jealousy crept up, like bile. Was his cousin the love of his life after all?

She had occupied her own heart with her babies. Marriages change, after all.

—————

Chloe complained to Angie about Peter: You coddled him, did too much for him. He has no internal engine left. She had a new therapist to complain to as well, a woman named Jane, and she liked Jane fine, liked her sense of humor, though Jane wasn't Hannah. She lacked Hannah's gravitas, her resonance with deep difficult feelings, at least Chloe feared she did and was reluctant to test her. In sessions she mostly talked about Peter, not the hysterectomy, or how she felt inadequate as a mother, and certainly not about Rosie. When she told Jane about Angie's auditory presence, and that she talked back to her, Jane smiled mysteriously.

The more she talked about Peter, the angrier she got. Jane suggested couples therapy and gave her a name. Chloe took it back to Peter. "I want to go to couples therapy."

"Come on. It's not that bad, is it?"

"Yes, it is. We need to go."

The couples therapist made a few stabs at Peter's relationship with Jenner, but Peter was such a laid-back dad, so devoted that it was hard to pinpoint something unhealthy about it. He didn't make much money, but neither of them brought up that. Chloe's demeanor, on the other hand, drew his attention. She felt misunderstood by the therapist, sure he assessed her as cold, driven, angry. She tried to correct his impression by showing other feelings, tried to be more sympathetic until it made her sick to do it. Pathetic.

Peter defended her. "Chloe's a great mother. No question. She's good with Jenner. Jenner's always been more attached to me. I honestly don't know why. That happens, don't you think?

Chloe found his assertions humiliating. She didn't need a defense attorney. They weren't in court, were they? "My hours at work don't interfere with my relationship with Jenner. Lots of parents work as much as I do. I just want Peter to work again."

"Hmm. This is unusual, a mother complaining that the father does *too much* with the child. You want Peter to make more money?"

"It's not about money. It's the waste. He had a growing production studio. He does nothing now."

"Except take care of your child."

Peter tried to point blame at himself, admitted he didn't work much. "It's just that Jenner gets upset if I take her to preschool. I think it's good for her to have a parent available."

The therapist seemed to ally with him more. Chloe hated the process. The therapist couldn't see her at all. What she couldn't bring herself to say was that she felt left out, that this family stirred up old feelings. She couldn't say she felt unloved. Being unloved made you seem unloveable. *Maybe you really are a problem,* Angie whispered.

After an especially frustrating session, she said. "This is doing nothing. I'd rather stay with my own therapy."

"Sure. Whatever. I never thought we needed therapy. We'll work this out ourselves."

---

She signed Jenner up for Saturday swim classes to have time alone with her. Watching her scoot under the surface of the water, her body undulating to the other side of the pool, she could almost feel the fluid silk of water on her own skin, the joy of supple motion. She hadn't been in water in ages and missed it. It was Jenner's element, too. The child was a fearless creature in the pool unlike some children. After class they went for sushi so Jenner could get maki rolls, her favorite food. "Do you like hanging out at Daddy's studio."

"Um-hmm. Except when it's boring."

"When is it boring?"

"When his friends are smoking. Their smoke doesn't smell good, and they get quiet. I like their music best. He lets me do the tambrine."

"Mmm. Yeah, I bet you're good with that. He says he's going to make a new album with some of those guys. Is that what they're doing?"

"I don't know but I played the tambrine with them on a song about a submrine."

"Can't wait to hear it. Should we go get ice cream?"

"Does a bear shit the woods?"

"Jenner! Where did you hear that?"

"One of the guys says it a lot. Is it bad?"

"Well, 'shit' isn't a very nice word."

"Okay. I'll try not to say it. Daddy says it, though, and so do you."

Chloe sighed. "Okay. But it's not a kid word."

When she got home, she went after Peter and threw Jenner's report back at him. He smiled ruefully.

"You're smiling. You think it's funny."

"Yeah. A little bit funny. Okay, I'll make sure folks go outside to get stoned. I'd rather they get arrested than have you mad."

"That's not funny, either."

Where had she wanted this conversation to go? Picking another fight, but it was tangled with feelings about Jenner and herself as a mother. Mother. She still didn't easily claim that word. That's what she should talk to her therapist about. Kath. She dreaded being like Kath. Then she realized she also dreaded losing her someday. That was a new thought. They were all getting older.

For a few weeks Peter took Jenner to her new school every morning and said he was placing calls at work, talking to musicians he used to know. Nothing was clicking so far. "Maybe I just don't have it any more. Maybe I should do something beside blues." He raised his arms helplessly.

Chloe offered to take Jenner to Asheville for a week so he'd have more time to think about music. He blanched.

"Don't do that. It'll happen." His face lit up. "Actually I have a new idea. I'll do an album of music for children. Covers of old songs. I'll introduce kids to our old music, and it won't take that long to produce. I know a couple of folks who'd be terrific vocalists on it. I'll call it *Ruby Bananaflower.*"

As he went to his office to send some emails, he was humming.

# CHAPTER 18

The drive to Nashville in July didn't go well. Brian was a high energy creature, and Willie couldn't keep him entertained. Andie fussed, Brian taunted her, "Big baby! You're such a big baby!" He pinched her until she screamed, and Jarrett snapped. "You better fucking quiet down back there." At a rest area he walked into the woods for twenty minutes. He apologized but Rosie was furious at all of them.

"I don't think we'll be driving over again any time soon," Rosie told Chloe. Chloe tracked their visits, five for Rosie and Jarrett including holidays at her parents. She'd been to Asheville nine times, with and without Peter. Rosie wouldn't drive alone with the kids, and Jarrett didn't like to come, although he and Peter were good friends now. It's me, Chloe thought.

"Unfair, I know. But please, as much as you can, Chloe, come. I miss you. I need to see you."

Thanksgiving, Chloe drove their new car after they passed Knoxville so Peter could sit in the back with Jenner. She'd turned cranky and clamored for Peter to sit next to her and sing. Chloe played his new album, which Jenner loved, but she still whined. "I need Daddy to sing."

Peter's voice suited a child. He couldn't do justice to blues or bluegrass, any of the adult music he'd worked with, but he could do voices children loved. He recorded himself on the new album, a version of "Stayin' Alive" on which he hooted and threw his voice up to a squeaky high level. Jenner squealed with laughter and made him do it around the house.

It was oddly warm for November, close to eighty. Rosie met them at the door with two-year-old Andie in her arms, mother and child rosy-cheeked in matching sundresses. Mid-life happiness still left her breathless.

"Oh, look at her. She's changed so much." Chloe eyed the child hungrily. Reluctantly Rosie handed her over to Chloe. Andie patted Chloe's cheeks, and Chloe kissed the top of her head.

"Put Jenner in with Brian," Rosie told Peter. "Andie still sleeps in our room."

"Jenner will want to be in our room," Peter replied.

"No! I want to sleep with Brian." Jenner dashed off in search of him as Peter carried the suitcases in.

Rosie tried to take Andie back, but she wanted to run after Jenner. "I guess we're not letting go until these babes are thirty." Chloe gave Rosie a look.

Rosie said. "I know. Hopeless."

Jarrett was in the kitchen chopping nuts for tomorrow's stuffing. He greeted them and cocked his head toward Rosie. "I've been telling her she needs to stop this twin thing with Andie."

"It's not a twin thing!" Rosie flicked her hand at him. "I just like these dresses."

"Yeah. And the matching tights. And the bathing suits."

Rosie threw a dishtowel at him. "It's not a problem. Don't make it one."

Aunt Laraine, in high-heeled sandals and red sundress, stood at the sink polishing a silver-plated gravy boat. "Don't be mad, honey," she said. "He can't help himself. You know he's got a protective streak a mile wide."

"Yeah? Who's he protecting?" Rosie asked.

Aunt Laraine kissed Chloe on the cheek. "Grand to see you again."

"What a great dress. You look fabulous."

"Just call me Mame," Laraine said, stretching out her hand to show off a gaudy ring, an enameled red rose on a gold band.

Rosie headed out the back door. "Let's leave James Beard and Mame to their work. Come see the new pool." She grabbed Brian's swim shorts off a chair and handed them to him, helped Jenner change while Chloe walked around holding Andie. Willie, sprawled in the grass and plugged into his music, waved lazily.

"All the work this house needs, and the thing we do is put in a pool. Are we crazy or what? But the kids love it." The pool was an amoeba-shaped thing that looked like a blue puddle to Chloe.

Aunt Laraine came out, pulled two chairs into the slight shade of the maple tree Chloe had given them, five feet taller now. Clusters of red leaves clung unseasonably to the maple's branches. Laraine patted the empty chair, motioned to Chloe to sit while Rosie ran upstairs to change into a suit. Andie looked ready to nod off so Chloe sat with her. The child lay her head on her right shoulder, put her hand on her neck and Chloe stroked her back, absorbing her lovely child warmth.

There was a lot of shrieking and laughing as Rosie tossed colored rings to the kids. Chloe considered joining them, but this was her chance to hold Andie, breathe her in. Besides, a pool you can't swim in seemed pointless to her. There was Jenner sliding under the water, kicking her legs one end to the other without coming up for breath.

Rosie waded to the edge and flicked water at Chloe. "I should put white rhododendrons around the pool area. Don't you think they'd look good?" Chloe pursed her lips to consider it and nodded.

"Have you ever seen anything like it?" Laraine asked Chloe after Rosie went back to playing with the kids. "They always need a home project. Both of them have so much need for family."

"Who doesn't?" Chloe said.

"I'm glad Hillie's in San Francisco. Honest to goodness truth, I don't know if Jarrett would've ever married if she were still here. Family can be too much. Don't you know?"

Chloe didn't know. Or maybe she did. Her family had been too much by being too little. All she really knew was that she missed Rosie more than when she first left. Even here with her, she felt the ache. Reluctantly, Chloe let Laraine take Andie in for a nap. Peter came out to see what they were up to, and the kids clambered out of the water and mobbed him. "Can we play Chutes and Ladders, Daddy? Will you play with us?"

"Sure thing. You go dry off, get dressed and we'll play."

The kids raced indoors. Peter smiled at Chloe. "Lucky you, you get to just relax for a while," and followed them in. Rosie climbed out of the water and pulled a chair close to Chloe.

"Talk to me."

"You talk to me."

"It is sooo warm today it's disturbing, isn't it?"

"Yes. Summer in November."

"Have you noticed how moody Jarrett is?"

"Umm. I don't know if he seems that different to me. I haven't spent a lot of time around him lately." She didn't say, he always seems on edge around me.

"He has these bouts of mania when he's feverish about work and gets so spiky. Little things set him off. I always wondered if he could survive in a family. There had to be a reason he didn't marry until his mid-thirties. I think he makes up research to get away from home. At least his book is out now, so he's not spending so much time time with those rappers in Atlanta. God knows what they got up to. He's started a book about mountain culture and all he wants is to get back up there. I almost see a little aura of guilt when he says he needs to go back, like he's fleeing us. Leaving me with three kids."

"Maybe he feels sidelined by how bonded you are with Andie?"

"I don't think that's it. It's stability that undoes him. How are things at your house?"

"The same, it's the Peter-and-Jenner story. I get her out of the house, and it's sweet, but at home it's like I hardly exist. I sign her up for things to get time with her. That's kind of our time."

"Why don't you and Peter adopt a child?

"Peter thinks Jenner's enough. He worries he might not love another child as much as Jenner. And I don't think he would. I know something about what it's like to be adopted by a family that didn't really want you."

"Like Kath was."

"Right."

"That's different, Chloe. Kath wasn't a baby, and her relatives weren't looking to adopt." She stretched her legs, shook out her wet hair. "But if Peter doesn't want to..." Her voice trailed off. "You haven't forgiven him. I don't blame you. I wouldn't either."

From the house they heard Andie break into a loud wail. Rosie leapt up. "I didn't think she'd let Laraine put her down. Sorry, I have to go in."

Chloe stared up at the maple tree after Rosie disappeared. This was the way things went these days, Rosie being pulled this way and that by the kids, while she sat alone and listened to Jenner and Peter laughing from the play room upstairs. She had the thought that her life was over and felt scared.

Her maple tree—she still thought of it as hers though it had been in their yard for a year and a half—would soon be as bare as the rest of the trees, a few leaves already falling while they sat there, while the heat weighed on her. Two different seasons at the same time. Her life felt unreal, too, not hers, not who she really was. She had a life someone else wanted. A nauseated feeling rose in her gut.

She thought of how she felt after reading a novel, how the characters lived on for her, and she wanted to know what happened to them afterward. They felt too real to accept that nothing more happened, that they didn't exist off the page. Now her own story was over, and she was off the page.

Thanksgiving morning, Chloe lingered in the kitchen as Jarrett stuffed the turkey. She resolved once again to do better with him. They joked grimly about summer hanging around in November, the lack of snow in the mountains, but too much rain. The climate was doomed. Was anywhere safe? The Bay Area, she thought, but did not say. Fear of earthquakes didn't seem as powerful now as the extreme weather in other parts of the country. The temperate climate in that part of California created a haven.

She gave Jarrett a high five once he got the bird in the oven. Peter and Rosie were on the back lawn with the kids, running around in a game of tag. Andie wriggled to get free from Aunt Laraine's arms and join the older kids. They all liked holding Andie. Willie hadn't even gotten up yet.

"I'll scrub the yams. How's your new book coming?"

"It's coming."

"I'm looking forward to it."

"It might not be your kind of book. Bad news about the South. You don't much like the South anyway, Rosie says."

Chloe bristled at the thought that Rosie and Jarrett talked about her. Had he read her mind about San Francisco?

"I don't like Tallahassee."

"Florida's not the real South."

"I know it's not. Tallahassee's really just south Georgia anyway. Nashville's not the same South. And the mountains aren't the same South, either."

"True, all of them are pretty different. So where *do* you like?"

"California, yeah, and I also like your mountains. I like Nashville, but it's hard to feel totally at home. I'd probably feel that anywhere, though." She looked up from her task of poking holes in the yams with a fork and smiled ruefully. He met her gaze, but his face was unreadable. It was an awkward silence. Jarrett wasn't one to talk about feelings.

"I like your writing. Your book selling?"

"Some. Taking off slow, but I hear there's a few reviews about to come out. If they're good, they'll help."

He was cleaning up his mess from turkey prep. "You should know the new book is not friendly towards wealth. It's about people who feed the county governments here and buy up the mountains, build big estates. I'm calling it *Midas' Mountain*. You might recognize a client or two on the wrong side of the divide."

"That doesn't mean I have no sympathy."

"It must be hard to live with contradictions like that."

"I try not to be righteous, but working with wealth, yeah, it raises questions for me, too." They both knew she'd moved into the category people would also call wealthy, even if not mega-rich like some of her clients. He added the yams to the oven, and she cleaned green beans in silence, snapping off the ends. She and Peter had picked up pies from a local bakery, Rosie had set the table that morning, cranberry sauce was made. There wasn't much left to do. Standing at the sink, she studied the people outside. How easy they were with each other.

The nauseated feeling rose again. Maybe she and Rosie never were really that close. What if their tie was simply wanting what each other had? She had gotten Peter when Rosie depended on him, she'd gotten career success, money, a daughter, a big house. Rosie got Jarrett, two more babies, her own big house. Rosie had surpassed her. They were not in sync, but headed to different fates. And Jenner—she was Peter's child more than hers. Would they have married if she hadn't gotten pregnant? She was tired of that question. The nauseated feeling rose again.

Determined not to leave the kitchen, she sat at the table and checked her office phone, sent a few texts, played solitaire. Jarrett opened the oven to give the turkey a dose of its juices, the aroma of roasting meat escaping. The pan slipped sideways as he pulled the rack out and trapped his wrist against the oven wall. He yelped loudly and swore. Chloe leapt up, grabbed two pot holders, lifted the pan to free him.

"I've got it."

His face puckered against the pain, age lines popping out like webbing. Chloe took a handful of ice cubes from the freezer and pressed them to the back of his wrist which was bright red. It would blister. He stared, grimacing, his eyes watery, then seized her shoulder with his other hand, looking bewildered. His eyes pinned her, he bent and kissed her. Chloe pulled back and gaped stupidly at him. Did he even know what he was doing?

"What the fuck?"

He moved his hand from her shoulder and turned away. Chloe closed the oven, retrieved the baster from the floor, tossed it in the sink, grabbed her phone and went out the back door. She waved to Peter who was scrambling in the grass with the kids.

"Can you help Jarrett? I'd like to relax with the kids."

Jenner jumped in the pool again. "Mommy, ride me on your shoulders!"

It just annoyed her, and she shook her head. "Sorry." Jenner only wanted her when Peter wasn't available. She felt rage at all of them. Was Jarrett out of his mind?

Laraine came around the side of the house carrying a tray of unbaked rolls from her car. "This heat is making me cranky. Here." She handed Willie the tray and reached for Andie. "Let me pick you up, sweetie." Andie waved fat fingers in her face and toddled away.

Chloe's phone rang. She walked across the yard to take the call. The woman taking care of Francisco while they were away was semi-hysterical. "I don't know how she got out, I was so careful, honest I was, but she ran out into the street, and..."

Chloe interrupted. "She was hit." The woman's silence confirmed it. "Is she alive?"

"I'm so sorry. I don't think so."

"Take her to the vet anyway. I'll pick her up when I'm home."

Chloe walked to the trail behind the house. No view along it now, only dense trees, scraggly and rough, bare, grey, a hillside you could call desolate. The mood overtaking her felt close to panic. Francisco, her companion. She began to jog. Jarrett was a dick. Peter, too. She wished he had seen it. She was finished with waiting for him to turn creative again. And if she had a spirit animal, which she didn't believe in, it was a black and white Maine Coon. What if she packed herself up and moved back to California?

Jogging fast, she felt despair creeping up. How had she ended up like this? Once she almost believed she was golden. What she'd achieved, the huge salary, big bonuses, big empty house—it was nothing about happiness. She'd gotten derailed. Jarrett was right about one thing: contradictions were a problem. Clearly he had no respect for her.

She lurched suddenly, shot forward, and slammed down into dirt. She tasted a mouthful of dust and a sensation of fracture radiated through her flank, splintering from shoulder to knees to twisted foot, but she got up, brushed off, eyed the exposed root that had sent her flying. Her body was okay, just scraped, one knee and her shins a little bloody, her insides shaken up.

It was not her body that was breaking. A slight limp, but she could walk back. She wanted to be alone with Rosie, no child tugging at either of their legs. She wanted to leave this place, leave Peter and Jarrett behind. She wanted to take Rosie with her.

Rosie was drying off Brian and Jenner beside the pool.

"Where did you go, Mommy? When are we going to eat?" Jenner hopped back and forth flinging her wet hair.

Chloe kissed on her the head and finished drying her. She wouldn't tell her about Francisco until they got home.

"Peter's setting up a game in the living room. We'll eat soon." Rosie shooed the children inside. She pulled a chair next to Chloe beside the maple, poured glasses of iced tea from a pitcher on the small wicker table.

"What's going on?"

"I needed a break. Almost got one." She extended her legs and palms which were dusty, scraped raw and bleeding a little.

"You're hurt! Let me clean you up."

"I'll wash off in a minute. I just need to sit here with you." She took a deep breath. Oh, she wanted to tell Rosie about Jarrett. She did. She looked at her open face, thought, *No, that's not what I want to do.* She took a deep breath. "Tell me again how you love your life. Is anything not right in it?"

Rosie laughed at her. "Not really. No secrets here. Jarrett's irritable, but we're used to that. Then he's sweet again. Just unpredictable. And they say women are emotional."

Her heart pumped out danger signals. "We've hardly had a minute to talk."

"I know. These kids! But talk to me now."

She poked her aching foot at the dirt. Nothing felt right any more. "I'm afraid I need to leave tomorrow instead of Sunday. That call was from the office. I haven't even told Peter. He won't be happy."

"Shit. I'm not happy either. I hate your work." Rosie made a face. "Sorry. I'm entitled to complain. I hate it that you have to go. Like you said, we've hardly had a minute. You have to come back soon, okay?"

"Hard to say. It's busy lately. I've got some traveling to do. We'll have to figure it out." She looked up. "I hate my work, too. Everything—the money, big office—you know. It's not what I want. Not to be melodramatic, but fuck, fuck it all. Really, what if I chucked everything?"

"I like that thought."

"I should just go back to California."

*Yes, you should go now. There are things for you there.*

The words resounded like they were bouncing around in her skull. No, like Angie was echoing them. She froze. Angie didn't want her here any more.

"Not that! Quit your work and move to Asheville."

"Do you hear much from Angie lately."

"Not really. I think now that maybe she was troubled after death. She was just too young to go. So she kept hanging around. She was always the overseer and couldn't stop that. Maybe she's more at peace now."

Chloe was silent, something frightening swirling inside her. She looked at Rosie, finally said, "I miss California."

"Don't talk like that. You're making me nervous. I'd never forgive you if you left. You know I'm not the forgiving type."

"You might need to be."

Rosie waved that aside. "In your dreams."

Chloe stood, "I'm going to clean my leg."

She'd tell Peter they needed to go in the morning. He and Jenner would be upset, but that wasn't her problem.

Rosie's words, *in your dreams,* echoed as she bathed her hands and shins in cool water, wiped blood from her knee. Hillie came to mind. Last summer Hillie was visiting when they were in Asheville. She and Hillie talked about books like they always did and discovered they were both into dreams. Hillie quoted a passage from Proust she kept on her nightstand: *If a little dreaming is dangerous, the cure for it is not to dream less but to dream more, to dream all the time.*

She needed to dream up a new life.

# CHAPTER 19

San Francisco in January was not really cold, just wet. Chloe didn't mind rain. She left her hotel, waited for a cable car to pass, pulled up her hood and crossed Powell. In Union Square everyone except the homeless people were scanning phones. She needed a look at Nike; to her the statue wasn't a war memorial but a triumphant woman with her own victory, independence. That's how she framed it in her twenties after she paid off her loans.

In a fine drizzle she crossed Post Street to Saks and stopped at the Clinique counter to buy new cosmetic brushes. The clerk was speaking to the woman next to her as she handed her a gift bag. "Just sign here, Yvette. It's always nice to see you." Chloe glanced at her. Yes, it was Yvette. Her Yvette, here in San Francisco.

"Yvette Doucette?"

Yvette looked at her blankly.

"It's Chloe. Chloe Berrit, from years ago in Tallahassee. I worked with you at Beckman's Deli. I was just a teenager."

"Sorry, I don't recall." The trace of accent was still there, the odd combination of French with a southern drawl.

"You taught me to drive. In your car. I probably ruined the clutch." Chloe said, embarrassed by how girlish she sounded. "You were going to have a baby."

Yvette laughed. "Yes! I remember you now. You were a very sweet young girl and with that lovely French name."

"Can I buy you a coffee or maybe lunch at the St. Francis where I'm staying. Please."

Yvette accepted. She took Chloe's arm and Chloe led her back to the hotel, almost giddy. She'd found Yvette—Yvette in San Francisco! Her mystique was still there, if a little shopworn. Yvette aged, but was still conscious of being attractive.

Chloe could think of no reason Yvette would care about running into her, and now as they took their seats dark feelings began to stir. She ordered a margarita though she didn't like drinking at lunch. Yvette ordered champagne.

"You look beautiful, as you always did."

Yvette closed her eyes, seemed not to like that.

"And your child? The child must be grown."

"My daughter. Colette. Yes, all grown, if twenty-three is grown. She's a singer like me, living here, too."

"I live in Nashville now and work with a lot of people in the music industry."

"My daughter is not a country music singer. She sings jazz and blues. Silky, jazzy blues."

"Jazz and blues are recorded in Nashville. Everything is. In fact my husband  produces blues." That wasn't true any more, but she liked to think he would in the future. "How did you end up in California?"

"A man. Of course. A wealthy man who owned a chain of sporting good stores. He came to Florida for sales events. I was singing in the bar of his hotel and, you know, one thing led to another, then he wanted us here. More appealing than Florida, you know. It wasn't hard to agree." She laughed and shrugged. Laughing at herself, Chloe thought.

"We moved to Sausalito with him. Colette loved it, I didn't. He didn't want me to work. I know better than to depend on a man, so I moved us over to San Francisco and taught French at a small school. But that was years ago."

Chloe nodded. This sounded like the same Yvette.

"Poor man. So sad. He died of a heart attack seven months later. I was broken up, *bien sûr*. I wept through his funeral like a widow. You know, it is easier to love a man after he's gone. And he left me some money."

Yvette went on about herself. Edouardo, sixteen years older, was the next one, an artist from Trinidad, married, so he wouldn't go out in public with her. They spent evenings at her apartment. Colette began to call him Papa Edouardo. "Finally she had a brown-skinned person like her. I wanted Edouardo to marry me. Can you imagine? Just because of Colette. In the end he wouldn't leave his wife. I threw his clothes, everything he gave me, into boxes on the sidewalk, and let strangers carry them off."

Chloe laughed with her. "Why did you even work at the deli?"

"Simon kept me in money for a while. When he saw the baby, that was it. Clearly not his. I sang in Paris when I was young, you know. I was good, so I began singing again. Always men, they mislead you of course. That boy in Paris who told me Florida was all sunshine, warmth, beaches, nightclubs. It sounded like the Riviera. After we got to Tallahassee, I saw. No beach, only hideous creatures that invaded my house—flying bugs, lizards, snakes that kill you. *Effrayant*. Oh, but the flowers! Trees with that spooky moss. It has beauty. You know. Alors, enough."

Yvette seemed a little worse for wear after all, the more she talked. She asked nothing about Chloe, not about her husband or child, why she lived in Nashville or how she became who she was now. The affected way she tossed in French words started to annoy Chloe. By the time they parted they were hugging each other, air kissing. Yvette invited her to a bar that night to hear her daughter sing.

"Lovely," Chloe said. An evening out with Yvette. Before she met with her client she went back to Saks and bought a clingy crepe dress like Yvette might wear.

———

Her daughter had an early gig at a bar on Vallejo. A blackboard outside read, "*Nobody's Business*/Jazz Trio: Colette Holiday, Paul Marsal, and Takeo Abe." They were late for the set. Colette was crooning with the keyboardist and bass player. She gave a little wave as they came in. Before her next song she murmured into the mic: "This one's for my mother, her favorite Billie Holiday," and launched into "God Bless the Child." Pretty good, Chloe thought, but young, she needed confidence.

Switching effortlessly between French and English, appropriately sultry in a tight black skirt, sleeveless charcoal top, Colette definitely had appeal. Nothing like Yvette except for the sensuous smile. Her skin was light brown, her hair short springy curls. After the set she came to their table, and Yvette leapt up, embraced her, then turned her toward Chloe, entwined herself around her from behind. "My daughter," she said. "Colette Holiday."

"Yvette gets confused," she said, peeling her mother off. "She thinks I'm one of her boyfriends."

Yvette dismissed that with a flap of her hand. "So American. How did I raise such a child? Chloe's in the music business. Be nice to her." She gave Colette a smile Chloe would call doting, but after finishing her drink she announced she had a date.

"She always does that," Colette said, once Yvette was out the door. "Comes late. Ducks out early. Hope you don't feel ditched." She did feel ditched.

Colette was headed to a club and invited Chloe to join her. They strolled North Beach, the night clear but chilly.

"You and your mother seem close."

"Yeah, sort of. I thought she was the perfect woman when I was younger. Not like other kids' moms. Sexy, she sang, she talked to me in French. I don't think I realized she was white or that I wasn't. You're white too, aren't you? Though a little ambiguous."

"Some mixed heritage back there. My father's people." Collette surprised her. Rarely did anyone read her that way.

"Aha. I can usually tell. We spoke French so people wouldn't understand us, and we went everywhere together: the beach, cafes, the theater. She had this sweetheart thing for me even then."

"It's charming."

"Yeah, well, charming until she parked me with random friends and went off for a week with a boyfriend."

"And your father...? Was he around?"

"The famous William Holiday. Never met the man. A figment of her imagination. When I was fourteen I forced her to admit she made up the name. After her idol, Billie Holiday. She claimed she couldn't remember my actual father's name."

"Wow. That's a revelation. So it's been mostly the two of you?"

"Yeah, for better and worse. Her boyfriends came and went. It was intense. A lot of screaming matches, and both of us throwing things. If I wanted to go out, she wanted me home. If I was home, she wasn't happy with what I was doing. Whether I had a girlfriend or a boyfriend, she found something wrong there and sulked. We'd make up, go out to a cafe, talk about music and art, men and women. We're better now."

Girlfriend? Was Colette bi? The fervor of their relationship made Chloe hungry—what would it be like to have a mother who adored you like that? Or a child?

"You don't know her that well, do you?" Colette said.

Chloe gave her a brief history, slightly embellished, of their relationship. She admitted to idolizing her.

"Me, too," she said. "Except when I couldn't stand to be around her."

How did she end up at her place that night, a small flat in Cole Valley? It disturbed and embarrassed her. She hadn't slept with anyone except Peter in years. But they'd danced together at the club, touching a lot, then she found herself kissing Colette. Making love with her brought up crushed desires; she thought of Elaine. Was she still in the Bay Area? Was she doing art? She would search online.

It racked up so much bad credit: her marriage, Colette's youth, Yvette. She made excuses for herself. She didn't usually drink. She was lonely, distanced by Peter and Jenner, out of sync with Rosie, hurt by Yvette's disappearance. And Colette was gorgeous. She'd agreed to meet her again that night.

She imagined Angie scowling as she took a cab home the next morning. What about Peter? I thought you were done with me, she whispered to Angie. *No one's ever done with anyone,* Angie replied.

———

She texted Hillie. *I'm in town. Love to come by the store* [emoji]. Hillie responded right away. *I'm here. Come.* [emoji]

Jarrett's book, *South City Blues,* was featured in the window of Uncommon Reader. Hillie was busy with a customer, so Chloe waved and browsed, picked up a few books for Jenner. A gift, Hillie said, and handed them back. She told Joy, her co-owner, they were going for coffee.

Over cornmeal scones they passed news from Asheville, but Chloe wanted to know more about Hillie's life. Hillie confessed she felt adrift. "Some people like being single, and some like being coupled. I don't do well with either. The best part of my life is this little family I have with my friend Celia and her daughter Lark. Celia's queer and single, so no relationship tensions there, and I'm like Lark's second mom."

"A second mom. Better than being a single mom," Chloe said.

"Her ex is part of it too. We all spend a lot of time with Lark."

A family of women, Chloe couldn't imagine it. "Doesn't she prefer to be with Celia?"

"Some days. Some days not so much. Children are amazingly flexible, happy to get love and attention wherever." Hillie said. "I wish I'd had a few other mothers."

"Me, too." Chloe smiled ruefully. "Me, too."

"Speak of the devil." A blond woman with bobbed hair walked in, waved, and came over.

"Joy said you were here with family."

"Chloe, this is Celia. Celia, Chloe. And we're talking about you."

Chloe's eyes locked with Celia's for a moment. "Nice to meet you. Are you part of the bookstore, too?"

"No way. I'm a therapist."

"Ah. Lucky for your daughter, a mother who's a therapist."

"You'd be surprised. I've had a few patients with a therapist parent. A mixed result on that. Let's see what Lark says in twenty years."

"I also have a five-year-old. I suppose Lark doesn't miss a father with all that family."

"Doesn't seem to. Of all the things she complains about, that's not one. There's enough drama for three of us. You know. A doll gets dropped into the wash. A sandwich cut across instead of diagonally can start a good wail. It's nice to spread it around."

"Yesterday Lark desperately needed purple pants. Life hung on a thread." Hillie laughed. They seemed to share every detail. Chloe felt not only envy, but other things she shouldn't be feeling, a flirtatious spark with Celia.

"I had a girlfriend in college." Chloe's face reddened. It was stupid to blurt that out, like a credential. She was not about to confess what she'd been up to with Colette.

"You're bi? But married to a man." Celia looked at her quizzically.

"Yeah. Afraid so."

They talked about the fluidity of relationships. It was the kind of conversation Chloe never had with other people, and it made her hungry for more. "I've even been in love with another married woman." She quickly added, "Not something that would go anywhere."

"Good to avoid that. Like walking down a dark alley," Celia said with a suggestive smile. "I've been there. Sigh. Love and attraction are such fatal afflictions."

Chloe laughed. "For sure." There was definitely something fizzy between them.

Jarrett's name came up. Chloe mentioned that they didn't do so well with each other. "Yeah, he's tricky, he's volatile," Hillie agreed. "I love him, but I know. He saved me when I was young. One of Laraine's husbands tried to mess with me, and Jarrett went after him. A lot of predatory men out there. Jarrett's in another category, though."

If you only knew, Chloe thought. She felt grateful for Peter—none of that with him. And with Colette she felt more like the predator.

Hillie was watching her and Celia, detecting the fizz. Chloe knew she was getting out of her lane, first Colette, now this. Celia rose to leave, prolonging eye contact with Chloe. Chloe watched her go with a wistful look that made Hillie say, "Really?"

"No. Not really."

Back at the store Chloe grabbed a biography of Emily Dickinson and insisted on paying. As Hillie rang the sale, her phone buzzed. Jarrett. Hillie said she couldn't talk, Chloe was there. "I don't know, business I think." Rosie didn't even know she was on the West Coast. Chloe felt caught. At what?

She promised to come by again the next time she was in town. Talking to Hillie left her feeling better.

———

It's not just jealousy, she told Jane. "Peter's too absorbed in Jenner. It isn't good for either of them."

Jane agreed. "And you're excluded."

"I'm used to that."

Since Jenner's birth, he'd put out only the children's album, which outsold all the adult music he'd produced. A bigger studio picked it up, and now he was making money, not a ton, but enough to feel successful, and he was planning a second one. "I need to get back to blues though," he groused, his hand stroking his head. Jenner was in kindergarten, he had no excuse except that he couldn't sustain interest in the work any more. The thought of introducing him to Colette crossed her mind. No way.

Chloe taught Jenner the alphabet at two, and Jenner was reading before she started kindergarten. She enrolled her in an early dance class and bought her the white tutu she'd wanted as a child. Peter preferred just to hang out with her. He got down on the floor with the Playmobil people, watched Nickelodeon and *SpongeBob*. As soon as Jenner could sit up, he laid a guitar on the floor and let her pluck its strings.

When she read to Jenner, it reminded her that she had no memory of Kath reading to her. She told Jane, "It's better now. We talk every few weeks. She actually calls me, I don't call her. Since I started talking to you, I've tried to forgive her. She couldn't help it. Never had a good mother herself. She just didn't recognize need."

"Like you?" her therapist asked.

Chloe put her head in her hands. "I don't know if I do any better with Jenner."

"That's not what I meant."

"I know. But if I don't know what I need, how can I recognize what she needs?"

She'd stopped pressing Peter to travel with her. He didn't ask why because he didn't want to be pressed. He still didn't like to leave Jenner, though she no longer protested, happy to be spoiled by Ruth and Frank, and once Peter's parents had come down. Chloe never asked Kath and Dee to stay with Jenner. When Kath called, she kept it brief. Jenner always wanted to get on the phone, but Kath protested. "She doesn't want to talk with me."

"She does, Mom. She asks to talk to you."

Peter had never been to Tallahassee. She didn't invite him the few times she flew down because she kept her visits short. They welcomed her, but were glad when she left, she was sure of it. She sent tickets to visit again when Jenner was two. That was their last. Now she sent money for a vacation or to splurge on something. They thanked her but were maybe embarrassed, and the vacation or the splurge never seemed to happen.

---

She texted Colette and returned to San Francisco late spring without contacting Yvette. The link to Yvette was alluring but also disturbing, she couldn't deny it; somehow being with Colette seemed innocent though, she had a pure air about her, young and open. Colette had hookups, as she called them, not relationships, and mostly with women. Being a hookup made Chloe feel a little younger. Wasn't Collette the perfect illicit lover?

They didn't risk going to a bar Yvette could frequent. Clubbing where a younger group would show up seemed safer. She liked to dance and paid for everything, but she didn't have Colette's stamina. The youth of the other clubbers left her feeling sleazy, an older woman with a young lover. Which she was, though she passed for younger. A *married* older woman. Nevertheless she loved the bump and grind, raising her arms and flapping her hands like she was used to it, and the drinking, too—what an easy release. Alcohol with lemon or mint was not bad. She was getting fond of drinking.

The next day she returned to Uncommon Reader, hoping to run into Celia again. No luck, but it was always good to hang out with Hillie.

———

Before her next trip she texted Hillie: *Let's have dinner. And invite Celia too.*⊠

They met at Cadillac, an upscale Mexican restaurant on the edge of the Mission. A few drinks in, Chloe asked Celia if it was hard to come out. "Not so much," Celia said, "not like for some people. I hid it a while, put distance with family, and we had been close, so they knew something was up. Then I realized my Aunt Amelie was a lesbian, someone I loved in childhood, and that helped me tell them. Amelie was my idol. She lives in Asheville actually. She used to own a bookstore there where Hillie worked when she was young."

"I learned the trade from her," Hillie said. "When I moved to San Francisco, she made me promise to look up her niece. That's how we met."

"Destined. I love that." She looked at Celia again. "What I meant is, was it hard for you to know?"

Celia laughed wryly. "Not hard. I always knew." She sipped her drink and eyed Chloe. "Are you questioning?"

"No," Chloe said quickly. "Just thinking back, my college thing, how that was anything but easy."

She'd hoped for something more from Celia, but what and why, she didn't know. The three of them found it so easy to talk, to laugh. Why didn't she have this in her life? Why didn't she have any friends besides Meera, with whom she only discussed work? Her life was not normal.

She and Colette went dancing again. At home she'd day-dreamed about dancing, loosening her body, feeling younger, freer. They stayed out till two, and the next morning the bed-room smelled slightly fermented. She tiptoed with her suitcase into the living room, changed into shorts and running shoes, filled her bottle with water, tuned into music, and slipped in earbuds.

She jogged past the Panhandle and made an easy loop around the lake. It was the third week of August, the dirty sea-son, no rain in San Francisco since April and none to come for a while. Dust of dry leaves and barren dirt drifted over sidewalks, into stairwells. Trees had a dingy cast. Ornamental cherries dropped fruit that got trampled into gory splotches and would remain on the sidewalks until rain fell in a few months.

Energy returned as her body began moving, and a breeze off the ocean cleared away fog. She trotted into the park, looped around Stowe Lake, then back. A woman in a tank top whizzed by on roller blades. The sky was bold, blue, the way summer sky looked in Nashville. She picked up pastries for Colette and herself.

Around ten Colette's cell rang, an electronic version of "Stardust." She silenced it. It rang again, and she answered. "*Not* now." Colette had that slightly sarcastic tone she used with her mother. Chloe began packing for a quick exit.

"I have company…None of your business. Come to Fredo's tomorrow night. I'm singing…Will you stay?" When she staggered into the living room, she mimicked Yvette's accent. "*'For most of your set.'* "

"I'm leaving soon anyway." Chloe was already searching for an earlier flight. She couldn't bear a furious Yvette. Watching Colette mimic her mother, it dawned on her that Yvette wasn't much different from Kath, except for the sexiness and big display of feeling. She once wished Yvette was her mother, but really, what did she give her? Her occasional and brief presence.

"So when will you come back?" Colette sat next to her, nudged her shoulder. When Chloe didn't respond she stopped. "Seriously."

Chloe gave her a funny smile, a little sad. "I don't think I'll come back."

"Why not?"

"Peter. Jenner. And your mother. I feel like we're incestuously related."

Colette jerked away, appalled. She went into the kitchen. Chloe followed, touched her on the shoulder, tried to kiss her cheek, but she stepped back.

"It was a mindless thing to say. I'm sorry, Colette. Really."

Colette faced her, puzzled and hurt. Chloe picked up her bag and her computer, hugged her gently. They were silent a moment. Colette seemed to understand something unnameable about her Peter never would, maybe that old sense of not fitting anywhere, and she'd wounded her, touched something too sensitive, made her feel her own shame.

She let herself out and went downstairs to wait. When she got home, she'd be swallowed in work again, but hooking up was not the new life she wanted.

There was a big task waiting for her as well. Jenner needed a strong mother, not a Kath or a Yvette. On the plane she remembered Hillie's words: Children are amazingly flexible, happy to get love and attention wherever. She turned her face to the window and wept. In her own way she abandoned her child. She'd stepped back and let Peter take over. Kath and Jenner had merged in her mind, made love sting so much she'd turned away from it.

PART FIVE

PLANET OCRACOKE

# CHAPTER 20

"Pedal hard until you find your balance. I'll hold on," Chloe said, running alongside Jenner on her new bike. Once Jenner pushed forward, Chloe retrieved her own bike and caught up. They stopped and started a few times, circled the park as Jenner's confidence grew. She thought of Yvette teaching her to drive. Yvette was a stroke of luck, pain and all.

The third time they passed a large sculpture new to Centennial Park, Jenner pedaled across the grass for a better look. She tumbled off the bike and walked over: five women in bronze, carrying signs.

"Why is this here?"

Chloe studied the statues and read the names out loud. "It's a monument for women's suffrage. They're marching, demanding the right to vote."

Jenner looked puzzled. "Why couldn't these women vote?"

"No woman could. Some men, not men like your father, thought women weren't equal to them."

Jenner spurted with laughter. "I can read better than any boy in my class."

Chloe nodded.

She picked her up every Wednesday now; they rode a bike path by the river, one along a greenway, and another on the shady Harpeth Woods Trail through a canopy of hardwoods. Jenner took to riding like she had to swimming; she liked to be in motion. When they ventured onto streets of their neighborhood, Chloe taught her to watch for potholes and parked cars whose doors might fly open suddenly. "Not every driver signals before they turn, either. Riding a trail is more fun, not so much to worry about, but you need to know streets. I was riding my bike to school when I was your age."

On a second trip to REI, they bought skates for Jenner and rollerblades for Chloe, plus gloves and kneepads, and went back to the park. Chloe landed on her butt as Jenner wheeled past, then turned back, collapsed on the path with her. "Are you okay, Mom?" They lay together on the warm pavement and talked as people skirted them. Jenner tapped her arm, pointed to a cloud with a puff like a curved trunk, an elephant's head.

"Those cottony clouds are called cumulus. The thin wispy ones way up high are cirrus."

"*Serious* clouds," Jenner laughed. Chloe loved the way Jenner laughed, low at first then higher and full-bodied.

"A cloud that covers the whole sky is called a stratus cloud and the rainy grey ones are nimbus. Sometimes there's light all around them like a halo."

"Nimbus! That's Maisie's cat's name." Jenner chanted their names—*cumulus, serious, stratus, nimbus*—as she rolled over to watch pair of crows fight over a piece of foil a few yards away.

This was what she'd missed, this was having a daughter. Chloe wanted to pull the child close, hold her tight, but it would spoil the moment. Enough that she liked being outdoors with her and was interested in nature.

After school she stood by the playground while Jenner named kids who were friends and introduced one, red-haired Maisie. Chloe always said hello to Maisie. Over ice cream they discussed who annoyed her, who got the teacher's attention and why, and all they did that day, things Kath was never interested in. Maisie came to the zoo with them, and Chloe heard Jenner say how good her mother was on a bicycle, but that she had beat her twice when they raced.

Chloe took every Wednesday afternoon off now for Jenner time. Rainy days, they went to the planetarium or the kids' studio at the museum where they made art and watched older kids create animated movies. Jenner wanted to do that, too, of course. She was different with Chloe, an older child who liked to venture into new places, learn new things. Peter preferred Jenner's younger self.

Thursday evenings were movie nights. Peter should busy himself with music, Chloe said, or whatever he liked. He shrugged. "Okay. See how it goes." If he thought Jenner would object, or that Chloe wouldn't stick to the plan, he was wrong. He kept suggesting Disney and Pixar movies—he'd purchased all of them—and sometimes Chloe acquiesced, invited him to join, but mostly she shooed him away, made popcorn and streamed her own choices: *Princess Diaries, Mamma Mia, Little Women* and, over Peter's objections, *The Kids Are All Right*. Jenner asked questions about that one. She choose *Little Women* often, to weep once more for Beth. When Jenner was enraptured by the movie, Chloe texted Colette: *Sorry about last time. ☒ If you have any interest in having someone listen to a demo of your group, let me know. I may know someone.*

Colette didn't respond.

---

Rosie told Willie she was going back to work. He announced that he wouldn't babysit for his brother and sister any more. Rosie snapped at him, he retreated, his door slammed. It stayed closed. Okay, he's angry, she sighed. Long overdue. It escalated until everything she did was wrong. If he did speak to her, it was a variation on "Stop fucking telling me what to do!"

What had happened? Her new job was a comparatively minor thing. No, it was adolescence. Adolescence had poured into him like a dangerous elixir. At fourteen he'd turned manly, with a body unfamiliar to her. Her tow-headed boy with the angelic face had been consumed whole by this creature with brown hair hanging in fringes at his neck, six inches taller than her. Girls eyed him at the mall or on the street, and Rosie wanted to turn their faces aside. She pictured a small evil creature that breathed angry, destructive maleness making a home for itself in a vulnerable organ in Willie, tiny tentacles grasping on.

Jarrett was freelance now except for the occasional column. His first book was moderately successful, but his second was taking longer to shape up. Rosie suggested he didn't want to finish it because he'd lose his excuse to run up to the mountains. That really irritated him.

A chance link to an older woman years ago, before they were married, had sent him on a path. He'd gotten lost, wandering off trail in the Smokies, and ended up on Janie Stickle's property. She invited him into her remote cabin, the walls covered with her own paintings. The next he heard of her, two years ago, her art had achieved cult status with an exhibit at the American Folk Art Museum. A collector from New York discovered her at fifty-seven. She accepted the money, not realizing how far it would take her into the public eye.

When Jarrett met her, she was still painting with cheap acrylics on plywood, a solitary woman whose son and husband had been killed in the first Gulf War, living alone on the back side of Newfound Gap. She was dead now, but he poked around the Swain County courthouse, located relatives. There was a life there, before the solitude, and there were letters, enough to flesh out for a biography that could anchor the new book's story of mountain culture and how money changed it.

Money was what they needed while he worked on the book. With Andie in preschool, Brian in first grade, Rosie was free to work. She signed an offer at a boys' prep school, then she woke at four a.m.—what was it like to teach only boys? She thought she understood adolescents after so many years of teaching, but what was happening with Willie undercut that confidence. And the age difference between herself and teenagers was greater now.

Her new students were academic jockeys—all they cared about was speeding around the track. Competition over college dominated their parents' minds and their minds, even in tenth grade. It's like factory work, Rosie concluded. Pointless to her. It pained her that she didn't love her students, but she liked having an income again, just hated how Willie leaked adolescent gloom.

All fall his closed door created a wall of silence. He needs a shell, she told herself, vowing to reach him over the holidays. Maybe the shell was necessary, like new skin. To break it open could hurt him. He needed to be remote, off in a private wilderness. When he caught a whiff of concern, he moved farther away, crossing her territory as rarely as possible.

Jarrett was interviewing, doing research in several counties, away in the mountains long hours, even days. Willie went twice to the Canton courthouse to look through records together, and they located the old cabin. Willie wasn't angry with Jarrett, his stepfather who was still awesome. "Willie's fine. I did the same at his age," Jarrett said.

"I doubt it. Anyway, Willie's not like you." Rosie's voice rose higher. "And what would you know? He still likes you."

"You think you're irritable because Willie's difficult. Maybe Willie's difficult because you're irritable."

Too much obnoxious music poured from his room to imagine he was reading or finishing a history paper. Their estrangement caused her actual physical pain. On days he wouldn't speak to her, she felt a fissure opening in her chest, gaping, a wound that made her feel faint. Her baby, her first child, the years of closeness flown away. She put her hand between her breasts and tried to imagine something soothing it. Those days she would call Chloe. Chloe understood things like that. Jenner's rejection had felt like she was throwing gravel in her face.

Chloe murmured sympathy. For a change she was having success after success with Jenner. Her daughter snuggled up, leaned on her shoulder while they watched movies, dropped to her lap so Chloe would stroke her hair. When she came home from work, Jenner ran to the door and tugged at her waist to show what she'd done in school. She'd ask if her small neat bit of homework looked good enough to hand it. Homework was nothing to Jenner, who was ahead of the rest of her class.

"Take a break from him," Chloe said. "Go away for a few days."

"I can't just go off somewhere."

"Sure you can. Let's go to New York and stay in a great hotel, see a play or two. The best revenge and all that. I'll pay for the hotel. And theater tickets." Chloe liked to spend money. Partner now at her firm, she earned an unimaginable figure. "Three days of sleeping late on fancy sheets, eating in fabulous restaurants, going to the theater, that would be a great escape."

Rosie didn't protest the money. She could use the MLK weekend and add a day. When she told Jarrett that Chloe offered to take her to New York, he scowled. He seemed to have a permanent grudge against her.

"Brilliant. Her money. Okay, go. It will be good for everyone to miss you."

------

Manhattan was a tantalizing interlude, a few days of finding another life out there. They shopped, went to MoMA, ate foods they couldn't pronounce. Affectionate, they touched each other's arms as they talked, and the thread of conversation never ran out, mostly thanks to Rosie. Chloe couldn't recall laughing so much in a short span of time. Over dinner before *Hamilton,* Chloe said Peter's petulance about Jenner just annoyed her now. "She doesn't need him as much, and he doesn't like that. He should be glad Jenner and I are better, but no."

"Being married has an inflated reputation," Rosie said.

"Necessary, I guess. But not sufficient, as my statistics professor liked to say."

"Sometimes I just prefer being with you. You need them for children, then what? What's their function? To make money, take the car to the shop? We can do that."

Over drinks after the play, Chloe said, "Remember the French woman I told you about who taught me to drive when I was a teenager?"

"The sexy one?"

"The sexy one," she nodded. "Yvette. When I traveled to San Francisco last year, I ran into her. Shopping at Saks."

"How cool. What a small world story. Is she still sexy?"

"Yes, twenty years older and the same."

"I wish I could say that."

Chloe's smile was flirty. "No worries, my dear."

They ordered another round, and Rosie remarked that Chloe was drinking more than usual. "I discovered the joys of inebriation."

"Since when?"

"Um, well, it turns out my Yvette has a lovely daughter who's a singer. I heard her at a jazz club, went with her to another place, and we drank, and we danced and had an amazing time."

"Whoa. Wait. That sounds like a date."

Chloe made a little innocent face, smiled slyly. "It was. I saw her twice more."

"You didn't, you know, do it, did you?"

"Hmm. Shouldn't have, but yeah, I did. You *cannot* tell Jarrett, of course. He'd tell Peter."

"I won't tell. You shameless thing, an affair with a woman. I thought all that was in the past. What was it like?"

"Are you shocked?"

"Of course."

"You think I'm terrible?"

"No. Jealous. Just be careful. So tell me."

"It was only a few times. She's just lovely and sweet. I can't say I'm proud of it. This is a confession, not a brag."

"So your travels are not all business."

"I also saw Hillie a few times. I wasn't just spending my time in bed. I like Hillie a lot. We've become friends."

"You and Jarrett both. I feel like she's part of our marriage. Why do I keep ending up in triangles? Triangles suck."

"Yes. They suck. When I was in San Francisco I googled Jamie, the guy from Florida, the one I got pregnant by. I never wanted to know about him, but then I did. He does research at Georgetown, not patient care. Guess what his special area is: chronic heart failure."

"Wow. He's a natural."

----

When Jarrett picked her up at Arrivals, Brian and Andie leapt out of the car and elbowed each other to get to her. Willie had stayed home. Back at the house she heard him in the kitchen. He poked his head through the door, muttered, "Hello," then headed to his room.

"Willie," she called after him. "I brought you a present."

He reappeared, slung himself onto the couch. She handed him a gift bag, but he didn't take it, so she laid it in his lap. He didn't even look up.

"*How was your trip, Mom?*" she mimicked. "Great, Willie, and thanks for asking." Willie didn't flinch. "Well, it *was* great. You would have loved it. I wish I could take you to New York. There are so many things you'd like."

He reached into the bag, retrieved a new phone. "Thanks, Mom," he said, heading back up the stairs.

Jarrett's bag held a backcountry GPS. "This stuff's expensive. Did you cave under Chloe's influence?" He picked up her suitcase and called Andie and Brian behind him. "You guys need to get into your pajamas."

Rosie listened from the living room as the commotion increased upstairs, Brian laughing his weird high-pitched way. She wouldn't go up there and pass Willie's door. And she wouldn't tell Jarrett that Chloe bought the gifts. After a little back and forth between them, she'd let her. He'd be angry and truth was, she was embarrassed that she *had* caved, just not in the way he thought.

Andie came back downstairs in her pajamas clutching the unicorn Rosie brought home. She curled into her lap. "I'm glad you're home, Mommy. I love you, Mommy." Rosie picked her up, carried her to her room and lay with her as Andie whispered. "Mommy, Aunt Laraine and I made a pie. We went downtown too. I named my unicorn Silver." Rosie stayed with her close to midnight. She missed Chloe already.

By morning she was back to yelling at Willie. The amount of rage she could feel over a wet towel on his closet floor or clean laundry that sat in the basket all week was unsettling. It left her smug and remorseful at the same time—what did she care about a messy room? Willie gave her baleful looks.

Late that night Rosie went to his room to tell him to turn off the music, go to bed. He startled when she opened the door, closed his computer with a swift motion, and stashed it under the covers where his other hand was, his face pink. There was a hallucinatory air in the room, the power of sexual fantasy at work. She backed away, closed the door.

Why was she shocked? He was fifteen now, for criminy's sake. What did she think he did in that room besides play nasty music? Once she'd opened his computer and saw words on the screen she didn't know he used. He'd moved into a beyond she couldn't follow.

# CHAPTER 21

"A week!" Rosie grumbled. "Leaving me with the kids a whole week."

Jarrett's plan take Peter to the mountains for a week and record local musicians sounded good to Chloe. Possibly it would jump-start a project for him.

"What about this? Jenner stays with Ruth and Frank. Laraine always wants to stay with your kids. You and I could go somewhere, maybe to the coast."

"What a fabulous idea. You're a brilliant woman. I'd love a beach vacation."

It was May when they drove across North Carolina in Chloe's silver Lexus. Rosie didn't mind stealing time from the school year. Wildflowers speckled the fields, trees were lusciously green. They took the ferry over to Ocracoke and settled into their rental, a house on stilts five hundred yards from Pamlico Sound with a wraparound porch and a wide hammock. Chloe's bedroom had a king bed, jacuzzi, TV on the wall, Rosie's had another TV, a Japanese soaking tub and overlooked the sound. She threw her things on the bed, inspected the house and stepped out to the deck to breathe in the air.

"Kind of a miracle being here," she said.

Chloe spent the first morning working on client files, making calls, moving money, reading reports, while Rosie walked to the village for a cappuccino and strolled a stretch of white sand as breezes whipped sweat off her body. Early afternoons Chloe jogged while Rosie napped. They went into the village the first night for seafood on the rustic porch of Blackbeard's Grill.

Watching the sunset Rosie said, "I'm not a bitch now like at home. You wouldn't believe how I complain about Willie. His wet towels everywhere, dirty clothes all over his floor. You'd think I really cared. If I could live like this even Willie might like me."

Over mojitos they studied the menu, Rosie reading aloud that Blackbeard used Ocracoke for shelter and was buried there. Chloe stretched her legs to the last rays of sun. Pink layered the horizon, and a line of pelicans flew overhead.

"A pirate's safe house. What a wicked place we came to."

They ordered a bottle of white Zinfandel, some crab cakes and blackened trout. Rosie's way of stroking her finger around the rim of her wine glass unsettled Chloe. As they teetered home along the beach, their arms wrapped around each other to steady themselves. On the deck they began kissing. Chloe was unclear who started it, but drunk as she was, she tugged Rosie to her bed where they kissed more, drowsy and passionate at the same time. They undressed, fumbling with buttons and dropping clothes on the floor.

Rosie whispered, "You're out of focus."

Chloe laughed, then suddenly felt scared. "I think we need to go to sleep."

"I don't think so. You taste like caramel." Rosie burrowed into the crease at her neck. Chloe sighed, but didn't turn toward her. Rosie fell asleep with her arm flung across her, tugging at her.

In the morning Chloe brought in a tray of toast, a pot of tea. "You might need this."

They didn't speak about the night. It was not exactly infidelity, Rosie thought, making out with a woman. They had gone no further than kisses and a few caresses before sleeping skin to skin. Chloe climbed back into bed and opened the novel she brought, but she didn't last long, asleep again until lunchtime. When she woke, she saw Rosie studying her.

"You're a beauty, you know. Perfect nose. Sweet, smooth mouth." Rosie touched her high cheekbones. "I was so intimidated by you at first. How smart you are. So skilled, so confident, but I've seen what's underneath, you know. You protect yourself, but you're really kind of defenseless. That's what makes me trust you."

They went back to Blackbeard's again the next night. "I'll have a Pinot." Chloe said. "Just a glass."

"That was nice, last night."

"Yeah."

"It's okay, I think, since this is a safe house."

Back at the rental they smoked marijuana and made out again lazily on the couch. The soundtrack from *The Hours* was playing through when Rosie whispered, "You are so hot," and slid off the couch, pulled Chloe to the floor and rolled over with her. "Let's go to the bedroom."

Chloe hesitated, then took Rosie by the hand and led her to the bedroom, threw covers on the floor, and they undressed each other. Rosie felt shy about her body, her flesh slack from childbearing and middle-age while Chloe was still lean, her single pregnancy leaving no marks, just that thin surgical scar. She pulled a sheet around her.

"No, you're beautiful," Chloe said.

Rosie laughed. "I'm not beautiful."

Chloe pulled back the sheet, stroked Rosie's nipple. "Oh, you are."

She kissed her way down her torso and stroked between her legs. When she put her tongue on her clitoris, Rosie shuddered. Chloe paused to look at her and Rosie nodded, her eyes closed. After she came, she wriggled her arms and legs around Chloe, shivering slightly in spite of her heat, and held her close. She turned her over and kissed her breast. It was the first time Rosie had touched a woman's body intimately. She was stunned at how much she liked it. Stunned it was Chloe. Chloe's orgasm was intense, but she turned away afterward.

How had this happened? Chloe asked herself. They'd fallen under the spell of sunshine, ocean, freedom.

The rest of the week was a delicious haze: days drenched in light, walking the beach, kayaking the sound, eating fresh shellfish. Chloe left her work undone. No rain, no cold snap. They bought small gifts, hand-painted tees for Rosie's kids, a necklace of handblown beads for Jenner, watercolors of Pimlico Sound for Peter and Jarrett.

The chilly ocean wasn't for swimming, so they lazed on beach towels and read. Chloe sat at the waterline building a drippy sandcastle while Rosie stretched her legs into the shallow waves.

"This reminds me of Gulf beaches. Come to California with me one day. The Pacific is nothing like the Atlantic or the Gulf. The waves are huge. Giant blue-gray beasts rolling in. The water's ice, no good for swimming but great for opening your mind."

"Hmm. One day." Rosie rolled over onto her belly and looked up. She told Chloe how she and Angie had pretended to be mermaid-dolphins one summer at Hilton Head and how, after Doug disappeared, Angie came over to tell her she was going to be fine because she was a mermaid. "She was right. I didn't drown."

Envy prickled Chloe even as she knew it was sadness that made Rosie tell this story. She sprinkled sand on her arm, brushed it off.

At night they slept together and made love, not talking about what was happening, shy about it, unsure what to say.

On the last day as they were packing, Rosie said. "I can't believe we did this. I thought I knew you, but now it's like we went to another planet. Planet Ocracoke. I feel like an adolescent. I love it."

"Planet Ocracoke," Chloe said. "For space travelers."

"Erotic space travelers."

Chloe nodded, wondering where Rosie would go when she came back to earth. Regret? Dismay? She had to say it: "I'm thinking about Peter."

"Me, too. Funny, isn't it. I feel like I'm betraying him, not Jarrett."

"Yes. Peter would be pretty upset."

"He'd be mad at you, maybe, but he'd hate me. After all we've been through together, I'm in bed with his wife."

"Peter could never hate you. Besides, Jenner's his love now."

---

Home again, Rosie was relaxed about the empty bottle of tequila she found in Willie's room. Jarrett challenged her. "You aren't upset?"

"He's not doing anything different from every other kid in his class."

"It's a bottle of *tequila*, Rosie. A whole bottle."

"Talk to him about it."

"I plan to. He's not legal, so how did he get it?"

"How did you get it at his age?"

The disorder Jarrett left in the bathroom, dishes in the sink felt comfortable to her again. She'd been amorous on her return, sexually looser than in months. Jarrett ran his hand through her swirl of hair, faded and grey-streaked. "The trip was good for you. What did you and Chloe do?"

"Relaxed. Both of us. It was amazing."

Why didn't she feel like she'd cheated on him? She couldn't make sense of it except that it seemed like making love with Chloe was a good thing, even for her marriage.

Peter was another story, a disturbing one. She'd trespassed on his family space, and there was a weight of wrongdoing in that. They didn't talk about feelings any more, didn't actually talk much at all, and his relationship with Chloe was a mystery. What was going on with him these days? Chloe was often frustrated, but what did *he* feel? He did seem to be all about Jenner, like Chloe said. Would he care? Would this thing she and Chloe had done be good for them? She shuddered to think she was hurting him. But would he really care?

And what would Angie think? If she wasn't happy about Jarrett, wouldn't she be furious about this? Yes. She'd gone silent for so long now, Rosie wondered if she hadn't imagined her visitations in the first place.

———

Even if she had never thought the actual thought or consciously wished for it, the wish was there, her wish for what had happened at the beach. There was nowhere to go now, though. Chloe listened to Peter walking around downstairs while she read to Jenner. Was her life okay now? She and Jenner were so much better, not that she didn't still opt for Peter a lot of the time, but she chose Chloe, too.

If Peter knew about Ocracoke, would it undo him?

She went downstairs and suggested a nightcap. They could play some music, catch up. She'd tell him about the beach, the food, the house they rented. It shouldn't seem like she wouldn't talk about the week, and he could tell her about the mountains.

"No thanks. I'm actually working. I have a tape from a woman Jarrett introduced me to, up near Santeetlah, an old banjo player and some of her family. It's a pretty special stuff. I hope she'll let me do more."

Good news, Peter at work, but it made her paranoid. He never decided to work instead of hanging out. He suspected something. Disapproval was in the air, settling over her, like Angie being around again. Angie would be inflamed by this.

She talked to Jane again about the crazy feeling of Angie's presence in her life. "I know it's not real, but it feels so real."

"You hear her voice?"

"No, I feel her, in my mind, sort of hear her without any external sound, like she tells me things inside. It's very weird. I know how weird this sounds."

"Good things? Bad things?"

"Both. She's helped me, sort of, but she also disturbs me, she disapproves of things I do."

"The things she disapproves of—do you feel bad about those yourself?"

"Sometimes. But you know I can always feel bad, it's my default. I don't actually believe I'm bad like I did when I was young, at least not most of the time, but some of that feeling creeps up on me."

"Blaming it on Angie might be a way to bypass your own disapproval. Doesn't that sound like projection?"

Chloe couldn't dispute her logic. "Sure. But it seems distinct, like her. I can't explain it. Once Rosie told me it doesn't matter what you believe. If something is, it just is."

"You believe Angie's in your life?"

"Of course not. That is, she's always been in my life since Peter. Not like that though. And yet I do."

Another triangle. Rosie was right. All of her relationships became triangles, too. She hadn't told Jane about sex with Rosie because she didn't want to risk her disapproval. She would have told Hannah, though. Someone, she needed to tell someone.

Hillie maybe. She and Hillie texted often since their conversations in San Francisco. But of course not Hillie. She was Jarrett's person, and Chloe was sleeping with his wife.

She asked Meera to lunch and over crab salads told her about Rosie, a leap to a level of personal intimacy she and Meera didn't usually have. Quickly Chloe knew she'd made a mistake. Meera was all about propriety. This was all about impropriety.

"A woman, Chloe? That's not right. I can't imagine women doing that. And she's almost your sister-in-law." The rest of the meal was terrible, with Meera telling her she never guessed Chloe was like that. "And you're married. You're a mother. What were you thinking?"

Chloe sat in silence as Meera rebuked her, knowing the friendship was over.

She would keep this to herself, encapsulate it from the rest of her life, and never let it happen again. She felt at great risk. All week she dodged Rosie's calls. When they finally talked, Rosie said again what an amazing week it had been, so *transgressive*. She said it with great relish.

"We were pretty daring, weren't we?"

Rosie didn't seem to share her confusion. She seemed untroubled, not that different than before. It was clearly a one-off thing with her.

———

Chloe mentioned that she had a meeting with a fund manager in Charlotte, and Rosie offered to meet her there. Chloe paused.

"C'mon, Chlo, let's space travel again. It's summer and I need to get away. I can drive down in two hours. You can't pay this time. I have money."

Now was the time to say they shouldn't do this again, that she couldn't do it. But a long weekend with Rosie, she couldn't not do it.

The three days in Charlotte were intimate and sexual again. Making love began to feel natural, inevitable. They went to the public market, ate fried oysters at a nearby restaurant, managed to walk the lake in the park, but also ordered champagne for the room and, except for Chloe's business meeting, stayed in bed a lot. Rosie whispered, "We're being really bad, aren't we?" Chloe didn't like that. It sounded like a childish romp, or worse, a sneaky undertaking, like her affair with Colette, which it was of course, but it wasn't, at least not to her. It felt like the most natural thing in the world. It felt more right than wrong.

They didn't talk about what it meant between them, as if it didn't mean anything that needed to be talked about. They didn't talk again about what it would mean to Peter or Jarrett, either.

"This is not real life, you know."

"I know. It's like a double life. Escaping real life's a good thing."

———

Rosie got a job at Emerson, a county school with a high percentage of at-risk kids where she felt at home, energized by their needs, and ready to tutor the willing ones after hours. By November Willie would voluntarily talk to her again, even joke around. Once he sat and graded papers.

Her students' ignorance about math dismayed him. It was a poor school, underfunded and understaffed. Half her sixth grade class didn't know the multiplication tables. When she described the chaos in the classroom as they neared mid-terms, he advised. "What if you let them use their books during the test? They're probably anxious."

"Hah. A lot of them wouldn't even find the right page."

"Give them a page number with every problem. Make it easy. I never understood why math has to be memorized. You're going to forget it anyway."

"Smart, Willie."

She and Chloe talked almost nightly, a sexual tremor passing through the phone. "I miss you," Chloe whispered into the phone.

"I miss you!" Rosie almost shouted. "It feels like things are coming together again. Willie likes me now. You believe in signs and cosmic influences. It's got to be a sign."

———

There was another weekend in Charlotte a few months later. Afterward Chloe dreamed she was spinning threads inside a small space, strands of silky blue-green, like a small creature who could produce beautiful sticky threads. She held them together, making a large covering for something, it wasn't clear what. She couldn't easily free her fingers from the strands and when she did, it was only to pick up more strands and find them clinging to her fingers again. Working the fabric was arduous. She worried how to finish it. She woke up tired and felt uneasy all morning.

# CHAPTER 22

Another Thanksgiving in Asheville. After the pumpkin pie disappeared seven-year-old Jenner climbed into Chloe's lap and put her arm around her neck, while Chloe rubbed her back and rested her head against Jenner's. Rosie raised her eyebrows, nodded. Peter started clearing the table then called a pingpong tournament in the basement for whoever wanted to play. Jenner jumped down and raced Brian to the stairs.

The next morning Jarrett wanted a hike at Chimney Rock. Rosie passed, tired from the fuss of the big meal. Chloe said she'd keep her company. They had behaved well, no secret looks, no touching, an implicit understanding not to breach their cover in Asheville. The men drove off with the kids and a daypack of turkey sandwiches.

"Should we be bad?" Rosie stroked Chloe's shoulder from behind her.

Chloe shook her head. "Not here. We can't."

"What's the harm? They're gone for hours. It's hard to be around you and not even touch."

It felt more than daring to Chloe, it felt confusing, really close to betrayal. She'd resisted asking what it meant that they were lovers but also resisted feeling it was that. Rosie's house was not another planet. Still, her "Not here" felt unsure to Rosie; she thought she could persuade her with some kissing. Chloe shook her head, but it was true, it was hard to be together and not touch. She remembered Hannah once told her to honor what she longed for. She had cordoned it off, tried not to think of Rosie at home. That wasn't good, either.

"Not in your bedroom, though."

---

Jarrett drove to Weaverville, basically a suburb of Asheville now, to show Peter and the kids where he'd lived before his mother died. The cottage was gone. In its place, a huge contemporary house of glass, wood, and stone, built for views from multiple decks and porches.

"McMansion. This is where Appalachian culture goes to die. We had a small house with lots of yard. They have lots of house with a small yard. An indoor life, not outdoor."

He doubled back the long way through Black Mountain for the scenery and burgers at Straightaway Café. When they parked at Chimney Rock, the kids jumped out and Jarrett told Willie to go ahead with them. "Wait for us at the Opera Box, Willie."

He halted Peter. "Let them have their own adventure." He picked up a stone and threw it into the woods.

"A shame about your old house."

"I didn't expect it to be there. Last time I looked, six years ago, the porch was rotting. Everything around it was changing. Shops, the little school, all gone. Only the church and cemetery. My mother's there. The big trees we had, they're mostly gone. They must have cut them to make room for more house. After the kids are grown, I mean to move out of the city into an area developers haven't ruined. Well, maybe. Rosie's not sure. She'd rather go back to Nashville. We'll see."

The kids were waiting at a flat area underneath an outcropping rock. "This is the Opera Box," Jarrett said, extending his hand to the view in front of them, an expanse of valley and mountains fading in color. "Too late for the leaves."

"But still pretty spectacular," Willie said.

"Spectacular," Brian said, loving the sound of the word. Willie wanted to go on to the highest point, the top of Chimney Rock. Jarrett told him to take the kids; he and Peter would meet them at the car. Peter looked uneasy, but he waved them off, and they trooped after Willie, Jenner right behind him.

Jarrett threw his arm around him. "Don't worry. Willie's more protective of the kids than either you or Rosie. The stairs to the top have railings up both sides. Kids do it all the time. He'll keep them in line."

Jarrett was happiest in the mountains. He'd pushed out the deadline for his manuscript again to interview people about climate change. "They had the highest rainfall ever in a few hollows this year, and that's after last year's record. Flooding washed out bridges and took some houses." He picked up another stone and threw it into the woods. "I talked to Molley Connell again. She turned eighty in September. They made it through the flooding okay."

Molley was the banjo player Peter met when they went to Santeetlah. He'd gone back once more with recording equipment and gotten new tracks of her singing and playing with her daughter. They were gold, he said. He met more of the family, all of whom played one instrument or another. He was trying to get an invite to one of their gatherings where they played late into the night and hoping to get them down to his studio for a series of recordings. It was the first project to excite him in years.

"Molley's not budging so far."

"Not surprising. She doesn't even come to Asheville any more."

"I might be able to get her daughter or grandchildren to persuade her. There's a great-grandchild who plays harmonica. That's four generations. I can't promise anything, but they could make an album that would be, in Willie's word 'spectacular!' It would bring in money for them."

"Yeah, well. I hope you succeed, but money might not be your best selling point, at least with the older generation. They don't trust city money for good reason, and you might not even be the first person to try. They're used to people trying to exploit them. It took me a while to get Molley to talk, but she likes what I'm writing now."

"I'm not waving dollars in their faces. But I do know it would sell."

"You might be better off talking about preserving the music."

"I might be better off if you came with me. What about that?"

"I'll give it a think."

"What if we collaborated—you write about the music, I produce recordings."

"Nice idea, but I'm still working on the book. Maybe afterward."

They walked in silence, enjoying the pleasure of being together. Peter liked talking to Jarrett better than his musician friends, most of whom were preoccupied with rumors and opportunities in the recording world. Once he'd been preoccupied that way, too, but not for a long time.

"So I have a thing I need to talk to you about."

Jarrett's posture seemed to tighten and Peter wondered if he was presuming—Jarrett didn't talk about personal things often. Men were so much harder than women when it came to that. He waited for Jarrett to nod or encourage him, but Jarrett showed nothing.

Jarrett was thinking of another Thanksgiving, thinking that Chloe finally told Peter about the kiss. He expected it one day and had nothing to say for himself. What was it about her that left him in a state when she was around? He didn't understand why he found her attractive. She was the kind of person he warred against, wealthy and making other people wealthier.

The attraction intruded even with Rosie, making him angry or difficult at times. Rosie's best friend. These were feelings he couldn't articulate even to himself, so he avoided Chloe as much as possible.

He'd had a brief affair once when he was doing an interview and ran into a woman from high school up near Maggie Valley. Twice, actually, but he considered it once, since it was the same woman, the same week. Well, actually there was one more time. But Chloe was different. She didn't like him much anyway, he could tell. He'd waited for Peter or Rosie to wonder why he dodged her, to accuse him, though they hadn't so far.

Peter continued tentatively. "You can probably see things are weird with me and Chloe. Is it okay if I talk about this?"

"Yeah. Sure. Go ahead." Jarrett pressed his fist into his palm.

"Maybe Rosie talks to you. I'm sure she and Chloe talk. She's unhappy, and I feel it. Of course it's my fault, the way Jenner and I are."

Jarrett relaxed slightly.

"I guess I've never gotten past losing Angie. Sad to admit. I never like being separated from Jenner. When Chloe and I went away, it was a special kind of torture to say goodbye to her. Jenner would be crying, and I'd start saying maybe we shouldn't go, and Chloe would be angry. But I didn't feel right leaving Jenner like that. I don't know how other parents do it. We'd go in the end, but the trip would be spoiled for a while, and I'd worry. Overanxious, I guess. Chloe started traveling on her own and now she's vying with me over Jenner. I don't know how to make things right with her."

Jarrett breathed deeply, nodded. "Yeah, you and Jenner. It's hard not to notice, to tell you the truth."

"I know, I know. I can't blame Chloe for traveling by herself. Always business she says, you know it's always business with her, but I worry, what's she really doing? You know your mind can trip you up. Again, I'd hardly blame her. After the kid's album I haven't pulled in much money, and my work doesn't seem to be going anywhere. It's embarrassing to think I've taken taken advantage of her income."

He looked at Jarrett, who kept nodding.

"That's part of the reason I want to do this bluegrass album with the Connell family. That, and I love their music, of course. It's really distinct, what they do."

"Ah. I thought maybe."

"I hate to ask this. But I have to. Does Rosie know anything, does she talk about Chloe being up to anything?"

"I don't know anything about what Chloe does. If Rosie knows, and I don't think she does, she wouldn't tell me anyway, not if Chloe didn't want her to."

"I figured. I'm relieved she travels with Rosie now. At least I know she's not, you know, meeting someone. I wondered once if she was lying, if Rosie actually does go with her or if it's some guy. You remember when I called and talked to you, the second time they went to Charlotte, when I asked to say hi to Rosie. I just wanted to hear you say she was away with Chloe so I could say, 'Of course, I'm an idiot, forgetting that.'"

Jarrett laughed out loud. "Yeah, I remember. That was weird. It gave me doubt for a minute, too. Of course Rosie goes with her. Those two are thick as thieves ever since they went to the beach. Rosie's always going up to the bedroom to talk to her. Can't imagine what they talk so much about."

"True. I'm an idiot, I know. Embarrassed I had to ask."

Jarrett squeezed his shoulder. "No worries. We all get caught up at times. Have you talked to her about this?"

"She'd be mad that I'm suspicious. I'm gonna do better on this Chloe-Jenner thing. I guess I should step back, but it's hard. I'm always thinking about Jenner."

"You said it. Back off a little. Let go a little more. Jenner's growing up fine and she needs a mother, too."

"Right."

The kids met them at the trailhead all talking at once as they climbed into the van. "They did great." Willie sounded proud.

"We could see all the way around in a circle." "We saw a really long river." "And a lake!" "All the way to Tennessee, I bet."

"Well, maybe not Tennessee," Willie added, "but quite a distance."

They chattered most of the ride home, growing quiet only when they entered the city. Andie fell asleep on Jenner's lap in the far back. Jarrett stopped for gas at the neighborhood station. He liked to leave the tank full for Rosie when he took the Jeep to the mountains.

They turned into the driveway and the kids piled out, raced to the front door. They couldn't open it, so they banged with their fists. "Mom! Open the door!"

"Sorry." Rosie unlatched the door after a couple of minutes. "Chloe just felt safer with the chain on after you were gone. She's not used to how we don't bother to lock."

She looked at Chloe, a sly look that said, *Sorry to blame you.* The kids bounded in, full of excitement. They had a story to tell.

Only Peter caught the look.

January, Rosie's principal offered a grant for the annual math teacher event in Atlanta. Rosie claimed it and walked out of the office to call Chloe. "Want to meet me in Atlanta in three weeks?" She'd attend enough of the conference, skip some, and they could have time.

"Hmm. I really couldn't come before Friday."

"Shit. Whatever, just come anyway. We'll have two days at least."

The weather was cold, snow possible. Rosie wanted to cloister in the hotel, luxuriate in a sweet retreat. They hadn't seen each other since Thanksgiving. Chloe's flight arrived late, one o'clock that afternoon, and she called from the High Museum at two-thirty, asked Rosie to come over. It was only a few blocks from the hotel and there was a special exhibit: Asian-American Artists. She had to see if anything of Elaine's was there. She'd discovered online that Elaine had sailed into the art world, her work shown in a few national exhibits. Miffed, Rosie said no, it was too cold. She'd go to another session, meet her in the hotel bar at four.

Over glasses of wine Chloe said, "I wish you'd come to the museum."

"Sorry. The only artist I really love is Frida Kahlo." She ordered sweet potato fries, then brought up the discrepancy of their incomes.

Chloe shrugged. "What does it matter? I do what I do, you do something different. Your work is more important, mine pays more."

"You're so rich now. You probably give away more than I earn. Doesn't it bother you?"

"Sounds like it's bothering you."

"You should see the kids I work with. Some have nothing. A couple are homeless. It pains me."

Chloe sipped her Chardonnay, looked away for a few minutes. "It should pain you, Rosie. You know I didn't grow up with much. My parents were cheap because they had to be. My father's disability is worse, he can't work at all now. I pay taxes on their house, I'll pay their health insurance until they get Medicare, and I send as much extra as they'll accept. I didn't want to have a family that lived on that edge, but yes, it bothers me."

"And you pay for almost everything with us. I was thrilled you wouldn't be paying this time."

"I get that. But why shouldn't I pay?" Chloe's wine glass trembled as she held it to her lips. "You're picking a fight. You're annoyed that I didn't come straight to the room with you. Is it because it had something to do with Elaine?"

"God no. But yeah, I'm annoyed. We have so little time."

"I can't move as fast as you."

Rosie raised her eyebrows and sat back.

"Since when?"

"Tell me something, Rosie—how is it you're so relaxed about being lovers? Our week at the beach, the first time, how was that easy if you've never been with a woman before?"

"I don't know. Maybe it just comes naturally."

"What does that mean? With Jarrett, too?"

"Sure. As long as it's someone I love. I can't make love with someone I don't love. I did that when I was young, and it was terrible. Sorry," she laughed, "but I don't have a slutty history like you."

Chloe flicked wine at Rosie. She shouldn't have told her about Colette. Rosie blinked. "I don't know. Because it's you?"

"Don't you need to understand this?"

"How? What are you suggesting? It doesn't feel wrong. Most of the time. Maybe when we were in my house. That was a bit too, I don't know, something. It's not like we're hurting anyone." She sighed, gave Chloe a look. "Okay. I'll go slower if you need to, Chlo."

They sipped their wine in silence. Rosie looked around. "You know one cool thing about having a woman lover is that I can sit here in a bar having this conversation with my teacher friends walking by and no one suspects a thing. I don't know, maybe things like that, it just doesn't feel like cheating."

Upstairs in their room, they smoked a little weed. Rosie gently pulled Chloe close. Her lips were soft, the kiss tentative. Rosie tasted sweet pungency: their curry dinner, the Zinfandel. Like sinking again, and Chloe wanted to sink deeper but she resisted, stood up, sat down, and kissed her again, a long kiss with urgency. They were both breathless, couldn't speak.

After making love they lay in a tangle of sheets. Rosie traced Chloe's arm and torso. "You told me a long time ago you'd tell me more personal stuff."

"Did I? I don't know why. It's not happy stuff."

"Tell me anyway."

Chloe got out of bed and retrieved the remainder of a joint, lit it and offered it to Rosie. "I told you what happened to my mother's family." She hesitated, scowled. "I hate talking about this stuff. You aren't my therapist."

Rosie said, "Come on, Chlo. Don't go there. I want to know everything about you. You've always known everything about me."

She looked at Rosie's face, so open and eager. "I've always been afraid of getting close to other people. I never had close friends. I used to believe something was wrong with me because my own mother didn't love me. Or didn't seem to, except a few times. Then she did. Having a mother like Kath, it was just hard.

It still is. She suffered too much. She gave me so little. I love her, I hate her."

Chloe looked at Rosie carefully before saying the next thing. "I don't think people like you who grew up in normal, happy families understand people like me. You can't. We're already set apart. There's a gap you can't cross."

Rosie started to object, but Chloe cut her off. "I know your family had its troubles, but it's not the same. What happened with your parents got healed, more or less, and things went on. They were okay. You were okay. What Tolstoy said about families is only partly true. There may be a sameness about happy families, but what he didn't say is there's another sameness about unhappy ones. We feel like outsiders. Things in our families never heal, can't be healed, and we know it. We can never be normal. My father's disabilities are physical, my mother's are psychological. Our families are different, and we come out of them different. There's no avoiding it."

"Chloe! That's so terrible, so painful. You think I can't understand you, but maybe I can. Give me a chance. Or do you just want to be around someone from a troubled family, too."

"God, no. I'm relieved you aren't. Like Peter. I want to be with people who are okay. I get a little more okay myself then. A little bit. I couldn't bear someone like me."

She teared up, more than she usually did with Jane, and looked plaintive. "I don't know, I wonder, am I enough of a mother myself? Especially after the hysterectomy. I couldn't understand how I let it happen, except maybe I knew. I wasn't meant to be a mother." Chloe's tears brimmed. Rosie sat quietly touching her leg, on the edge of tears herself. "You told me once that Angie tries to tell us things we don't see ourselves."

"I said that? I don't think that way now. Now I think she was a troubled spirit. She died too young. She hadn't finished what she meant to do. She was scrambling, she still wanted to be in control. She kept at it by trying to take care of Peter, making sure he had someone. Someone who'd give him a child."

"Using me."

"Maybe. I don't know. She knew you'd be good for him."

"But she didn't care if he was good for me."

"I don't mean that. Just that her attachment was to me and Peter. She might be finished now."

"What about you? Is she finished with you?

"I don't know. I hope so. I hope not. She scares me."

The next morning they slept late and lay entwined in bed, not making love, just holding each other for a while before they ordered breakfast in the room.

"Funny how little we know about people, isn't it? Even people we're closest to. All that you told me last night. It's so much." Rosie touched Chloe's face, but Chloe flinched. "You're somewhere else now. Is there more I don't know?

"Hard to say. Tell me things about you."

"You know everything. I spill all the time. You're the one who's mysterious. If there's something I should know, you'd tell me. Right?"

Chloe shrugged, nodded.

At the airport Rosie saw Chloe board her plane, walked to her own gate and made it home in time for family dinner. She was not interested in sex that night, confused as well as comforted being with Jarrett.

Chloe's and Jarrett's bodies were so different, both athletic, well-muscled, fit, but Chloe's had suppleness, soft breasts and buttocks, while he was firm everywhere, except his waist and belly which had a new layer of flesh. She wondered if his body was headed toward softness, too—she didn't want that. She wanted them different, Jarrett on one side, Chloe on the other— not literally, no, the thought horrified her. She liked a nice piece of geography between them, their beautiful mountains.

# CHAPTER 23

Chloe didn't call for weeks and sometimes let Rosie's calls go to voice mail. She apologized: things were frantic at work as the economy rebounded, plus she'd signed up to assist Jenner's soccer matches. Rosie suggested they go back to Ocracoke for spring vacation. Chloe suggested a spa weekend in Highlands instead. Rosie hesitated—the Blue Ridge was Jarrett's territory. He loathed Highlands though, everything so posh and expensive. She wouldn't feel she was trespassing on his turf. So what if Jarrett would sneer when she told him?

Two days before they were to leave, Chloe called. "I'm sorry, but Jenner's sick."

"Shit. You know I won't be able to get away again until summer."

"I know. I really am sorry, but I'm not leaving her when she feels so rotten."

"Yeah, of course. But it sucks."

During her break Rosie sank her frustration into a vegetable garden in the back yard. She bribed Willie, offering good money if he'd help her turn the soil. Good for him to get his hands dirty another way. They created an eight-by-twelve foot plot, and Willie helped with bags of manure. "Yuck, gross," he yelped as he spread it with his hands. That drew Brian out, but Brian didn't want to work, and Rosie was glad—this garden was hers and Willie's. Together they put in seeds of tomatoes, squash, peppers, bush beans.

Days later Willie launched himself into the house with a whoop. "Come look, Mom, there's new shoots. Another thing's coming up!"

Over the next weeks rows of beans, spirals of squash, tomato and pepper plants sprouted, grew taller, produced flowers. "Way cool, these green things just keep growing," she heard him say into his phone as he helped her edge the garden with lobelia. He seemed to have girlfriend, though he hadn't said and she hadn't asked.

———

Chloe and Rosie met in Highland late July. Chloe reserved a two-bedroom cottage and brought a stack of reports. She put her things in the smaller bedroom. As they walked around town deciding on a restaurant, Rosie found fault with Chloe's choices, and Chloe seemed indifferent to hers, preoccupied.

"What's up with you Chloe?" Rosie asked. "Things are not the same. What's changed?"

"I had a terrible week, too much work, a big fight with Peter. The only good thing is that Jenner complained a lot when I left. It's pathetic how much that means."

"Oh, sweetie. She's shifted, hasn't she? I told you she would."

"I'm going to assist her soccer coach again. Ridiculous for Peter to be the soccer dad. I'm not enjoying work much anyway."

"Good for you. Throw those reports down the mountain." Rosie's mood lifted.

Chloe said she hadn't slept well all week and need to go to bed early, alone. She got up early, too, put in a few hours on her computer before they went out for breakfast. "Sorry. I had emails from clients I had to respond to."

After lunch they hiked Chinquapin Mountain, a steep root-rutted trail that skirted and crossed a rocky stream several times. They took off their shoes and waded into the water, sat on a flat boulder in filtered sunshine listening to the stream trill over a small waterfall. Rhododendrons with faded magenta blossoms edged the bank. Chloe shifted away abruptly. Rosie saw her wipe her eyes and put her hand to her shoulder.

"I don't know what the matter is. But I can guess."

"I doubt it."

"You want to stop this, and you're afraid to tell me. I knew it last night when you didn't sleep with me. You're done with this little fling we've had. I suspected it. You haven't come to Asheville, you don't want to go to the beach. I've tried to give you room, but you could have told me before we came."

Chloe put her head on her knees, turned toward her, snapped, "That's not it, Rosie."

"Don't talk to me like that. I can't stand it when you're hard."

Chloe put up a hand to stop her. "There's nothing you could say that hurts like *that*, and you know it. Of all people you know I'm not hard. All I seem to do is cry."

"I'm sorry. But when you won't talk I can't stand *that*! Tell me. I can't take silence. I'm a grown-up, Chloe. I've dealt with worse things than being dumped."

"You *aren't* being dumped.."

"So, what? Tell me *something*."

"I don't know. Maybe it's Jenner."

Rosie nodded. If the amorous weekend wasn't to be, it wasn't. She was confused, disappointed, hated that it had gotten complicated, that they quarreled now, how Chloe seemed not to want her any more. Rosie clasped Chloe's waistband as they walked back down the trail. At the inn they had massages waiting for them.

After dinner they walked uphill to their cottage. Rosie took Chloe's hand and said, "I've thought a lot about our conversation about Angie's mischief. Remember? When I said the dead must have a different morality."

"I remember. I hoped you'd laugh or say I was crazy. Not that she really might shadow me."

Rosie described how she used to go to the Shelby Street bridge and imagine leaping, how Angie saved her. Then Angie almost killed her when she was driving home from Asheville, before she married Jarrett. They reached their cottage, Chloe carded the door, and they went in.

"So I thought that's a crazy thing. I don't believe our lost ones are malevolent. Like Victorian ghosts. Anyway, it can't be that she tried to save me then tried to destroy me. It doesn't make sense. I told her to leave me alone after that. And she did. I didn't like that either. Please don't look so horrified. I've never told anyone all this. I just chew on it."

"It scares me, Rosie, that you thought of doing such a thing."

"It scared me, too. I was grateful to her, then furious. But what I came to is this: if she does anything at all, and I'm not really saying she does, she tries to make me see things. She wanted me to know I wanted to live."

Rosie closed the sliding door to the balcony. The mountain air was cool at night, and Chloe clicked on the gas fireplace. She pursed her lips, shook her head and collapsed on the couch. "I don't know. You can't think I wanted a hysterectomy. That's what she was showing me?"

"Well, nooo. But, I don't know. You said yourself you didn't know about being a mother. I'm just saying."

"That's horrible. *What* are you saying?"

"Maybe it wasn't about that at all. Maybe it was something about you and Peter."

Yes. That was it. Chloe shuddered. It was about her and Peter.

They slept together again that night, but something was missing. Heart? Enthusiasm?

———

Driving home the next day, Rosie's phone buzzed outside Sylva. Jarrett, she thought. She hadn't told him when she'd get in. It was Chloe though. "Find a place to pull over. I have to talk to you, and I don't want you driving. I'm in the parking lot of a Denny's myself." It was hot, and Chloe had parked in a rear corner hoping no one would hear her with her windows down.

"Okay. Give me a minute. There's a pull-out just ahead. Here it comes, I guess." She parked beside a mossy outcrop, turned off the car. "Tell me."

"I'm really really sorry, Rosie, for being difficult. You were half right, it's you and me." She could hear Rosie breathing heavily in the silence. She wanted to stop herself and wanted to comfort her at the same time. "It isn't that I want to end it. I've thought of that, plenty. I can't seem to. It's that I'm in love with you, Rosie. It's more than what I feel for Peter, or ever did. I imagine running off with you. Honest to God, I'd figure out how to do it if you would."

Rosie froze. She sat silently, waiting, thinking, panicking.

"Tell me what to do. You think I'm crazy. Say it. I couldn't tell you this in person."

"Oh, Chloe. I don't know what to say."

"That's not how you feel, is it? When you told me it doesn't feel like cheating, I knew. For me, it's cheating. It's serious. It's not a fling."

Rosie didn't respond. Chloe put her hand on her chest, her lips quivering. "You don't have to say it. I know already."

"But you. You've had other lovers before. You wouldn't be satisfied with just me. You'd want Peter, too, or another man."

"You're wrong. It's complicated. I've been afraid of this for years. You don't know how long I've loved you. You're the one who wouldn't be okay with it."

After more silence Rosie pleaded. "Don't get off the phone, Chloe. I do love you, you know that. I just want to go on the way we've been."

"I can't. Almost equal is no good any more. You have to understand that. I just can't do it this way any longer."

"I *don't* understand. What about Peter? Or Jarrett? I couldn't leave him. Not even to mention the kids. I could not. I couldn't betray any of them like that, and I don't believe you could, either. You wouldn't leave Peter or Jenner. You're her soccer mom now." She laughed. "I'm sorry. It's not funny."

"We'd take the kids with us. I don't know what I'm capable of. It's terrible to think of it. But I think of it all the time."

"They would not be okay. Willie would never forgive me." Rosie winced to think of it. "You're just feeling desperate, Chloe. This could be about Peter and Jenner more than about me."

"It isn't, and that's insulting. It makes me mad."

"Sorry, but what if it's true? Neither of us could do it."

"You don't know about me. I needed to hear you say it. I have to go home and get my head on straight. You shouldn't call me right now. Wait for me to call you. I love you, Rosie."

She hung up, dropped her head against the steering wheel and closed her eyes. She hadn't intended to be so either/or, but there was no other option out there. She couldn't go on this way. Maybe it was the talk about Angie last night, realizing she and Peter were bankrupt.

What was Rosie feeling now? How would she feel when she got home? Angry. Sad, confused, dismayed, unable to believe Chloe could think she'd leave Jarrett, leave Asheville. Rosie was all about holding onto people. She'd never tear her family apart. Except. If. One day her kids would be older.

Willie would be off to college soon, Brian and Addie teenagers in a few years. And Jarrett? Chloe suspected he slept around on his trips into the mountains. Possibly he had someone there or just met women in a bar. Hillie had spilled his history, how he'd played around a lot. That bizarre kiss in the kitchen that day. If he could imagine she'd welcome it, he could do anything. An unpleasant thought broke through: what he wanted to do with her was exactly what she had done with Rosie.

Peter. She had given not thought to Peter. She pictured Jenner's face as she told them she was dividing the family. Peter's devastation. He didn't love her like Angie, but there was still caring there. She cared for him.

"Excuse me. Are you okay?" An older woman stood at the window of the car. Chloe lifted her head. "I saw you when I went in. It worried me to see you still here. If you're just sleeping, sorry to bother you. I wanted to be sure you're okay, that you don't need help or anything."

"Thank you. Yes. I'm fine. Just tired. Resting before I drive back to Nashville."

"Okay. God bless."

Chloe watched her walk away. Yes I need help.

---

She'd brought the curtain down. At home she was snappish when Peter asked about the trip. "We ran into some trouble. Time will have to sort it out."

"Trouble between you and Rosie? Tell me." She watched alarm take over his face and wondered if it was for her or for Rosie.

"Too hard to explain. I'm too tired. Don't worry. Rosie's okay. Or will be soon."

"And you?"

Nice of you to ask, she almost said. It would be easy to target him with anger. She had been doing that for a while. Polite anger, most of the time. Now it was turning cold.

"Like I said, tired. I'm sleeping in the guest room. I need a good night."

He looked hurt, then upset when he realized Jenner was watching. Chloe hugged Jenner tightly and said, "Let me put you to bed tonight, sweetie. I missed you."

"I missed you too, Mom. I wish you wouldn't travel so much. Why don't you get a different job."

"Not a bad idea. I should think about that."

Jenner read fluently, but she still wanted to be read to before sleep. She brought her worn copy of *Anne of Green Gables*. "Read me the part where Marilla starts to love her."

Afterward Chloe got her things from the bedroom and went down the hall. It was hours before she slept, and she was wakened by Jenner asking if she could sleep with her. "I had a dream." She lifted the covers for Jenner to crawl in and put her arms around her. Jenner hadn't asked to sleep with them in a long time. She really had missed her.

Someday Rosie might want to be free. Could she wait for her?

———

Rosie was moody at home. She threw Jarrett's dirty things from the floor onto his side of the bed and cut him off when he asked about Highlands. No calls to or from Chloe at night. When Jarrett turned to her in bed, she shrugged away. Brian and Andie left her alone because her mood was dark. Brian was about to turn nine, not close to puberty, but if he was going to be like Willie, she couldn't endure it. Andie, seven now, seemed to be going on twelve, planning her own play dates, reflexively independent. They had all grown away from her. Did they even need her? Did Jarrett?

She thought of Chloe constantly. What was she doing? How was she feeling? Should she call anyway? What if she loved her but wasn't brave? It occurred to her that Jarrett might have been unfaithful. He was the guy who couldn't sustain a long relationship before they married. Their passion cooled a few years ago. She didn't know what he did, but the question had been in the back of her mind a long time.

Willie did have a girlfriend. Zoe. He wanted to go to State when he graduated and to study sustainable agriculture, in love with growing things now. Zoe planned to go UNC. "That's still a year away," Rosie said. "Lots can happen in a year. In a day sometimes." He hugged her sometimes now, but he was out at Zoe's all the time, and she hardly saw him. Life moves along, she told herself. He probably would be fine without her. It was Chloe she missed, an ache that didn't disappear.

Jarrett came home early one afternoon and found her immobile on the garden bench, glaring at the peppers as if to catch them in the act of failing. He asked what was wrong. "Nothing." She looked up at a long branch of the red maple. "It's blocking their sun." He went to the garage, pulled out the ladder and long-handled loppers to prune it.

"Don't you dare." She took the loppers from him. That was Chloe's tree. It was a presence in the yard, her presence. Jarrett's glance at her was plain: you are so weirdly ornery lately. He slammed into the house.

Go on in. I'm not coming after you. I'll prune the goddamn tree myself when I'm ready, she thought. Thinking of it was enough to make her weep again.

PART SIX

THE ONLY ONE WHO GETS IT

# CHAPTER 24

The thwack of a branch breaking, the impact of hard ground, an explosion of red, Rosie remembered only that. She must have lost consciousness, the sun was higher. Or lower. Which? She felt no pain, but when she tried to sit up she discovered she couldn't, except for a little head movement—and there was the pain, a dagger at the base of her skull. A stirring of panic began, and she called out.

No answer. The children would still be at school, and Jarrett—where was he? Away. Panic swelled, propelled her voice with a rasp. "Can anyone hear me?" It exhausted her. She closed her eyes, squeezed them to make the pain stop, felt her cheeks burn, her mouth taut. Why couldn't she get up?

She's felt lightheaded, anxious this morning, feelings common the past two months, but worse today, and she'd called in sick. Then she felt better and decided to prune Chloe's tree, symbolic as it was. She pulled the ladder out, found the long loping shears, climbed. Nothing after that.

A mourning dove called. She opened her eyes again. A pair of squirrels chased through pines overhead. She couldn't judge time, time was stalled. She was out of time, drifting. Her body, absolutely weightless, hardly seemed to exist. Except for her head, which she wanted to flee when the pain struck again. Her breath stopped against it.

More time. How much? Maybe she'd passed out. The sun tilted over a pine tree, but she couldn't recall how far it had moved. A child yelled, there was the soft whirr of bicycle tires.

Kids riding by? She tried to call again, as loud as possible. "Help. Can someone help?" The words sounded weak and distant.

Nothing. She was somewhere else, younger, lying on the ground after a fall. Angie peered into her face. The dove called again, another answered. Rosie let her voice out and held her throat open as long as possible, a guttural hawking croak. Clouds floated in circles over her head, trees stirred, bending in a circle. Time.

An audible motor, it turned off. Angie was there again, holding her hand, speaking, but Rosie couldn't hear her. Then a blur of people, unsteady movement. She was traveling, wheels on road. The woman peering into her face and holding her hand was not Angie. She looked Indian. She wore a blue work shirt with a patch—Allied Services. A laminated photo clipped to her pocket, her name: Leela Chowdhury. Rosie's brain wrapped around that. Hurry. Hurry.

"You awake?"

She tried to nod, but it hurt too much. She moved her lips, a whisper. "Yes."

"Do you feel my hand holding yours?"

Rosie didn't feel it, she saw it. She closed her eyes, retreated to wherever she was before the woman spoke. She wanted Angie again. Rosie floated high and below her was a plum-colored ocean. The woman spoke again. Rosie fluttered her eyelids, hoping that was sufficient. Where did Angie go? Suddenly she was in a room of too-bright lights. She remembered this room—she was looking for Angie. A hospital. She needed to find her in here. Angie was in trouble. Fuck the harsh lights. They hurt her eyes though her eyes were closed. Angie was near. Ahh, moving toward her in wavering light, that same purple hue.

A man stood next to her, the lights draining color from his skin. "Vitals?" he asked. He was speaking to someone she couldn't see. Rosie tried to turn her head but couldn't, the dagger still there. She tried to lift her hand, but the hand wouldn't obey. Her body had a mind of its own or no mind at all, just fire running through, metal things on fire inside, places she couldn't locate.

"Unstable. Low BP, tachycardia, possible fractures of C4/C5," a woman's voice responded. "Respiration stable. We're setting up an MP drip and taking her to radiology. She's grimacing, may be in pain."

They were talking about her. "Yes," someone who sounded like her said, "pain."

The man leaned over her. "You'll have relief very soon. It may not be much comfort, but it's a good sign. Tell us where." He spoke matter-of-factly.

"Hot things. In my head." Her voice was stronger. "Don't know. I can't tell."

A woman in scrubs came in with an IV pole and hovered over her arm.

"Can you wiggle your toes?"

Rosie tried. "Did they wiggle?"

"They kind of twitched," the man said, smiling at her. Was he lying? The nurse was working on her right arm, but she didn't feel anything.

The first woman spoke again. "I'm Dr. Schwarsky. I'm assessing your injuries. We'll be making decisions soon." She wrote in a chart. "Dr. Gleason's taking over, but I'll be back."

"Decisions?" Rosie repeated, trying to be alert. "Decisions? God, my head hurts."

The doctor gave her a smile, left her room. The IV pole was attached to her arm, and the nurse left also, brisk, like a TV nurse. A soap opera. She was in a bad episode, starring role. Here was the handsome doctor lifting her eyelids and shining a light into her eyes. He asked her to count backwards from one hundred. "Ninety-nine, ninety-eight, ninety-seven, ninety-six, ninety-five. Can I stop?"

"Try it from fifty."

"Fifty, forty-nine, forty-eight. Silly."

"Yes. I'm going to do more silly things." He was fooling around at her feet though she couldn't tell what he was doing. He gently lifted her arm, caught it himself as he let it drop. "Are you hot or cold?"

"I'd say...cold?"

"Good." Was it her imagination or did he wink at her? Another brutal wave of pain trounced her. She tried to squirm away but her chin was propped, her head held in place like it would topple off. The rush of pain subsided. "What's at my chin?"

"You have a cervical collar." The nurse was back, leaning over her other arm, and seemed to be injecting her with something.

"What's wrong with my neck?"

"We'll know more soon. We did some X-rays. We'll be doing an MRI."

"MRI?" Angie had an MRI. "I'd like Angie to be here."

"We need phone numbers for next of kin."

"What time is it? Is school out?"

"Not yet." He was waving someone in. "You have children?"

"Yes. Call Jarrett. And Laraine."

"She'll get your information." He inclined his head toward a woman with a clipboard. Everyone else left as she asked questions and Rosie gave answers—cell numbers for Jarrett, Laraine. Alert now, feeling no pain, she could think. She told her to ask Laraine to pick up her kids, keep them until Jarrett came.

She was exhausted. Numbers floated on the ceiling. She closed her eyes, she needed to drift again, back to that ocean.

Cold. She took Angie's hand and it warmed her, like sitting in the sun. They seemed to be floating together, not anchored and not moving. *We have to plan.* Angie spoke calmly. Rosie gave a little push on her arm. You always plan. You know I never plan. Angie wrote a series of phone numbers in a notebook and Rosie watched, the joy of being with her a perfect thing happening, familiar and new at the same time.

Another man, not the handsome doctor, stood beside her. "Hi, Rosie. Can you tell me if you feel relief from the pain? Keep talking to me, okay? Tell me what happened."

His voice was warm, more intimate than the others. "I don't know. I was on a ladder. Am I okay?" Her voice sounded so small again.

"We don't know yet." Was he was lying too? Did they all lie?

"Who's *we*?"

"My name's Danny Reilly. I'm the nurse anesthetist. You have a neurologist looking after you and the attending physician from the ER. The neurosurgeon's coming soon. We're deciding on the surgery. I'll do the anesthesia."

"Surgery?" Why hadn't she felt afraid?

"You injured your neck. You have trauma to your head, possibly a bleed. We don't know when you were injured. I'm hoping you can tell us more."

She was slipping into the waves of light, the sea of purple. "In my backyard."

"How long did you lay there?"

"I don't know," she whispered, slipping back into that watery space.

———

She and Angie were in a chamber, though nothing seemed wet, only smooth and clear like water, or light, except the surface far above them which was roiled and distorted. It was not easy to breathe. Angie was wearing a white shawl. Rosie couldn't remember if she'd seen it before. She passed pink lilies to Rosie, red gladioli and closed white rosebuds. Her hair was light and glossy. *You hold the flowers. I'm making notes,* Angie said. *We're going to change.*

Clothes? Rosie asked.

*Sure.* Off to the right was a swirl of other beings.

Clothes? she asked again. She could see into the dense mass, a dazzle of colors. Angie disappeared abruptly and Rosie was bereft. Angie? Angie!

She opened her eyes. Voices, words drifted in from the hallway...traction...surgery... can't accomplish...damaged...could prevent...A debate. Where was Danny Reilly?

"Where's Jarrett? My husband."

"I don't think they reached him. Cell phone seems to be off." Dr. Gleason again.

"Out of reach. Happens all the time."

"How's the pain?"

"No pain. I need to talk to Angie again."

"Who's Angie?"

"My sister."

There was a mirrored surface. She could see herself in it, her gardening pants, her grubby loafers. She shook off the heavy gloves, wiped her cheek, which was smudged with brown. *You need something nicer to wear.* Angie walked into the drifting mass of color, returned with something in her hand. *First we should play Scrabble.* Angie always loved games. *Here are your letters.* She gave her a Q, a Z, a T, an S, a G and a W. Then she handed her two more letters. *But just use these.*

Rosie put the two letters on the board, an N and an O.

She offered to get clothes for Rosie. *After all, you can't walk.* Rosie waited a long time but she didn't return. The chamber had become horizon again. There was the sound of the mourning dove. Angie. Rosie called. I'm looking for you. I can't see you now.

Danny was speaking to her about surgery.

"No. No."

"The neurosurgeon's very good. He won't operate if it's too risky."

"No surgery. No surgery. I can't walk. Tell me the truth"

"The images show fractures in the neck vertebrae. Nothing conclusive. Surgery may be able to fuse them."

"I'm paralyzed."

"We don't know."

"You know. No surgery."

"You might not have a choice."

"I have a choice. Uh-uh. I don't consent."

The doctor came in and Danny left. "Look Rosie, I'm afraid you really *don't* have a choice."

"I have a choice."

"Look, I don't know how else to say this. Your life is in danger."

"I am in danger. I want Danny Reilly."

He left and she waited, a long time, it seemed. No more Angie. When Danny came in, she looked at him, pleaded with her eyes.

"Angie gave me the N and the O."

"Angie." Danny cleared his throat. "Rosie, we asked the social worker to locate your sister. Your aunt said the only sister died years ago."

"Yes. We're twins. We don't look alike. But she was here."

"It's easy to get things confused after an injury like this."

"She was here. I touched her, I put my hands in hers, she was warm. We talked." Tears dripped from the corners of her eyes down toward her ears. Danny wiped them with his hand. "I've missed her."

"Rosie, you  need to stay awake if you can. We're getting information as fast as possible. Let's see if we can get Jarrett here."

Rosie wasn't listening, she was concentrating, still weeping, looking for Angie. "I don't know what to do," she said. "Tell me what to do."

"You need the surgery."

She looked clearly at him. "You say. I'm already ruined. You know it. Talk to me. I had a friend in grammar school named Danny. Angie and I played board games with him."

"I had a friend in grammar school named Rosie."

"Like we're old friends, ha ha. You tell me. How paralyzed am I?"

*Stay with me, Rosie. It's better here. Mermaids.* Angie spoke in the most beguiling way. She could talk the feathers off a bird. *I've missed you so much. Remember, you wanted to, before. It would be easy now. Remember. You wanted to.* Angie turned her face away. *We can't forget each other again.*

Rosie was shocked. I never forgot you. Did you forget me? You did, didn't you? You were the one who left.

Angie wouldn't answer. She had a cryptic expression on her face. A mystery woman. Rosie wouldn't let her go this time, no matter how elusive she tried to be. But Angie was fading anyway. She was speaking through a void.

She opened her eyes. There was Danny still. She tried to bring his mind in more clearly. She and Angie used to do that with each other, wordlessly. She recognized the sensation with an involuntary twitch, almost a shudder.

"Do you have a sister?"

"I did. Mine died too. Years ago also."

"Were you there?"

"Huh?"

"Were you with her when she died."

"Yeah."

He thought she wasn't lucid, but she was. She was lucid all right. "Tell me what happened."

He was resisting. She pressed him as hard as she could, with only her mind working. "You're afraid you're dying, Rosie, but I think we'll save you."

"I'm not afraid. Do not save me." He looked distressed. She could feel the void left by Angie, but also the space Danny occupied. "Did your sister talk when she was dying? Did she tell you what was happening? You were there."

Danny looked exasperated. Medical people, they shut out these spaces.

"Angie and I, we can hear each other think. Tell me. Tell me about your sister. Did she want to die?"

"Maybe."

"And you let her."

He looked really disturbed now. Maybe he was angry with her.

"I'm a goner. I know it. You know it. Help me."

He leaned toward her, and she looked in his eyes. She was so clear about this. Wasn't she speaking to him with ordinary words? He could understand the whole of what she meant, she knew he could. He just didn't want to. "What happened to *you* when your sister died?"

He was remembering.

"I held her hand so long I had to lift her fingers off."

"Yes. What else? Don't look away." He felt her now, she was sure. He was an ally, even if he didn't want to be. He spent time with dying people, unconscious people. He'd been in sight of that boundary. "The mind keeps something apart, doesn't it? It can move, out and back, can't it?"

She felt him wanting to leave the room, and she let him go. He was at the door when a woman bumped into him. "What about the husband?" he demanded.

"I was just coming to say. I finally reached him. He was near Canton. He'll be here soon. I talked to the aunt again. She's got the children."

Rosie groaned. Andie. Brian. Willie. Andie. The light around her heaved like water, eddied. She could easily drown. Not the same as dying. To think of her children would drown her. She heard Danny in the hallway, talking.

"She's refusing surgery. I think she's hallucinating. Not able to make a decision." He hesitated. "She knows she could die. She's wanting to go. You don't see that when someone's got kids."

He came back into the room, and she beckoned to him, but he didn't seem to hear her any more. Her bed had been cranked up slightly and she could see him clearly. "Time to decide," she said.

"Yes."

"No," she said. "What we'll wear. We're deciding if we should wear the same dress."

"Rosie, stay awake."

"I'm so awake. The sun on the water's amazing. Indigo. Violet."

"Keep your eyes open."

With effort she held her eyes open. "Okay."

"We may be able to repair some of the vertebral damage."

"May? Some?"

"No guarantees. Jarrett will be here soon."

"Don't let Jarrett in. Send him home. He has to be with the kids. I don't want him here." She panicked again. Jarrett. A sucking pull from the watery light, a whirlpool of misery. She couldn't feel him and stay afloat. He'd drag her out and she'd be a limp fish, flopping on sand the rest of her life. All of them tending her. No life for them, no life for herself.

"You need to consent. Just verbally agree."

"No. Won't do it. Not to them." She closed her eyes. "It would be bad. Very bad." She was pleading with him. It was hard to reach him again. The urge to disappear was so strong.

"Rosie, think. Your family needs you. The surgery may save you."

"I can't move. Don't lie. I don't want them taking care of me. You know. Please." It was so hard to keep looking at him, to penetrate his resistance. A great effort, everything available, but he was unsettled again, she could feel it. "Okay?" she asked. She was losing control over her eyes, they kept going dark, seemed to close down, and tears leaked out that she couldn't stop. "Speak to me. I'm losing ground. My children will be okay. Angie said. Jarrett will be okay." The words came out with a gasp.

Chloe? What about Chloe? Chloe. Chloe. A shudder passed across her face. She could feel her mouth twitch. *Chloe can't have you.* Okay. I know. You don't like her. *I like her. But she's not yours.* I don't know what to do, Angie. I don't know how to leave them.

Someone said to get her to the OR now, the brain stem was at risk. Danny reported that blood pressure was dropping, respiration poor, pulse racing. She was having trouble breathing. Rosie listened. Her ears were working.

"She's still refusing."

"We've waited too long already."

Her eyelids flickered. He was sweating, she could almost hear him thinking. "But she refused."

The surgeon snapped. "You said she was hallucinating. Get her ready."

People whisked around the bed, pulled her hair to the side, put something cold and moist on her scalp. She heard Danny snap. "I'm doing what I can." Was he talking to her or them? She fluttered her eyes. She didn't need long. A flurry of sounds, activity in the hall. Danny was speaking to someone.

"She won't survive the anesthesia."

Rosie drifted off. She'd won.

She was brought back to the room by a woman's voice. Monitors in her room began beeping, people were running. A flash of lights and popping noises, it was like a party, champagne corks and distant fireworks, muffled the way those little Chinese poppers sounded when they tossed them on the street the year she and Angie went to the coast with their parents for New Year's.

---

Jarrett's voice was calling down the hall, demanding where she was. She was already safe. A doctor spoke. "I'm so sorry. She died before we could get her to surgery. I'm afraid she broke her neck in the fall, what we call a complete cord injury, complete paralysis."

His footsteps came like thunder into the room. An enormous wave rushed toward her. She felt him at her side, bewildered. "Rosie," he whispered. He sounded so weak. He put his hands on her shoulders, his forehead against hers. "You can't go. You can't go." He lay his cheek on her breast, murmuring her name. When he lifted his head he spoke. "She's warm."

"Yes, she's warm." It was Danny's voice. He was removing the IV line.

Jarrett was agitated. She tried to touch him, but she couldn't. She'd thought she might be able to move again once she stopped breathing, but no, she was still paralyzed. She grazed him with love, the kind they felt only during their deepest intimacy. He had to feel that.

"I'll leave you a while," Danny said.

Jarrett was sitting on the bed, kissing her face and hands. "Rosie. Rosie. I love you so much."

She could feel his shock. She tried to soothe him, to hold him with her mind. He wanted to pull her into his arms, but the neck brace interfered. *Take it off.* Danny fumbled with the closure at the back of the brace and removed it. Jarrett lifted her and held her against him. "Stay with me. Stay with me." He held her like that, and the flood of his tears spilled into the sea around her.

*Jarrett. It's okay. I'm okay now. I'm right here. I am. You know me, Jarrett. I know it confuses you. But it's me. I love you.*

That was all she could do, just that. She said goodbye, she would have to go. But it wasn't as easy as she thought. She tried to pull away, go where she belonged now, wherever it was. She felt like one of those balloons in old British movies, metallic war balloons, giant silver things tethered with heavy ropes so they couldn't float away, anchored to a building, or however they did it. She couldn't release herself and drift off. Jarrett held her. It would wrench her too much. Her mind—this wasn't consciousness, but whatever it was now, bigger—would be twisted, fractured. She had to wait for him to let her go.

Or was it herself holding on? To leave was impossible. Jarrett. Her children. Chloe. Peter. Another thought like that and she could never let go. Where would she be? Jarrett, the children, they were off in their own safety, and maybe she'd be able to watch them, maybe that was allowed. Like a movie angel watching loved ones. Being dead was so new—what was possible? Was she only half-dead, neither alive nor dead, not able to return, not able to leave?

Danny came back. He stood by the bed with Jarrett in silence until Jarrett spoke.

"She's gone. I felt it when she left. She was here when I got here. I felt her. She was here. Her body gave a little shudder when I touched her."

Danny nodded. "That happens sometimes after death."

"That's not what I mean. She was here and then she wasn't, and I couldn't get her back. You understand?" He sat with his head in this hands. "How do you know a person dies the minute the heart stops? How do you know that? You don't *know* that." His voice pinned Danny like a wrestler.

Rosie wanted to shake him. *I'm still not gone yet. You don't understand either. I've just lost transmission. Incommunicado.* Surely this wasn't what being dead was.

Danny shook his head. "You're right. I don't know. We only know what happens to the body. The rest, we don't know about that."

He dimmed the lights, the air in the room as violet as twilight, pulled a chair over for himself and sat with Jarrett, his arm around him.

Terrible anguish, the feeling that had been waiting to swamp her all this time. When she was giddy, when she was disturbingly calm, even when she was panicked, all of it was a screen against this letting go that would knock the final life out of her. After that, maybe peace, maybe ever-presence, maybe even Angie. Maybe nothing. But this anguish was bearing down on her like a tsunami, the pressure in the air changing as it got closer. It would hit her in a moment. Then she'd be gone.

# CHAPTER 25

"Terrible news, Chloe." Peter's voice on the message was thin and high, like a wire stretched tight. "Rosie fell off a ladder. She's in the ER. Laraine called. She may have broken her neck."

Chloe shut her computer and called to her assistant. Racing home she ran a stop sign before she turned onto her street. Peter was packing a bag for Jenner. She threw things in a travel case, but before she snapped it shut, the second call came. Not even Jarrett got there in time. She stared at Peter as he told her, standing in the doorway of their bedroom. Her head jerked to one side like she didn't understand what he was saying. He stared back, unable to speak further, and sat on the bed, gaped out the window.

She sat on the bed with him trying to process what he said but couldn't do it. She walked downstairs to her office, shut the door. No, she couldn't be in there. She walked outside, made her way around the block, seeing nothing. Back and upstairs she went to the guest room where Rosie slept when she visited, a shuttered space that made the world outside dark. Rosie gone? That wasn't possible. Gone? She sat on the bed, smoothed the pillow case with her hand and lay her head on it. Rosie's pillow.

The pain of the last months had been eased by one thought—*someday, when your kids are older.* Awareness descended now in stages as she lay there, slamming her each time. She'd lost her twice. Like a mental door clanging shut over and over, trapping her in a small dark space.

Punishment. For which of them?

Rosie fell because she couldn't face the choice. What if I said nothing? Chloe thought. She had told someone how much she loved them, and this happened. As it grew darker outside, she dialed Hannah, got her voice mail. "Sorry to call after all these years." Her voice was small and hesitant. "I need to talk to you."

Half an hour later Hannah called back. "I have some time."

Chloe began speaking and couldn't stop. She told Hannah who Rosie was, told her about Peter and Jenner, told her she'd fallen in love with Rosie, and what she'd done, the history Hannah knew nothing of. Mostly she talked about Rosie. "I knew, Hannah, finally. I knew what I wanted. I went for it. That's why this happened."

Hannah listened quietly. It didn't feel like silence, it felt like presence. She said Rosie's death was not Chloe's fault. "Life is cruel sometimes. No reason. We don't control things. I'm so, so sorry. You're suffering so much right now. I hear it in your voice." Chloe began sobbing and Hannah waited.

"You're strong though, Chloe. You don't know what to do. You have a terrible load of grief. I know what that's like, Chloe. Remember though, you learned to think of the life you want. Your life is not over. You should call me again whenever you need to."

She'd go see Hannah. She burrowed into the bed, tried to quiet the howling inside. Peter and Jenner were calling her, but she didn't answer. When Peter came in, he turned on a small lamp. Her face was wet, her body limp. He asked why she was there. She lifted her hands and dropped down them again. He sat on the bed with her. They needed to drive to Asheville in the morning.

"No," she said. "I need another day."

"Okay, we'll wait a day."

The memorial was its own ordeal. They sat behind Jarrett and the children, Hillie. She watched them wipe at tears, watched them move their shoulders together. Ruth and Frank huddled also—they looked so much older, both of their daughters gone now. Grief etched their faces. Too many people spoke, but Chloe could not. If the situation were reversed, if she died and Rosie was the mourner, you couldn't have kept her from the pulpit.

Andie went forward and read aloud from *The Night Garden*, a book Rosie read to her at bedtime. Hillie guided her back to her seat when she broke into tears. Everyone was in tears. Andie was so like Rosie—her cheeky face, dark hair a curling bit of chaos, Rosie's high-spirited ease with people, too, emotions all on the surface and unashamed. That's why she loved them both. Loved Rosie from the beginning if she was honest, even before she married Peter. She was always late to recognize her feelings.

It was unthinkable to be attracted to Rosie, so she hadn't thought it, just stepped into it, blindsided with her eyes open. Now the bright autumn day was surreal. Rosie couldn't actually be dead. Likely she'd show up soon.

On the way to the house afterward, Chloe exited the Interstate at Merrimon. "We need to stop for flowers."

"We already sent flowers." The flatness of Peter's voice echoed hers, but she couldn't comfort him.

"Funeral flowers. We should bring something they'll want two days from now." She was just stalling their arrival. Next she drove to Bentley's, sent Peter and Jenner into the bakery to pick up a lemon cake. Alone in the car she leaned against the door, her palms pressed to her eyelids. Who thinks up these rituals?

Latecomers now, they parked far down the street. So many were at the house already. Of course there would be. Peter turned into the long front walkway, Jenner on tiptoe behind him, as if she needed to be quiet in spite of the voices, even laughter, drifting from the open windows. To an nine-year-old, death is strange and awesome and also nothing, Chloe thought. To herself, only that same question: how could Rosie be *gone*?

Jenner picked nervously at the corner of the cake box. The three of them looked like any family, Chloe thought, but really they were strangers. At least she was. At the door Jenner handed the box to her. "Would you carry it, Mom?" Chloe took the cake and Jenner took Peter's hand.

Aunt Laraine opened the door, put her arms around Peter as he entered. "Thank the Lord you're here. The man Jarrett needs. Jenner, sweetie, go out back to where the other kids are. Look at that—lemon cake. I used to get those for Jarrett's birthday. From Bentley's, no less. Who told you that was Jarrett's special cake?"

"Rosie did."

Aunt Laraine patted Chloe gently on the shoulder and held up the flowers. "Look at these blue orchids. Where the heck did you find them? I might take them home myself."

The house was crawling—neighbors, teachers from Rosie's school, friends, all unfamiliar to Chloe. It was Rosie's house, but where was she? People chattered in the living room, spilled into the hallway and up the stairs. The oak dining table was covered—casseroles, biscuits, cornbread, slices of ham, plates of fried chicken, barbecue, green beans, macaroni and cheese. A Southern funeral was always a feast day. People milled around picking at their plates. There was touching of hands, quiet joking. That was what the ritual was for, not to be alone with death. She was alone.

In the kitchen Jarrett put down his bourbon and reached for Peter when they entered. The two men hugged, pressed their hands to each other's back. She could not do it yet. She put the cake on the counter, next to a chocolate one and a peach pie. A woman walked through listing gifts of food in a little notebook.

"We'll be talking a lot," Peter said to Jarrett. "I'm here with you."

"I guess you're the only one who gets it," Jarrett replied quietly, but Chloe heard him. That Peter's first wife died young, that's all that mattered, as if Peter hadn't moved on, as if their marriage never existed. And Chloe was standing right there. She left the kitchen.

There was wine, beer, bourbon, gin, and bottles of tonic on the sideboard. She mixed a strong gin and tonic. People kept coming. They all seemed to know each other. Jarrett's old crew from the newspaper with a deli platter, another plate of ribs. Not one person she knew, other than the family and kids in the backyard, who felt like pieces of herself she couldn't remember. The most important piece now was invisible, unknown to others. Rosie had held more pieces of her than anyone.

She could whisper to Jarrett: Guess what? I'm really the only one who gets it. What would he do with that? Anxiety pumped up, and she focused herself, her chest practically rattling out loud. You couldn't say a cruel thing to someone who was stunned with grief. Even if you were stunned, too. Her secret created unspeakable pressure because it was unspeakable itself. She took her drink to the front porch swing and decided to get drunk.

It was a party Rosie would have enjoyed. Chloe hated parties. When she met Peter, both of them were hiding out at a party.

Not one person knew. Rosie surely told no one, certainly not Jarrett or Peter. No one on this planet knew. Except one, who wouldn't tell anyone. A month ago Peter had gone to the mountains with Jarrett for another recording session, and she felt so alone, so acutely aware that Rosie was also alone in Asheville, she ached to call her and almost did. Instead she called Kath and told her the whole story. She spilled it out and cried over the phone while Kath listened. She was likely shocked, but she didn't show it. She seemed upset only for Chloe. Chloe felt her sympathy again. Kath remembered Rosie. She said it sounded impossible for both of them. That was a lot from Kath. It helped.

She'd ended the call with another thought: I'm not totally alone. Where was Jenner? She'd found her downstairs watching *Divergent* on her computer. Peter wouldn't have allowed it, but Chloe joined her until it was over, then made cups of tea, and sat down. She would tell her Kath's story. Jenner should know her grandmother's history.

------

When she went inside to refill her drink, she spotted Ruth and Frank talking with another older couple and stopped to touch Ruth's arm. Both of them hugged her. That felt painful. She was raw, as if all her skin were gone. Touch felt like a burn. She took her drink back outside, walked up and down the driveway. The rawness was inside and out, and she didn't want to be touched even by Peter or Jenner. She hoped alcohol would seal her off.

People were leaving now as well as arriving. When her glass was almost empty, she went back through the kitchen door. Laraine was there with another woman whose hands were in dishwater. The woman turned to her.

"Hello, Chloe. Remember me? Celia."

"Of course. I didn't recover you, I mean recognize you."

"No wonder you didn't recognize me. I'm totally out of context on this terrible day. Lark and I came with Hillie. She's out back with the kids."

Embarrassed by her inebriation, Chloe picked up a towel and began drying. Laraine chattered as they worked—who brought food, who didn't, who stayed too long, who didn't stay long enough. "I've got a list of what everyone brought. Hillie's going to have to help write thank you's. You're not taking her back until she does."

"I'm leaving tomorrow," Celia said. "She'll be all yours."

"All mine," she snorted. "Are you kidding?" Laraine had complained about her daughter for years. A large platter slipped from Chloe's hands, a chip flying off the edge as it hit the floor.

"I'm sorry. I'm so slippery. I mean, it was slippery. I'll get a new one for whoever it belongs to."

"No need. It's an old thing of mine. Somebody gave it to me a long time ago, I don't remember who, and I never liked it much."

"I should replace it for you."

"I do not need another platter, Chloe. At my age it's time to let go of things. Besides," she winked at her, "it's not a big chip. I'll probably use it again."

Chloe acquiesced. Too drunk to handle dishes, too drunk to speak. Where was Peter? She hadn't seen him since they arrived. Or Jenner. Neither would be missing her, and she wasn't missing them. She walked back through the house. Too drunk for dishes, not drunk enough to be in Rosie's house. She spirited an open bottle of wine and a glass outside with her, drunken thoughts jigging with words: red wine, all mine, all fine, hot line.

Back in the porch swing, she watched the October evening advance into a perilously beautiful night, stars popping out above the trees. So many stars, Rosie. Are you that far away? The habit of talking to her was familiar, what she did when they were apart. What she'd been doing these past months when they hadn't talked. Easy to imagine her attentive face, her body, to remember how nicely they fit each other, Rosie meatier, curvier. She caught her breath, thinking of them together.

Rosie left her feeling like an egg cracked open. Cracked totally open, exposed, all messy inside. The vacant spaces, what lay behind all that lovely armor she spent her life acquiring, were exposed now. Unarmored. Unamored. Unmoored. How could you do this to me, Rosie? I need to run away from myself. Where can I go? You left me nowhere.

Celia came through the front door, arched her back to stretch it, saw Chloe and sat next to her. "Jarrett looks ready to collapse."

A brown-skinned woman with two kids in a stroller and a white husband trailing behind walked up the sidewalk. Celia looked startled, then went down to greet them, talked intently to the woman for a while. The man took the stroller to the backyard.

When Celia returned to the porch she said, "That's a woman I knew in another life. Her husband was the anesthetist. He was with Rosie when she died. It's a bit of a shocker for me to see her here and married to him. Are there only really fifty people in this world and the rest is smoke and mirrors?"

Chloe startled. She wanted to talk to that man. "I should go see how Jenner is in the back yard."

"Lark has glommed onto her."

"Lark."

"My daughter."

"Of course. I'll introduce myself." Chloe hadn't paid attention to the kids all afternoon. She walked back through the house, drank a big glass of water and went to the bathroom.

After she peed she considered throwing up, but decided against it. *No more alcohol.* She needed her head.

In the backyard Jenner waved, "Mom! Come meet Lark!"

"Hi, Sweetie. And Lark. I know about you from your mother, or mothers. I'm so glad you're here."

The man was talking to Jarrett so she stayed near the girls. His wife had parked the stroller with the twins near the maple tree and the girls knelt beside them playing a finger game. "Five little monkeys sat in a tree..." they chanted as the twins wriggled their fingers. The man was headed over so she approached him and introduced herself.

"You were the nurse with Rosie, weren't you? Could we speak for a minute? My name is Chloe. I'm a close friend."

"Of course. I'm Danny."

"I want to know whatever you can tell me. How was she? Was there pain?"

"She was on a morphine drip, so not in pain."

"Did you talk with her?"

"Yes. We did talk." He looked a bit awkward.

"Tell me something. Anything."

"Hmm. We talked about our sisters. We both had sisters we'd lost."

"Angie. She was talking about Angie?"

"Well, to Angie actually. Yeah. That's not unusual. Morphine can do that. She seemed quite peaceful. You should know that. I don't think she suffered."

Angie. Of course. Angie. This was Angie's work. Angie didn't want Chloe to have Rosie.

"Did she talk about anyone else?"

"I shouldn't be speaking about what she said. I'm sorry. I know it's a great shock."

"Yes. I understand." When Chloe's tears started up, Danny put his arm around her.

"No pain, really."

"Not pain, torture. It must have been torture for her to know she was dying, leaving her kids without her, and Jarrett. And other people."

"No, really, she was, I don't know how to say it, accepting. Letting go. I believe the sister helped."

Danny sighed. Distressed. Chloe knew he'd spoken more than he should have.

"Thank you. Thank you for coming to the house. I'm glad you were with her."

Chloe squeezed his hand, walked away. Angie did this. She looked toward the sky. How could you?

Rosie couldn't leave her family for her. She left them for Angie. Shaken, Chloe imagined Angie and Rosie reuniting like holographic sweethearts, a ghoulish, sad, ridiculous image. Both of them had played her. She cast off the image—that wasn't Rosie.

# CHAPTER 26

Celia was still in the swing, gently rocking. "Did you find Danny?"

"Um-hmm. I met Lark, too. She's lovely. She and Jenner are playing with your friend's twins." Chloe retrieved the bottle beside the swing.

Celia rolled her eyes and made a face. "Oh, the irony. Olivia with twins. She's an ex of mine, as you probably guessed. She didn't want a child when we were together. That's why we broke up. It's impossible that I'd run into her here, connected to these people, but there you have it. The world is way too small. And I'm not done talking with her either." Celia laughed dryly. "But thank you. Lark is herself. Sit with me." She stopped rocking and patted the place next to her. Chloe remained standing, the bottle propped between her legs. "Poor Rosie. Such a horrible freak accident, so terrible for Jarrett and the kids. What will they do? For you and Peter, too."

Chloe eyes flickered, she looked to the darkening sky, then at Celia. "You have no idea."

Two men came out the door, talking in low voices.

"What a mess he is."

"Yeah, trying not to show it."

Chloe's voice croaked. "Sorry I said that. Please ignore me."

"No worries. I have no idea what you meant, but you're gonna spill that bottle." She reached to take it, and Chloe held onto it, gave a little laugh, and finally sat. Celia leaned toward her. "Do you mind if we take Jenner back to San Francisco with us?"

"Take her. She'd love it. Take me, too. I don't want to be here. I don't know what I'm doing here."

Celia paused, thinking. She watched Chloe close her eyes, open them again, try to refocus. "It wasn't Rosie, was it? You said back when we met that you were in love with a married woman."

Chloe stared at her. Celia touched her again, and Chloe shuddered.

"This must be incredibly hard."

Chloe put her hands to her face. "I might be coming unglued actually. Sorry."

"Of course you are."

"God, you sound like a therapist."

"I am a therapist. You forgot. Don't worry. I'd never ever say anything. I've been there myself, more or less."

"The woman with Danny? Olivia."

"No. But you're not far wrong. You should come to San Francisco. It's a good place to flee to. I did, a long time ago, from her."

Chloe started to pour more wine but put the bottle down.

"It's okay to get drunk on a day like this." Celia reached for the bottle, too.

Chloe stood again, wobbly. She leaned back against the railing and looked at Celia. "Rosie and I took some trips together. That's when it happened between us. No one knew. She's my husband's first wife's twin sister. I know how that sounds. Yes, I was in love with her. I was ready to run away with her. I shouldn't be telling you this, but I can't help myself." Chloe wiped her eyes. "You must think I'm mad."

"Love's hard to control. It's like that in the queer community. This one's ex is that one's former ex and so on and so forth."

Chloe's mouth twisted. "You think lesbians are messed up."

Celia snorted. "No. I think humans are messed up. Not really messed up, just that love's hard. Look at Hillie. She can't figure it out. Now she's thinking about staying here with Jarrett, giving up her life in San Francisco to help him deal with this. Giving up the bookstore, all of it. I keep thinking I should stop her. Her mother, Laraine, will be terrible for her. They don't do well together. Laraine will take over, and she favors Jarrett. Her nephew, not her own daughter."

Chloe didn't want to think about other people's complications. "She'd leave Lark?"

"She says Lark's old enough to visit, and that she doesn't need her as much. That's not true. And I need her. She's running away. Or maybe he was always the one she loved. Craziness. Like I said, we can't help who we love."

They watched a few more people leave. "If you want to quit this town and move to San Francisco, you could run the bookstore for Hillie."

"What an idea." Chloe was startled to hear herself laugh. "I would live in Parnassus Books in Nashville if I could. It's where I go to be happy.

"I'm glad you talked to me, Chloe. I can't imagine what you're going through. I mean I really can. Call me, you know, if you need to. I'm good at discretion."

Peter came from around the back and stepped up on the porch, halted, sensing awkwardness. Chloe sat down again and Celia got up, wrote a message on a crumpled napkin she had in her pocket, smoothed it out and put it in Chloe's hand. Chloe dropped it in her pocket.

"What's up with you two? Haven't seen you all day, Chloe. You okay?"

"No."

She saw pain in his eyes, his reddened face, worn from weeping. Her heart went out to him this time. It *was* almost like losing Angie again. She sighed. "I'll go get Jenner."

"No need," Peter said. "They're all in the family room. I'm giving her a little more time, okay? I promised to play ping pong with her and Lark." He turned to Celia. "Lark's your daughter, isn't she? She and Jenner seem to be instant best friends."

"I know. But I need to get her going. She has to chill a little bit or she'll never get to bed."

Peter went in with her, leaving Chloe alone. What would Rosie think? She'd told someone. Chloe had hoped they'd get caught sometimes. Now someone else knew. She thought about Peter with remorse. This must be so hard for him. He was a good man, a good husband, even if he didn't love her the right way. And she didn't love him right. Either way, their marriage had hit a dead end, but he and Jenner depended on her financially, if not otherwise. She and Jenner were closer now.

Peter came back out with Jenner. "No one wants to ping pong any more. We should get out of here. I told Jarrett we'd be back tomorrow. At least I will."

Jenner eyed her mom, curious, unsettled. They could hear Celia and Lark in the living room, Lark's plaintive "*Why?*"

Jenner picked that up. "Why can't Lark stay?"

"How's Jarrett?"

"Terrible." He gestured his head toward Jenner. "Let's talk about this later."

"I managed not to speak to him all day. I need to go find him. I can't leave without speaking to him."

Peter gave her a hard look. "Yeah. You stayed pretty far away."

Jenner slipped back into the house.

"I thought, um, it seemed like people were with him the whole time."

"Um-hmm. So go talk to him if you want. You know what you want to say? Just say you're concerned for him. I think you're a little too drunk. Be careful what you say. You want to tell me first? He's fragile right now."

Did he suspect something? Did he know? He couldn't possibly know, it was just her inebriation. He knew about Elaine. He could have figured it out. Figured out at least that she was in love with Rosie. She was so impaired that she didn't feel guilty talking to Celia, telling her things she shouldn't have, but she would not say anything to Jarrett. Of course not. Didn't Peter know that? The way he was watching her, worried about her talking to Jarrett. He knew.

Still standing, she swayed the swing with one hand. "Maybe I won't tonight. I'm too wasted. Okay? Maybe you corral Jenner, and we'll get out of here."

Peter nodded, headed back inside, letting the screen slam. Her mind raced on alcohol and suspicion. If he knew, had known for a while, what did it mean? He had let it pass. He hadn't cared? Maybe it even took pressure off of him. Maybe he knew and didn't want to know.

So he knew how undone she was. He was undone, too. A repeat, the two of them, grieving for the same person, like with him and Rosie. No, not like that—of course they couldn't share it. The tie he had with Rosie, it was too late for that with them, and a violation of their marriage anyway. So many places they never got to.

It occurred to her that *impossible to leave* was a state of mind. Maybe she could leave, and needed to leave. Maybe she needed to take Jenner to see Lark and hang out with Celia and talk to Hannah. This thought lifted and devastated her at the same time. She could go to San Francisco for a little while at least. She could take a break. If losing Rosie didn't kill her, didn't kill Peter, maybe it would free them.

Chloe woke late the next morning, her head ready to split and her insides bathed in acid. What a bad idea to drink so much. What a good idea. Peter was getting Jenner ready. She waved them off and didn't crawl out of bed until eleven when her coffee and toast arrived from room service.

Her mind roamed over the previous day. Rosie. Rosie. The funeral, Jarrett. Peter. Rosie. Jenner. Hillie, Celia, Lark. She located the note Celia slipped her: *If you come, you can stay with me.* That was interesting.

Not speaking to Jarrett: she had been a coward, daunted by the war between truth and compassion. She wanted to fly back to Nashville now, leave Peter to drive home with Jenner. How wrong would that be?

When he hadn't returned or called by two, she decided to go. No reason to pretend normalcy, and the thought of driving home with him, unable to talk because Jenner was in the back-seat and would hear everything, even with earbuds in, settled it. Peter didn't answer her call, so she left a message, took a cab to the airport.

He called after she made it home to say they'd drive back the next day, probably get in late. She told him she needed to go away for a while. He didn't reply.

A game plan, that's what she needed before he arrived. The next day she sorted things in her closet, packed two bags, then sorted out her office, really so little there she needed to take besides her computer. She backed up everything. She tried to sort things in her mind, plans loosening and racing forward. She felt, no, heard, time ticking, insistent drumming. How to talk to Peter, to Jenner?

One thing she was sure of: she couldn't go back to work feeling like this. She called her office to tell the senior partner she was taking a month's leave, at least a month, maybe longer. He was hostile, someone she'd always had a bit of trouble with.

"That's impossible. You cannot take off abruptly for a month or longer. You have important clients."

"We've had a death in the family. It will take a while to sort things. I'll work it out with clients from San Francisco and be available if anything comes up. And I *can* do it."

She didn't care what he thought, but she did care about her clients, at least most of them. Of course the firm wouldn't want to let her go, but they couldn't fire her. Then again it might be best. If he wanted to terminate her partnership over this, she'd resign, she wouldn't fight. Maybe she'd close things out and resign anyway. She needed to think. She could do this. She really could. The heavy thing in her chest lifted a notch.

There were funds to be liquidated, money to be moved—enough cash into their account to float Peter for a while, enough into her own to last her. She felt a storm inside her, winds picking up, a sense of liberation growing, along with terror, unstoppable, sweeping into something unknown, better or worse than the known, which she could not endure any longer.

She searched Airbnbs in San Francisco. Off-season, a small flat in Bernal Heights was available with a deck. No view. She didn't need a view, she needed a place to be. She booked it for as long as it was free, six weeks. Better not to stay with Celia. She was in enough trouble as it was, and Jenner could stay part of the month if she had her own place. How bad could it be to miss a little of third grade? She was ahead of most other kids.

She would see Celia, though, spend some time with her. Lark and Jenner had bonded.

Thoughts rushed forward again. A month, two months, to know what to do with the rest of her life. She imagined a few things. Manage money for her family and perhaps some clients, not all of them. She had money. Money was not what she needed. She called Hannah, left a message asking for her earliest appointment. She went to the garage and pulled out her bicycle, then rode for an hour to calm herself and think. One piece, then another. She had a place to stay, a therapist, an income. She could do this.

She began to see how she and Rosie were never in sync, their paths not even going in the same direction. All her life she headed forward; there was somewhere she needed to get to. Even in her dreams. Something was unfinished in her and she kept trying to finish it. Or rather, it was a matter of finding something—finding what she needed, finding herself. Her direction was future, a second life. She kept thinking she'd found it, but she hadn't, not yet. She was still living in the shadow of her first life.

Rosie, like Peter, was headed toward the past. What she really wanted was the past, her first life. She got closer, sort of, with Peter, and with Andie, but really she was waiting for Angie to retrieve her.

She and Rosie crossed in time. Their present lives overlapped. Rosie didn't want a second life. That was not to say they didn't matter to each other. They loved each other, they moved each other, in important ways.

———

Peter and Jenner arrived late. She feigned sleep, in bed in the guest room, Rosie's bed. The next morning she took Jenner to school, though that was Peter's job. When she got home, she poured coffee for them and told him she'd taken a leave from work, she didn't know for how long. He looked confused. He told her she was off her head right now.

She agreed. "I'm going to San Francisco for a while. Get my head back on straight. I want Jenner with me, at least part of the time."

He threw his coffee in the sink. "You can't be serious. You can't even think of taking Jenner, especially now. Haven't I lost enough? It would just be cruel."

"Haven't I? Things are wrong at the heart of us. You know it. Everything feels cruel right now, for me, too. It's Jenner you love. If Jenner stays here, you wouldn't care so much, would you?"

"You know I would. But you can't. She wouldn't be okay with you. I mean without me."

"I know what you mean. What you said the first time. And maybe she wouldn't be okay without me either."

"Is this about Rosie?"

"Yes, it's about Rosie."

There she said it. Did he hate her for it? Did he even hate for her to go? Could she rip a marriage apart this fast? They would never ease apart because of Jenner. She'd give him time, not take Jenner immediately. Jenner was the price. She'd bring her out for a week, maybe more. She was old enough to fly by herself, though Peter wouldn't think so. Or she'd fly her home if needed.

She had been cruel before in love. She could be cruel again. Which would she be: cruel to him or to herself?

———

She lay awake for hours that night, rigid in the old way she used to sleep, when she was young and terrified, not knowing what was ahead, no secure life to rely on. She was trying to build something new and had no base again. She talked to Rosie in her head. "I'm doing it, Rosie, but without you...You'd like it in California. I can't believe we never went together... What did you really feel about being with me?...We seemed so happy together, really, we had everything: love, sex, the outdoors, a history. You would have been happy if we had the kids with us."

But who knew? Rosie herself didn't think so. Though maybe she was just afraid. It would have torn a lot of relationships apart, a mess, maybe ugly. More ugly than now? She couldn't say Rosie was wrong or even that she could have done it herself, really, in the end, at such cost. Yet she had, she was.

"I miss you so much. Are you free from all these human feelings? Sad as I am?"

Rosie didn't talk back. She didn't sense her presence the way she had with Angie. Why? Was her head too busy with plans? Was Rosie busy herself, reuniting with Angie? Talking to others besides her? Had she imagined Angie's presence after all? She sensed Angie was done with her now, maybe done with all of them. She'd gotten what she wanted. Rosie.

She wouldn't contact anyone from her old life other than Hannah. She'd get Jenner out there. And if she stayed, Jenner might choose to be there. She'd be so excited, seeing Lark again, discovering the city with her. The white crocodile at the Academy of Sciences, the room full of butterflies, the Exploratorium, the ferry to Alcatraz, Victorian houses.

Chloe knew she wasn't coming back any time soon. She'd have to tell Peter at some point she was returning to California indefinitely. Would he want a divorce? It would all be devastating. She couldn't sort it out, she just knew she couldn't the face the days ahead here.

And Kath. At some point she'd get Kath to California. Dee had been sick a lot. He probably didn't have long. Kath's future solitude weighed on her. Spending time with Kath terrified her unreasonably, but everything terrified her now. She wanted to heal and wanted Kath to heal, too. She couldn't make that happen, but she could do something.

She talked to Rosie again. Whatever you're doing, wherever you are, just speak to me from time to time. I need that. Maybe you know what I should do.

# PART SEVEN

# EPILOGUE

Jenner lived with them most of the time. She didn't go to Lark's school, a small alternative one nearby; she wanted a big city public school with diverse students. It was good for them to be in different schools. They spent so much time together at home, and adolescents now, their social lives were likely to diverge soon.

Her relationship with Peter was embattled. He spent many holidays with them, she spent time in Nashville, but tension was always there. He didn't fight well, which made Jenner fight harder. She wanted him to be okay, with and without her, but he wasn't.

Kath had visited, awed as Chloe knew she would be by the city. On her first visit they sat in Union Square so Chloe could show her the statue of Nike. Kath secured herself on a sheltered bench and watched the people warily, as if ready to dart off, a cat in a strange space. The cacophony of voices around them, languages from across the world, also awed her. She liked the park best, a few blocks from their house out on the avenues, and walked alone there for the solitude and quiet.

After Dee died, Chloe worried about her isolation. Getting her to California, even for Christmas, took negotiation. She guided her in and out of shops, held her arm when Kath wanted to buy presents for Jenner and little Hana. She was stunned by prices. Chloe assured her chocolate mochi balls would be the one thing they'd definitely want and reminded her to get them for Lark, too. They stopped for scallion pancakes and ramen at Marufuku,

She vowed to get Kath to move to California. She'd balk, but in the end she might agree. Puzzled that she accepted Celia so easily, Chloe asked her how. Kath simply said, "Remember, I told you, it doesn't matter who you love. Being loved is the important thing."

———

When Covid closed everything, the bookstore stalled. Joy had hired help after Hillie left, but Chloe came to the rescue, investing in it, finally buying Hillie's share. It gave Hillie some money and Chloe a project with a small income. They consulted frequently, by phone and text. Now the store had a book garden on the back patio with mobile shelves, seating, and self-serve coffee. It wasn't thriving. Chloe made little from it, leaving most of the small profit to Joy who ran the place.

She still managed investments for some old clients as well as her own and a fund for Jenner, Lark, and Hana. Free of the pressure, she enjoyed it now. She also enjoyed playing bookseller, Uncommon Reader a slow-paced oasis. Having time to read anything she liked: nonfiction, fiction, poetry, offered an antidote to financial documents, which she didn't read much any more either. Once, closing a novel she loved, she had a thought: I'm no longer off the page.

She talked to Rosie, especially at first. You'd like San Francisco. Could have been yours, too. We wasted a lot of stupid time. Sad, don't you think? Do you feel sad or are you free from all these human feelings? When she looked at apartments her first year, before Celia, she couldn't help but think whether Rosie would have liked this one or that one. Same for restaurants, people she met.

After she and Celia got married, then Celia had Hana, Chloe thought of Rosie less. Peter was her biggest ache. Doing better now, dating a new woman, he said, though it was not clear if it was going anywhere. His last two albums did fairly well. Bluegrass, old-timers who had millennials following them, a niche that Spotify and Apple promoted. He was making money. Really, it had not been good for him that she supported him so long.

She never heard Rosie speak to her. She kept a space on her desk like a tiny altar: a photo, a fresh flower, often a red or yellow one from the Chinese lantern bushes in their back yard, plus a shell from the beach. Sometimes they got moved around. Celia swore she never touched them. The girls and the woman who cleaned their house knew Chloe's desk was off-limits, though you never knew, especially with Hana, who loved to handle small things. Rosie was situated somewhere and maybe wanted her to know it. She would not want to be left out.

Photo by Ellie Waxman

# ABOUT THE AUTHOR

BEVERLY BURCH is the author of two nonfiction books and four poetry collections. Her books have won a John Ciardi Poetry Prize, a Gival Poetry Prize, a Lambda Literary Award and were finalists for the Audre Lorde Award and Housatonic Award. Her short fiction has appeared in many literary journals. She lives in the Bay Area with her wife. www.beverlyburch.com

# ACKNOWLEDGMENTS

Everything comes from solitude first, then community; nothing from one person alone. The encouragement of editors and first readers meant everything as I wrote this book. Thank you to the following journals who first published parts of this novel in story form: *Southern Humanities Review, Ascent, Briarcliff Review,* and *2 Bridges Review.*

Amy Zhang, Heidi Pitlor, and Wendy Tokunaga gave miraculous insights to my drafts and revisions. Their close readings helped the work evolve from linked stories into a novel. Thank you for your amazing literary minds. More thanks to the best beta readers ever, Robert Thomas, Julia Levine, Zack Rogow, Carol Jenkins, Joan Bonnar, and Linda O'Brien who believed I could make the leap from poetry and nonfiction to writing a novel. Their keen interest in the characters assured me there was a story here. The women of WOM-BA support, sustain, and suggest strategies to sister writers for getting a book out into the world. Nina Schuyler, Sasha Vasilyuk, and Frances Dinkelspiel each gave me a vital point or two of direction as I moved from one publishing world to another.

A huge thank you to the women of Sibylline Press for creating such a perfect home for this book. Their creative vision and industry know-how have smoothed the path in many ways. A community of women writers, wow. Julia Park Tracey and Vicki DeArmon are geniuses at this.

Nashville and Asheville, cities that matter to me: I want to come back.

Especially I thank Linda who put up with many occasions where I raised my hand to say, Don't talk to me right now. She also created the playlist for the novel. We keep finding the rhythm of separateness and togetherness which lets each of us do our work. I love you.

# STUDY GUIDE QUESTIONS

1. What pulled two women so different as Chloe and Rosie together—circumstance or chemistry?

2. How do you think Chloe's relationship with her mother impacted her? How do you feel about Kath?

3. How did Rosie's relationship with her twin, Angie, alter her? How do you feel about Angie?

4. What did having children mean for each character?

5. Have you ever experienced grief the way Rosie did? Peter? Chloe?

6. Did Chloe's relationship with Elaine shape her love life afterwards? with Jamie?

7. Do Nashville and Asheville, two different cities, reflect something of the characters' personalities?

8. Andie's birth propelled Rosie in one direction, then Willie's rough entrance to adolescence propelled her in another. Would she have been different without her children?

9. Yvette, then Colette, ushered in a big shift in Chloe's life. Do you think they triggered it or reflected something already in motion?

**Sibylline Press** is proud to publish the brilliant work of women authors over 50. We are a woman-owned publishing company and, like our authors, represent women of a certain age.